I0666404

The Dream States

Jonathan DeLeon

Beyond Normal Books LLC

I dedicate this book to the friends and family who have filled my life with splendid memories and joy. Special thanks go to my wife, Sarah, without whom this story would not have been possible.

Contents

PROLOGUE

S arah's eight-year-old eyes burned into her mind the night that would change her life forever. Cracks of gunfire pierced the air as the humid dark erupted in flames and violence. She was crouching behind a tree stump, ankle deep in the Louisiana mud, scared and cold. Shifting her position to keep the swamp water from getting inside her boots, she turned to her father and whispered, "Dad, what do we do?"

Her father, the man everyone called "The Master," was crouched beside her, looking out at the fighting through glossy eyes. "We have to go," he murmured back under his breath.

"But—" A blast of gunfire interrupted Sarah as bullets rattled through the swamp. "But what about Mom and Miss June and everyone else?"

The Master hunched over, looking into Sarah's eyes. "Kiddo, I'm sorry, but they aren't coming."

Sarah's eyes filled with tears. "But Dad."

"I know. I'm sorry." The Master hugged his young daughter to his chest as she broke down.

Between soft sobs, she squeezed out, "Why? Why is this happening?"

"I underestimated the programming. I thought he understood. No, I know he did. I just didn't think the power of that code was so... I don't know. I thought he'd be able to fight it, but he couldn't. But at least he held out long enough to bring this back to us." The Master pulled a small flash drive from his pocket and showed it to Sarah. "Do you remember what I told you about the mission everyone just went on?"

"You said,"—Sarah thought for a moment—"they were looking for a key?"

"A key code, the key code that we can use to set you free."

"This is happening because of me?"

"Oh no. No, of course not. You did nothing wrong. The world is just, it's sick, kiddo. Everyone believes that to find life, they must go to the Dream States, and that there is nothing else for them. They don't realize they are missing out on the best part of it all. Everything they need to experience, feel, and live is right here." The Master pushed Sarah's hair out of her face. "They don't need endless simulations. They need one actual connection." Taking a deep breath while staring into his daughter's eyes, the Master could see something was missing. Sarah had lost that innocent gleam of youth. Steeling his nerves, he continued, "The people who run this whole corrupt system they know the truth. They know that genuine connection, genuine love, like you and I and your mother have, is better than their program. Because of that, your mother and I knew that those who run the Dream States would come for you. You're proof that their system isn't enough. That's not your fault. It's theirs. This mission was to ensure they can never get you. I'm sorry to tell you all of this. I wish you could live a few more years without having to think of the dangers out there." The Master shook the flash drive, bringing Sarah's attention to it. "But now we have the key to keeping you safe, and everyone else we save. With this code, we'll be able to make sure you never have to feel like this ever again. But first we need to get out of here. Okay?"

Sarah nodded. Tears were still pouring from her eyes, creating tracks through swamp mud that had splashed onto her face. "I want Mom."

"I do too. Come on." The Master reached his arm under Sarah's legs and cradled her. One careful step after another, the Master, with Sarah in his arms, walked through the dense marsh.

She reached her arms around his neck, holding tight, and asked, "Where are we going?"

"I know a place. Somewhere that we can hide. There, we'll be able to rebuild and wait."

"Wait for what?" Sarah's voice was waning, exhaustion from the emotion of the night taking its toll.

"The right person to wake up."

CHAPTER 1

KEVIN ALTAIR

Phillip Welsh opened his eyes for the last time. For the past two months, Phillip had been lying in a hospital bed, unable to walk, and sleeping most of the day. Yet the sudden failing of his health hadn't had a similar effect on his happiness. Never in his eighty-five-year-long life had he felt more loved.

Handprint paintings, made by Phillip's grandchildren, hung taped to the hospital room's window. Framed pictures from his life covered his nightstand. Happy memories were brightening the room as his life waned.

In these last minutes of his life, Phillip let his gaze move from frame to frame. Each picture immortalized an amazing piece of his existence. Together, they played out the movie of the last eight and a half decades.

His eyes fell on a picture of two young kids standing next to a large oak tree with a homemade tire swing. It pulled Phillip's mind backwards in time. For a moment, he was twelve years old, playing with his sister, taking turns pushing each other on the swing, smiles on their faces. He could feel the cool, humid Wisconsin-autumn air bite at their cheeks, turning them blush red.

Phillip's eyes moved to another frame, pulling from that memory into another. He had never seen a sight as beautiful as Margaret walking down the aisle of their wedding day. The sun shining through the stained glass had set a strange and mystical pink hue to everything. Margaret had chosen him; Phillip never understood why, but always gave thanks. Her smile had enchanted him every morning. That toothy grin had warmed his heart and made him love her even more every day. Soon that affection and her smile multiplied. Somehow Margaret had passed it on to their four children.

Phillip looked at a Christmas card from a few years back, before Margaret had taken her rightful place as an angel in heaven. He would reunite with her soon.

Phillip's eyes felt heavy. He watched dust particles dance in the afternoon sun. Thick beams of light shone through the metal shutters. Phillip allowed his eyes to close for the last time. So much love had been his; now he was ready to move on.

At 5:45 p.m. on a Tuesday, Phillip Welsh died.

Bright light burned his eyes, sending a shooting pain into the back of his skull. He reached up to shield his vision from the luminous assault, but something stopped his hand before he could reach his face. Looking down, he saw the IV tube and needle taped to his palm stretched to their limit. Looking closer, he saw a tattoo on the inside of his wrist:

ID# 925387

Understanding dawned on Kevin. He remembered. It took only a few seconds for it all to come back. Kevin knew where he was and what the death of Phillip Welsh meant.

Vacation was over.

A soft creak drew Kevin's attention to the door that led into his small square room. In stepped a nurse dressed in metallic blue from head-to-toe. Robes covered almost every inch of her body. The only part of her he could see were her eyes—orange and black. Kevin did a double take. He had heard of this trend but hadn't seen it in person.

The nurse moved quick, not returning his glance. She was working. Kevin was one of fifteen people she had to unplug. It always seemed like they came in waves. However, this facility demanded a higher level of customer service, so she forced out some small talk as she pulled the IV from Kevin's arm. "Welcome back. How was your life?" she asked in a typical upbeat customer service tone.

"It was good. Real good. I don't think I've ever had a better one." Kevin was about to say more before the nurse cut him off.

"Well, that's good," she said as she typed a few commands on a computer.

Kevin's bed rose to a more elevated position in response to the command she had entered.

"Your scores will display in a minute. Please look them over, and when you're ready, please proceed along the blue line." The nurse crossed back to the door, stopped, and turned. "Oh, and thank you for visiting DS 7. We appreciate your stay. Please come again." With that, the nurse disappeared out the door. She had left so fast that Kevin couldn't say thank you or goodbye.

Kevin sat up more in his bed. He wished she had moved slower or stayed a minute longer. This life of Phillip Welsh had been such an amazing experience. Kevin wanted to share it with someone, tell someone about it, before it was gone forever. But that was the curse of The Dream States, a great vacation, but alone.

The wall across from Kevin, one massive projection, lit up. There was Phillip Welsh staring back at him—the last picture of how he looked in his last days. Looking into Phillip's eyes, Kevin felt unnerved. It was a strange thing to look at someone else and yourself at the same time. As the visage of Phillip disappeared, scores scrolled in from the bottom.

NAME: Phillip Welsh
YEARS LIVED: 85.55
TOTAL MONEY MADE: $10,434,382.09

PERCENTAGE OF LIFE DISCOVERED: 85%

"Oh, come on!" Kevin said with an unbelieving disdain. Eighty-five percent was not a bad score; it was the highest he had ever achieved, but it still felt like it was too low. The love he had felt as Phillip died deserved over eighty-five percent. Kevin sat and watched as the screen scrolled up from the bottom, listing the statistics of his life as Phillip Welsh. It was strange that every event that had meant so much to him boiled down to buzz words.

ACHIEVEMENTS:

FIRST STEPS
I CAN TALK
HONOR ROLL
YOUTH SPORTS STAR
FIRST LOVE
WATCH OUT! NEW DRIVER
HEARTBREAK HURTS
HIGH SCHOOL IS SO OVER
MET YOUR MATCH
COLLEGE GRAD
MARRIED YOUR MATCH
I'M A PARENT
...

The list continued to scroll for over five minutes. Each term sparked a memory in Kevin's mind. Even after the list had shifted to the negatives, Kevin was reminiscing. When the negative of **LEAD FOOT** came onto the screen, he thought back to the first speeding ticket he, as Phillip, had received.

He had been so afraid the cop was going to arrest him for speeding so blatantly while trying to show off for his first girlfriend. She had wanted a rebel, and he was trying hard to be it. Racing down a forty-mile-per-hour road at sixty-five miles per hour seemed like a good way to prove that. The high-pitched whine his voice turned into when the officer handed him the ticket erased any badass status he had built. Soon after that, the girl had left him. It took years for Phillip to understand, but that ticket had shaped his life. He chose in that instant not to be a wild child, but to be himself. Here it was on a list of negatives. It didn't deserve to be there. It had been a positive to him.

As the final negative scrolled off the screen, Kevin scooted to the edge of his bed, his feet hanging off the end. Now was the time. Now was when he would receive his score. He had been so close last time. This had to be his last time spent at DS 7. If Kevin could rank just one level higher, then he could move up to DS 8.

DREAM COMPLETE.
READY TO COMPILE?

Taking a deep breath, Kevin centered himself. "Yes."
The screen showed an animation of numbers adding together and whirling. Category scores shot forward.

TOTAL KARMA SCORE: 8
...
LIFETIME ACHIEVEMENTS
AND NEGATIVES SCORE: 8

"Yes!" Kevin pumped his fist in celebration. Considering both scales were from negative ten to ten, a score of eight on both gave him an awesome chance of getting into DS 8. He needed an Overall Rank in the eighties to make it in, and these scores gave him hope. Kevin wiped his sweaty palms on the blanket, nervous. The numbers whirring on the screen were taking too long. Then it came.

OVERALL RANK: 82

Kevin jumped out of bed, throwing his hands overhead. He screamed, "Yes!" As he did, he almost fell to the floor, his legs feeling strange underneath him. It had been a while since he walked in either life. He leaned against the bed to balance. The screen lit up with an animation of numbers exploding into fireworks. After the show, a new text appeared on the screen.

**CONGRATULATIONS!
KEVIN ALTAIR, ID# 925387
YOU'RE NOW A LEVEL 8 DREAMER!
ON YOUR NEXT VISIT,
REPORT TO DREAM STATE 8.**

Kevin stared at the screen. He felt so proud of himself. Most people his age were level 6 or had only recently gotten to level 7. Not him though, he was a level 8. Now all he lacked was someone to celebrate with. He thought back to when Phillip and his wife had celebrated their twenty-five-year anniversary.

There had been a roomful of people clapping and dancing. Here was Kevin, alone in a sanitized room with no windows and no love. For a moment, Kevin felt the victory robbed from his heart, but only for a moment. This was too big an achievement not to feel amazing about. The screen went blank, and the lights in the room got brighter. A voice came over the ceiling speaker.

"Thank you for your visit. Please change into your clothes, in the locker in the corner of the room. Take it slowly. Your muscles will feel strange at first. Electrical stimulation has kept them active, but it will take approximately five minutes for you to feel normal again. When you're ready, follow the blue lighted path to out-processing. As always, thank you for visiting DS 7. Please come again."

I'm not coming again, thought Kevin, full of defiant pride. This was the last time he would see DS 7 because he was a level 8 now. He changed back into his clothes from the hospital gown, a pair of retro vintage blue jeans and a classic white button-up shirt. He smiled as he laced up his remake Converse All Stars. Most people laughed at his choice of clothing, but he liked his style. It was why he always chose the 2000s as his period to dream in. Most people went either further back in time or dreamed in an alternate version of today's world. Modern style and life weren't as appealing to him as the openness of the period of history known as the age of freedom. Kevin stood and stretched his entire body. This was it. This was the last time he would walk out of a DS 7 dreaming room. As Kevin opened the door, a lighted path on the floor shone blue. This LED line would lead him down an expanse of hallways to his least favorite part—the burn.

It took Kevin near thirty-five minutes to walk the long maze of hallways from his room to out-processing. Kevin had passed hundreds of doors, yet on the entire trip, he hadn't seen a single person. He felt a strange sense of eeriness throughout the entire walk. Finally, he had seen the double doors that led to out-processing and pushed his way inside.

Now Kevin sat in a plastic chair in a room with twenty other people, waiting for an out-processing room to open up. Surrounded by others just like him, all having just woken from dreams they wanted to talk about, and yet it was still silent. Kevin wanted to reach over to the closest person next to him and talk about the dreams they had just woken up from so badly, just a quick conversation to share something about their lives, but it was strictly forbidden. Kevin would not risk his newly achieved level 8. So he sat there, semi-patiently waiting.

"ID number 925387. Room 9," the computerized voice commanded over the loudspeaker.

Kevin rose and walked to the door with a large red 9 emblazoned on it. This wasn't Kevin's first time doing this, and it wouldn't be his last, but he hated going into these rooms. He stepped inside and closed the door behind him. The magnetic seal clicked as it locked.

"Let's get this over with."

Kevin walked to the center of the room. As he did, he looked around, surveying the plain, medically hygienic walls of the DS 7 burn room. It was rumored that DS 8 rooms had couches and attendants—a vast improvement over his current habitat. The only thing that broke up the whiteness of the walls, floor and ceiling was a shiny, metallic, black cushioned chair. The seat back had a round bowl attached to it by an arm, which held it over the head of whoever sat in it. It looked like the devil's salon hair dryer.

As he lowered himself into that chair, the bowl-shaped bell descended over his head, all the way past his chin. Pitch black engulfed Kevin. The only light he could perceive was a small reflection of white penetrating the bell from below. He braced himself as a red dot began blinking in front of his eyes. It blinked faster and faster until it was almost steady. Here it came. Kevin let out a breath as the burn built in his mind. His brain was being set on fire. Kevin shook in the chair as the blaze stoked inside him. He tried to relax as Phillip Welsh disappeared from his memory.

As a kid, Kevin learned about the risk of fighting a memory erase. It was dangerous to hold on. Plus, it made the pain ten times worse. It was better to sit there and let it happen. Focus instead on something tactile, like the feeling of the chair or a pinch, to distract the mind. The burn, while painful, was a necessary evil. Humans couldn't handle the psychological burden of multiple lives. Their minds would crack. Kevin had seen videos of them, drooling and confused. Poor souls suffering hallucinations and memories from different lives penetrating reality without control.

For some time, there was no way to dream without losing your mind, until a brilliant young inventor created the mind chip. This small mental implant acted like a reset button for the psyche. While the burn machine erased your mind, this chip would save and store all your actual memories.

After the burn erased all you were, your mind chip restored you. It also stored your Overall Rank and Karma

Score. Your rank allowed for nicer facilities, while your Karma allowed for a better lottery life ranking.

Kevin smiled as happy memories passed through his conscious mind. The last memory to pass by before he fell unconscious were the letters DS 8.

Damn right I am, thought Kevin as blackness overtook him.

...

...

Kevin snapped back to reality from a dreamless zone with the sound of the magnetic lock unsealing. He was still sitting in the burn chair. The bell had risen from his head and now sat back in its starting position. It took a few seconds before he felt the rush of his memories gushing through his mind. The mind chip was reinstalling his identity.

He felt a strange tingle and dull pain as the mind upload burned memories back into his brain. Kevin closed his eyes as the pain intensified. He allowed himself to be pulled from memory to memory as his entire life restored to his consciousness. He saw a green chalkboard, smelled the wooden desk he sat in, and watched as a blur of white letters were drawn and erased on the board. The blur was so fast he could hardly make out the form of the teacher writing them. A few moments later, he saw blackness but knew writing, reading, and language.

"Mr. Altair!"

Kevin opened his eyes into a memory. He had fallen asleep in math class. The teacher stood at the front of the classroom, at a whiteboard filled with formulas.

"Mr. Altair, since you know this already and can take a nap, how about showing the class how to solve this formula?"

Kevin was pulled back into the blackness. He knew mathematics. He could remember everything from addition to differential equations and advanced quantum physics.

Kevin continued to be drawn in and out of memories, learning athletics and life skills. He let them fly by, not getting attached to any one memory.

Images of coding flew by as he learned advanced computing language. Kevin watched himself sitting in a chair, a cord plugged into his mind chip. Code flew by as pieces turned red. Next, his memories turned to white noise. Fear filled him as he felt something wasn't working. The mind chip struggled with a broken piece of his memory. Kevin's awareness came back as the memory of driving into Dream State 7 re-uploaded. A slight blur led him to the dream room, followed by a flash of black, and all the way back to sitting in the burn chair. Text appeared in his mind as the memories finished uploading.

KEVIN ALTAIR
ID# 925387
CURRENT RANK: 82

Hell yeah! DS 8! Never coming back to this place again, he thought as he saw the text.

Kevin sat for a moment, trying to remember the dream life he had just lived, but he couldn't. It was gone. So weird how quickly something like that could disappear. But it existed no more, no use trying to bring it back now. The burn was over. Time to go.

Kevin walked to the door and opened it. This time, the floor lit up with a green line leading him down another hallway.

As Kevin walked out of his burn room, he looked at the group of people still sitting in the waiting room. *See you never. I'm out of here. Maybe someday you'll see me again in your dreams, but you'll be looking up at me. I'll be coming from DS 8.*

He walked for a few minutes until he reached a large metallic door with massive hinges built of solid steel. It was out of place in a building that was otherwise unspectacular. As Kevin approached, a red laser light scanned his entire body. Kevin raised his arm, showing his wrist to the light so that his ID barcode could be visible. A beep sounded, signifying that it registered his identification. The door slid open with a groan as powerful hydraulics forced it to swing. Kevin didn't wait for it to open all the way, instead squeezing through the small available opening. Two guards stood just past the door, their backs to Kevin. They were there to make sure no one made a dash inside. Over the years, some lower-DS-classification individuals had tried.

Kevin strolled past the guards armed with automatic rifles and headed into the main room of the lobby. He observed the lobby of Dream State 7 for the last time. The large open room had white-tile floors, white walls and a white drop ceiling ten feet above. The white cushioned chairs, lined up in parallel rows, had small white tables separating every third seat. Posters on the walls provided the only pop of color in the entire area. Each poster was a marketing image of the happy dreams people had lived while being part of DS 7. Kevin glanced at the intake desks, four of them with a folding chair positioned in front and a nurse working behind. New dreamers occupied every desk at the moment. Kevin passed close enough to two soon-to-be dreamers to overhear their conversation.

"I didn't know you could buy bonus Karma points?"

"You can't, but you can buy Karma multipliers here. It's a risk though. If you're good, then you get to advance faster, but if you're bad, you may be back in DS 6."

Kevin laughed to himself. *If you need to buy bonuses, then you're never going to make it.* Kevin couldn't remember his dream life, but he knew he must have been something amazing. He had advanced to rank 82 and never once bought a multiplier. Kevin pushed open the door leading outside. A chill in the night air greeted him. It was fall in the Dream States, and the brisk winter was soon coming.

The dark outside was engulfing. There was no horizon and no stars in the artificial sky. The only light came from a spattering of lamps illuminating a small parking lot and one large spotlight shining on the two flags of the country.

One flag was the symbol of the Dream States. A half-cybernetic, half-organic brain diagram represented the union of technology and mind. The Dream States motto, *through our dreams we truly live*, inscribed across the bottom.

The other flag was that of the Reborn States of America. An eagle with wings spread was a throwback to a past image of freedom. It had been years since anyone saw an eagle alive or dead. The mind chip that it held in its claws was the real symbol of importance. It reflected the truth about the country. Without that chip, people would be slaves to memories of the past. It was the mind chip that gave all citizens true freedom, the ability to dream.

Passing a wooden sign on his way to the parking lot that said, **THANK YOU FOR VISITING! SEE YOU ON YOUR NEXT VISIT!** Kevin scoffed, "No, you won't."

The lot only held fifty vehicles in total. It was small for the massive facility that it serviced, but it was mainly used by the nurses and other employees. Most of the dreamers arrived by train. A few dreamers arrived by bus, having reached a new Dream State rank in their last dream, and having enough Z-credits to dream again right away. This was common practice in the earlier Dream States, but not as common with the higher ranks as it took longer to level up. There were only a few citizens who got permission to drive themselves.

Kevin looked past the lot to the train station that lay at the far end of the complex. It was small. An all-glass-walled building served as the waiting area. The current train was just finishing loading its passengers, which left the station empty. The windowless train came and went every thirty minutes. It constantly brought in new dreamers and took out those who had finished for the time being.

Kevin smiled as the train pulled away. He had ridden that train before. It was terrible. There was nothing worse than the trip back from a dream vacation surrounded by others who were just wishing to turn around and stay. The dream world was so much better than anything the real world could offer. Ahead of them were weeks of work without sleep or rest; behind them was freedom and fun. The ride would be quiet. The train car was a box of silent zombies staring at the seat back in front of them, trying as best they could to recollect one image from their past lives. It was a waste of effort. The burn was too efficient.

Kevin shook his head and walked down the row. There, under a streetlight, spotlighted with a red glow, sat his car. It was a vintage Fifth-Generation Electric Ford Mustang, one of the last of its kind made. Kevin had obtained special permission and even forfeited two dream trips to learn to drive and get the Mustang. It was completely worth it.

Everything from the exterior to the faux-leather steering wheel was stark white. It was a true classic. The red light of the streetlamp tinted its color, but it was not enough to mask the purity of the car.

"There you are. Did you miss me?" Kevin slid his hand across the hood of prized possession. It may have been a social faux pas to drive himself to the Dream States, but he didn't care. It was a little piece of the dream he got to live out for real. He grabbed the silver handle and pressed the button. With a click, the door opened, swinging on the front hinge upward, with a slight magnetic whine. Kevin sat down and felt the auto-conforming seat mold around him as the door descended back shut.

Kevin adjusted the rearview mirror. There was little need for it. Only the occasional bus would be on the road at the same time as Kevin. But it was the right thing to do, and if he was going to remember anything, it would be how to drive this car. As he grabbed the mirror, he looked at himself.

The face looking back at him was both correct and strange. Kevin studied his face. His medium-length black hair fell to the side of his forehead, sweeping and tucking behind his ear. His green eyes shined bright in stark contrast to his pale skin. Not seeing enough sun had turned his pigment. The only part of his face that wasn't albino was the five-o'clock-shadow beard that had grown during his dream. Kevin reached into his glove compartment and pulled out his laser razor. With a couple of quick passes and the smell of burning hair, he was clean shaven again.

"That's better." Kevin admired his now-bald, prominent chin. Satisfied with his appearance, he returned the razor to the glove compartment. He pressed two buttons on the top of the steering wheel, and the car came to life. A large screen turned on in the center console, and an automated voice spoke to Kevin as the screen displayed the same text.

"Welcome. Where would you like to go?"

Kevin responded, having practice with the commands. "Cancel auto drive, display directions Z-Bank ES 3, mute voice, enable pedal controls, tune media station news preset, dim screen brightness level 1."

The computer thought for a moment. The interior lights dimmed to a near-off level, news began coming through the speakers, and two hand pedals attached to the steering wheel lit up, one green and one red. This Mustang was the last car to have pedal control, the reason Kevin wanted it. Most vehicles only allowed for speed input or auto drive—where was the fun in that?

Kevin grabbed the steering wheel and squeezed the green hand pedal. The car pulled forward with a silent drive, its motors engaging. He pulled out of the entryway to the small parking lot and down the main drive. A large bus drove past, going the opposite direction. Only four faces in the large passenger bus pressed to the window.

Welcome to DS 7, Kevin thought as he drove by. *You can have my spot.*

Kevin watched the massive blue-neon Dream State 7 sign disappear in the rearview. He wondered what his dream life could have been like to jump him to rank 82. The thought still occupied his mind a few minutes later as he turned onto the mass-transit interstate.

As usual, he was alone. Few drove on these roads anymore. The only vehicles would be a truck moving some kind of equipment, a bus of upgrades, like the one he had just passed, or the red-and-white vans shuttling nurses in and out for their shifts.

The long trek had begun. It would be a long twenty-hour drive. As he sped down the dark highway, he listened to news radio.

"Which is why Z-notes have been on the rise in value lately."

"On another note, the DS board has approved the creation of an ultra-exclusive DS 11. That's right, 10 is no longer the highest rank. Eleven will be for only a select few and will include complete pre-dream detail selection."

Wow, thought Kevin. *Pre-dream detail selection would be awesome. I could choose to be born as a genius or with the genetic traits to be tall. I wonder how far they can go with that. Could I be born a superhero?*

"When asked about how this new Dream State would affect the current rankings, Norma Fultoe, press secretary, had this to say. 'DS 11 will be so exclusive and only handle such a select group of dreamers that most of the population will not be affected. The only rankings that may see a quicker elevation will be those currently ranked 81 or higher.' So it looks like those of you who are up there in rankings already you may be in for a treat in the form of..."

Kevin didn't hear the rest of the statement. He was too busy doing a little celebratory dance. His rank was riding the fast track. Already at level 8 and now getting a jump-start on his journey to level 9, he was more than ahead of the curve. Kevin was a shooting star. Kevin turned off the radio to celebrate without the monotonous voices of the news.

Kevin was celebrating, hitting the steering wheel out of joy, as he passed the sign for DS 6. He remembered when he thought DS 6 was amazing. Now the sign itself showed the lower quality of its dreams. It wasn't the neon glow of DS 7; instead, it was back lit plastic. Simple high-density polyvinyl and three colorful letters lit brightly in the night. *I wonder what DS 8's sign will look like*, thought Kevin, as his brief outburst of joy ended. Now back to the drive.

Kevin glanced as he passed the off-ramps for each Dream State. DS 5 took another hour to reach from DS 6, DS 4 another hour later, DS 3 thirty minutes after that, DS 2 thirty minutes after that, and DS 1 another five minutes after DS 2. Each sign became simpler until he reached DS 1, which was a simple road sign lit only by one light—the second had burned out some time ago. He could still see the reflective paint of the well-lit sign for DS 2 down the road. These first two states were for first-time dreamers and youth education.

A few minutes later, he saw the sign:

HEADLIGHTS ON MAX.
NO SERVICES FOR 1,000 MILES.

The drive through the non-dream lands was boring, to understate it. This long stretch of lightly used and even more lightly maintained road led through a land of near darkness. Overhead, the solar cloud, created a few hundred years earlier from nanotechnology, soaked in all the sun's rays, converting it to electricity for the Dream States. Kevin looked at the clock on the car dial: 08:00. The sun would be up by now, if he only could see it. Instead, he drove the lonely road, headed not home but to work. His mind wandered as the road barely even twisted. He thought about what his next life could entail. Would he be rich? Would he be a powerful man? Would he find love? Kevin's mind stuck on this thought.

What is love? He thought to himself. Kevin could recite a definition of what love was, but he could not even comprehend for a second the emotion or feeling of what love would be. *Have I ever felt love? I can't remember my dream lives. Did I ever fall in love in any of my dreams? Even if I did, does that count as actual love? Can a computer program even mimic authentic emotions? If it can't create and show love, how can I possibly know if anything about that past life ever even happened?* A lone tree in a field caught Kevin's attention. A crack in the solar cloud shone down on it. Green leaves soaked up all the light they could. I should report that, he thought. As Kevin watched that tree disappear into the distance, he knew he never would.

Looking for distraction, he turned the radio back on.

"Dream State 6 was the most recent victim of vandalization by the public-menace group known as 'The Awake.' Today we have Calvin Jardley, an agent for the Coalition Corporation, here with us to talk about this string of increasingly daring acts by the group. Calvin, thanks for being here."

"Thank you for having me."

"Mr. Jardley, the painting of the words Stay Awake! on the entrance sign to Dream State 6 is only the most recent action taken by the Awake. What is going on? Why are these people acting against a resource that is so vital not only to our economy but also to the full expression of the minds and lives of, well, everyone?"

"Well, first you have to put yourself in the shoes of these terrorists, and know they are terrorists. Aside from painting this sign and other acts of vandalism, they have also kidnapped a number of people from the Dream States, some of whom were actively dreaming and in the process killed several security-force members who gave their lives in the defense of these innocents. So, as difficult as it is, you must try to understand them."

"Do you understand these monsters, Mr. Jardley?"

"Not only that, but I actually pity them."

"You what!"

"Please, let me explain. These people who call themselves 'The Awake' are a group of people who are cursed with the inability to dream. Something about their brains doesn't allow them to stable dream, at all. You put them in DS 10 with the best doctors and prescriptions, and their minds will kick them awake like that." The man snapped his fingers.

"That can't excuse them for kidnapping and murder, though."

"I'm not saying that it does. I'm just saying you have to understand why they hate something so pure and so vital to our way of life. Somehow, in their minds, they have made the association that because they are un-linked to a computer, their lives are better for it. They have twisted their weakness into a positive. Now they are taking people and trying to fight against the dream to convert others to their mission."

"What are you saying, Mr. Jardley?"

"I'm saying that they believe they are in the right. They believe that the Dream States are not a blessing but a curse on this land, and they are the ones to cure us all of our addiction."

"So, how do we reach them and make them understand and respect our way of life?"

"You can't. The only way to stop terrorists with complete and utter belief in their cause is to either outlast their will or end them."

"Wow. Thank you for coming on, Mr. Jardley."

"Thanks for having me."

"That's your 0-900 update. Be sure to stay tuned next for the market news with Gail Suthers."

DS 6! Wow, I must have just missed it! Excitement made Kevin's heart race a little. He reached and turned off the radio again. *Unable to stable a dream, how terrible that would be. What would you do with your, well I guess you wouldn't need Z-credits if you couldn't dream? What would you do with all your extra time? The real world is work and monotony, and boring. The dream is your real life. You can be anyone, anything, anywhere.* Kevin smiled, realizing he had just recited the marketing brochure that Eli and Anders had used to sell people on the idea of stable dreaming.

"Autopilot engage." Kevin leaned back as the car's automatic driving system took over. He laid the seat back and reached for the serum cord that fed from the door. He plugged the cable into his arm and felt the familiar pump of chemicals. Kevin closed his eyes as the drug-induced sleep overtook him. The last thought that crossed his mind before he fell into a dreamless sleep was, *I wonder if they feel love.*

Kevin's black slumber ended as the small reservoir of drugs hit empty. He opened his eyes to find sunlight penetrating the horizon ahead. He adjusted his seat back to a normal position and rubbed his eyes. *Wow, that's bright. I forgot how it is, coming out of the Dream States. I feel like I always forget that.* He laughed to himself.

"Computer, how long until arriving at destination?"

The computer chimed back. "Ten hours, thirteen minutes."

"Argh..." Kevin let out a sigh of aggravation as he laid his head on the top of the inactive steering wheel.

CHAPTER 2

ERROR CORRECTING

T en hours and thirteen minutes of driving later, Kevin climbed out of the driver's seat and stretched his back. It had been a long drive. He had parked in a small lot on the outskirts of the tree line that surrounded the modern city of Z-York. The surrounding forest had overtaken what used to be suburbs. Only this small lot, meant for emergency parking for security forces, was maintained. Kevin had gotten special permission, at the cost of a boatload of Z-credits, to park his car here.

He climbed up a set of two-story stairs that led to the elevated platform of the maglev train that sat at the corner of the lot. Kevin checked the schedule on the wall. He had gotten lucky—only a ten-minute wait. Kevin stood staring into the distance until a shine from the left caught his eye. The train approached quickly and slowed suddenly. The computer seemed surprised to be stopping at this wayward, seldom-used station.

With a soft click, the magnetic locks released and opened a large sliding door on the side of the train. Kevin stepped inside. He found a seat on the far side, between two people, and sat down. He heard the magnetic lock reengage the now-closed door as he rested in the cushioned seat. His neighbors on the train were looking at him, confused about why he would have gotten on at this station. Kevin just stared straight ahead, looking at the back of the seat in front of him with a practiced disinterest. He took a little hidden pleasure at their curiosity. The train pulled away, continuing its journey into Z-York. Fifty minutes later, the train's AI conductor came over a set of speakers hidden in the ceiling.

"We are now pulling into all-forks station. All passengers exit here. Only Z-Bank employees, level 30 or higher permitted on the train past this stop. Punishment for improper train usage is Z-fines and demotion."

The train slowed as it entered the major switching station of Z-York. Kevin maintained his stare at nothing in particular. The only break his gaze encountered was the passenger seated next to the window pushing past Kevin. He could feel others looking at him as they disembarked at the station, still trying to unfurl the puzzle of this late train entrant. He imagined they must think that something was going on with a high-ranking Z-Bank employee. What rank could this mystery man be? Kevin smiled to himself. If only they knew he was only a Level 42. He had ascended to a high rank compared to many, but it was still a mediocre position in the ultra-exclusive Z-Bank workforce. The Z-Bank had been named as a callback to earlier days when banks were the center of the financial heart of the world. Now this Z-Bank was the nucleus of all computer memory. On the outside, it was a massive, 150-story, gold-plated building that shined bright, reflecting the sun. Inside, a massive structure of interconnected servers and networking cables ran all the Dream States.

A few minutes later, the train stopped at the level 30 Z-Bank station. Kevin stood and fell in line with the few other train occupants who had stayed. As the door opened, they each held their arm out, letting a security guard scan their barcodes.

"Welcome back," the guard said to Kevin, more out of practiced casual courtesy than actual enthusiasm.

Kevin nodded to the guard and headed up a large white-marble and gold-embellished staircase that led from the train platform to the employee entrance to the Z-Bank. The Z-Bank's employee entrance at this higher level was on floor 30. It serviced workers from floor 30 to floor 45. After a few more promotions, Kevin could move up to the entrance at floor 46. There wasn't much of a difference as far as entrances go, but the locker room would be nicer. Kevin glanced to his left as he reached the top of the stairway. A motivational poster hung on the wall. He had seen it many times before, but he still stopped and admired it. He read the words written across the bottom of a picture of the Dream States flag. It flew in a pitch-black night sky, lit only by a spotlight. *Only in our dreams do we truly live.*

Kevin looked down the wide hall he had just reached at the stair top. *How true that is*, he thought. In front of him was a plain, white-floored and white-walled walkway. At the end of the hall were double doors that led to the editing room, where he was now employed as an error corrector. A door to the right led to the locker room. There was no life ahead of him here, only work—just the same thing he had done for the last twelve non-dreaming months. He shook his head. *Just make it through, get back to the Dream States and you can have life again. I wish I could remember those lives. They had to have been better than this.*

Kevin walked the short distance to the locker-room door and reached his arm under a scanner, allowing it to read his ID barcode. *Beep.* He flinched as he felt the barcode activate. The guard's scanner was a simple reader; this scanner was more powerful. It activated the bioelectric link from his barcode to the mind chip. It was verifying the security clearance to access this level's locker room and sending a strange sensation the length of Kevin's arm. He flexed his hand twice and shook off the sensation. Kevin walked inside and pushed the now-unlocked door open. A minute later, he was at a locker, opening it with his eight-digit code.

"The prodigal son returns!"

Kevin flinched, as the yelled proclamation was only about four feet away.

"Whoa, jumpy much? Did you get murdered in your last dream?"

Kevin smiled, seeing Thairn's familiar toothy grin, round face and shaved head. "I don't know, but if I was, it must have been an assassination or something like that. You're looking at a level 8 dreamer now."

"Shut up." Thairn's mouth was agape. He sat down on the wooden bench that was bolted to the floor between two rows of lockers, shaking his head. "I don't understand. You work two weeks at a time, dream without bonuses, and move up faster than any of us."

"Maybe I'm just better than you?"

Thairn's wide smile highlighted the sarcastic tone in his voice. "Or you're cheating."

"Really?" Kevin returned Thairn's the playful tone.

"I'm just saying,"—Thairn put his hands up—"we were the same work and dream ranks a few cycles ago. I've moved up in work faster than you, so I get to buy bonuses, yet somehow your dream rank has skyrocketed. Something doesn't make sense. Wait, are you working three weeks and spending the credits on special multipliers?"

"No way. Work here for three weeks? That would be terrible." Kevin scrunched his brow at the idea.

"It's not that bad. I mean, at least we get to be in the dream network. Error correcting is the best of the jobs. We get to walk the dream and solve puzzles. If you ask me, fixing a few extra broken code instances to get those bonuses, I'll do it," Thairn said, shrugging his shoulders. As he stood and opened his locker, he continued. "Besides, working for longer has been shown to result in longer dreams. It's not like we have anything else to do. Can you imagine what it would be like to have a house to go to or a family, and just waste time doing, well, nothing?"

Kevin shook his head. "No, but I guess judging by the people we help in the dream network, that we all spend a lot of our dream time doing just that."

"We don't help people. We help the dream." Thair corrected him.

"Yeah, you know what I mean. Either way, I'm not spending more days working than I need to. Time in that pod doesn't pass like it does there, you know that. Three weeks of real time in a drug-induced semi-awake state doesn't interest me at all."

"It honestly feels the same as two weeks, man." Thairn stripped off his clothes and hung them on the hangers inside the locker. He pulled out the tight, wire-coated jumpsuit that would connect his body and consciousness to the dream. He slid his feet inside and pulled it snugly over his body. "Besides, man, it definitely beats working for a month in the security section, just scanning wrists, or in the bankers rank, typing accounting numbers into a computer, or the production states, just quality control, checking mind chips and converting the protein-plant hybrids that the agriculture section grows into liquid to feed everyone. Those poor agriculture people have to spend three months working just to dream once." Thairn zipped the side of his suit up, securing its fit. "Oh, and not to mention the maintenance and energy workers who have to scale the top side of the solar panels. Have you seen how scorched those guys get?" He shook at the thought of their sunburnt faces. "Can you imagine being so un-pale?"

"Never."

"Only job I'd take other than programmer is Eliander," Thairn said, laughing. "Maybe I'd be the head of this whole place. I'll take that office on level 150."

"Yeah, I'm sure that'd be nice. Just a little DNA change and you'd be good to go." Kevin threw his clothes into a pile at the bottom of the locker and pulled out his jumpsuit. The diode-coated latex material fit tight as he pulled it over his body. He reached back and plugged the small cord at the neck of the suit into his mind chip.

Thairn closed his locker, ready to go to work. "Well, man, if I never see you again, dream well."

"You too. Although, somehow we both always end up in the locker room together, so I'm sure I'll see you again."

Thairn laughed and shouted over his shoulder as he walked out of the room. "If you're lucky!"

Kevin smiled to himself. *If friendship was a thing that existed in the real world, Thairn would probably be my best friend.* Kevin closed his locker. He turned and walked back to the main hallway. A minute later, he pushed his way through the double doors and into the main level of the programming room.

Kevin had seen this room many times, the exact number he couldn't remember, but it still made him smile. The entire programming hall was a massive three-dimensional web. The head managers for this area were in the center nucleus, about twenty feet above the floor of the room.

A massive glass column shooting straight up from the floor supported this central orb. Inside its clear walls, fiber-optic cable glowed a bright bluish-white light. It tinted the room an artificial UV, while running up through the ceiling another twenty feet above the top of the room. Kevin began weaving his way through the tangle of staircases that connected the web of programming orbs. He glanced up each staircase, seeing how it led either from the floor to the center orb or from the ceiling down to the orb. A number of spherical programming stations dotted each. People sat in most of them, working in the dream network, error correcting.

After a short walk, Kevin began the ascent up a short, steep staircase near the center column. He was soon on the small ring around the manager's center orb. A man inside gave him a polite nod. Kevin nodded back and turned to climb a long stairway that led to the top corner of the room. Most people, as they grew in seniority and gained the ability to choose their programming pod, would vie to be closer to management, hoping to be noticed. Kevin, however, chose the highest sphere. He enjoyed looking down at the room, having a solid wall to his back. It gave him perspective and a sense of security. The downside was the climb. Sure, during Dream State visits, electronic stimulation maintained muscles, and oxygen pumps kept cardiovascular systems healthy, but climbing a flight of stairs still took Kevin's breath away.

"Phew," Kevin let out as he reached the top corner of the room. Hunched over to avoid hitting the ceiling with his head, he turned and sat on the step for a second, looking down at the room. He could see the pods lining the stairs he had just climbed. A pair mounted on either side, separated by just enough room to give space for maintenance workers. Kevin smiled, looking at the pod to his left. It had an *under repair* sticker on its door. It had been "under repair" for as long as he could remember. Kevin liked it that way—just another hint of privacy. Kevin looked to his right at the pod that he would call home for the next two weeks. It sat dark, a glass ball with a cushioned lounge chair inside. He reached out and typed his code into the small keypad. A circular door rotated open, and the ball illuminated, displaying a control panel across the front of the glass. Light turned on below Kevin's feet. Through the gaps in the metal steps, he could see the light from the fiber-optic cable connecting his pod to the central orb. He followed the light until it joined with the other cables from the closest pair of programming pods. Kevin took a deep breath and slid into his programming sphere. He sat in the lounge chair and reached back, checking that the cord from his mind chip was securely connected to his suit's cable. Then he plugged the cord leading from the chair into another port in his suit. The wires in his suit lit up for a moment and then dulled down.

>>>**CONNECTING**>>>
>>>**CONNECTED**>>>

Kevin read the text on the screen that was the entire glass wall in front of him. He grabbed the tube for sleep serum that hung from above and inserted it through one of his nostrils, his gag reflex making the process difficult. Kevin then reached back and found the headset mounted on the back of the lounge seat. He put it on. It was a helmet that looked like it had been cut in half. It covered one eye, leaving the other open to see the programming screen. Kevin's thoughts manifested into code.

>>>CLOSE POD ACCESS
>>>POD ACCESS CLOSING>>>

Kevin heard the circular door swing shut and the ventilation system engage. He cracked his neck, preparing for the next step.

>>>LOGIN
>>> QUERY>>>
>>>ID>>>
>>>925387
>>> LOGIN INITIATED >>>

Kevin felt his mind chip engage as the system logged him in. A mild headache began as the helmet increased its power. To program, a person had to split their consciousness. It was a strange and unnerving feeling to have one half of your brain in the dream network and the other half awake and alert. Kevin had gone through intense training to master this feeling. It had taken a few tries, but now he was fairly used to it. Still, the initial split was less than fun.

>>>LOGIN COMPLETE>>>

Kevin blinked his eye that wasn't in the helmet. He read the code on the control screen. Using the thoughts on the exposed brain side, he entered code into the control screen.

>>>OPEN VIEW WINDOW

A black screen opened to the top of the control panel. It was a live look in on what his dreaming experience was like. At the same time in his dream, a small window showing the coding screen opened as well.

>>>SHIFT AWARENESS TO DREAM 100%

Kevin's mind jumped into the black dream state, but he could still see the coding window now floating in the top right of his view.

>>> ID 925387 LOAD ASSIGNED TASK LIST

In the small view window of code, a list of tasks and error corrections began scrolling through. After a few seconds, it stopped scrolling. Kevin read through the tasks.

>>>12: YETI PACIFIC NORTHWEST 1975>>>
>>>13: POSSESSION UNITED KINGDOM 1653>>>
>>>14: APPARITION BROOKLYN 1880>>>
>>>15: TIME TRAVEL NEW YORK 2008 TO 1912>>>

Kevin stopped reading there. Ghosts and glances of impossible creatures were issues that needed fixing, most often caused by an error in the code showing a creature or a memory from a past life. But time travel was more serious. That meant a dreamer's code had slipped from one dream era to another entirely, not just in their own network. That threatened the stability of the dream. The knowledge a dreamer could bring into another era could cause overlap errors and overload servers, as each era had its own server farm. Connecting dreams from both date stamps could cause conflicts that could lead to more issues and possibly even a network crash.

>>>OPEN TASK 15: ID 925387

Kevin's mind and consciousness leapt into the Dream States, circa 1912.

Kevin stepped out of the rain and shook it from his over-coat as he entered T.E. Fitzgerald's Bar. He scanned the room until he found the man he was looking for. Kevin sauntered across the room, his leather shoes clicking against the tile. He sat down on a barstool next to a man with his head firmly planted in his hands. Kevin looked him up and down. While his hands covered his face, Kevin could see his neck-length blond hair laid messily over his shirt collar. The man wore a classic black tuxedo that was wrinkled from recent use.

"What are you drinking?" Kevin asked the man, who hadn't even acknowledged his presence. Before the man could respond, the bartender answered for him.

"He's not drinking anything. Just taking up a barstool."

"It's not busy," the man said through his fingers.

"Puritan?" Kevin asked the man.

"No," he answered.

"Ha!" the bartender injected. "This man's crazy. Don't waste your time talking to him. He claims to be from the future."

Kevin turned to the bartender. "Well, that's not some-thing you hear every day."

"That's what the man says."

"Did he tell you anything interesting about the future? Are the Highlanders going to do well this year?"

"No, but even I could tell you we're going to be mis-fortunate." The bartender shrugged his eyebrows. "Just tried to pay me using some plastic card."

"Plastic card?"

"Yeah, he said that in the future, they don't carry money."

"I'm right here," the man interjected, annoyed that the two men were talking about him like he wasn't even hearing them.

"So you are," the bartender snapped back. "That stool is for paying customers. I think it's time for you to move on to another establishment."

"I don't—" the man started.

"I'll buy two beers, please. One for me and one for the man from the future," Kevin said as he slid a dollar bill across the counter.

The bartender looked at the dollar and walked away. He returned with two beers and Kevin's change.

"Thanks," the future man said. "I'm Tyson, by the way."

Kevin took a sip of his beer. "Tyson, that's a unique name?"

"Yeah, it's like the chicken." Tyson took a rather large swig of his beer.

The bartender jumped back into the conversation in disbelief. "Like the chicken?"

"Yeah, you know Tyson chicken. The huge meat company," Tyson replied.

"What is wrong with you, son?" The bartender turned to Kevin. "Sir, I think you may not want to give any more charity to this man."

"I'll give charity to whom I please."

The bartender shook his head and walked down the bar to greet a new group of men who had just entered.

"1935," Kevin said, slightly above a whisper.

"What?" Tyson asked back, more confused than hard of hearing.

"It's 1912. Tyson Foods won't be founded until 1935."

"How?" Tyson's eyes grew large.

"How long have you been here?"

Tyson blinked. "Uh... like half an hour. Wait, how do you know—"

"No, not how long have you been here in this bar? How long have you been in 1912?"

"Uh, like six hours. Wait, how do you know about Tyson chicken?" Tyson's voice was becoming almost desperate.

Kevin smiled out of the corner of his mouth. "What? You think you're the only time traveler?"

"You?" Tyson's eyes grew wider than he thought possible at the implication.

Kevin just shrugged his shoulders. "You could say that."

"Oh, my god. Thank God. How, how did this happen? How are we here?"

Kevin turned and took a serious tone. "I'll explain that later, but first you need to tell me exactly what you've done since you've been here."

"Uh, I mean, I've just been walking around."

"No. Not good enough," Kevin pressed. "What exactly did you do? Did you leave anything from the future here, in this time? Where's your cell phone?"

Tyson blinked, a little surprised by the sudden tone shift.

Kevin grabbed Tyson's wrist, hard. Tyson flinched to pull away, but Kevin gripped it tighter and spoke with an anger in his growl. "Look, time travel is dangerous, not just for the future, but for you. If you brought anything back and the wrong people find it, they will come after you. If that happens, I won't help you. You'll be a pincushion in a lab someplace until you finally break." Kevin let go of Tyson's hand, shifting to a sympathetic body language. Kevin had played this part before. His act was well rehearsed. "I'm sorry. I don't mean to be so aggressive. It's just," Kevin paused for effect, "my brother and I used to time travel together, until one day, he made a mistake. They took him, and no matter how much I time leaped, I couldn't stop it. Some things just lock in."

>>>INITIATE SYMPATHETIC SINGLE TEARDROP RIGHT EYE, FALL SPEED MEDIUM-SLOW, EMOTIONAL ENERGY VIBRATION OUTPUT MAX>>>

Kevin mentally entered the code to induce his dream persona to cry. He could put on a good act, but the one emotion he couldn't fake were tears. Something inside him had died at a young age. It was the trait that had gotten him the editor's job. He couldn't cry, even when dreaming.

So he had to hard code that emotion in. The effect had achieved its desired goal.

Tyson swallowed hard. "No," he said and took another swig of the beer. "I woke up this morning in my apartment, or I don't know. I woke up, and I was in an old bed in a room with all this antique stuff in it. My phone wasn't on the nightstand where I had plugged it in the night before. I thought—" Tyson started laughing, cutting off his speech.

"You thought what?"

"Last night, or whatever you want to call it, I had a late night." Tyson placed particular emphasis on the word "late."

Kevin motioned to the tuxedo Tyson was wearing. "A wedding?"

"My ex-wife's wedding."

"Oh." Kevin pinched the bridge of his nose.

"Yeah. I didn't ruin it or anything, but I guess it hit me hard. So when I woke up in that room, I thought at first that I had fallen asleep at one of those boutique hotels or something. Then I walked outside and kept walking and kept walking. After a few hours walking in a living history lesson, I needed a drink. So I came in here, and you know the rest."

"Interesting."

"So, are you from the government?" Tyson asked in a suspicious tone.

"Why would you say that?" Kevin answered with the same reluctance.

"I'm a police officer, a detective, to be specific. I can tell when people are lying. That whole story about your brother and those tears..."

>>> **DISABLE SESSION TRACKING**
>>> **RUN MASK ALTKEVSESS2501**

Kevin watched the code stream, hiding his actions from the simulation tracking and management.

>>> TERMINATE EMOTIONAL BUFFERS/ALL
>>> DISABLE PERSONALITY MATCHING
>>> DISABLE NLP REVERSE PROGRAMMING

Kevin's appearance and facial emotions altered subtly in response to his code entering. He was breaking protocol by being one hundred percent his true self. It was against regulations because introducing your true self into the Dream State simulation could cause interactions in your mind when you dreamed.

Tyson was intently watching Kevin, noticing the change in him. "What just happened?"

"You want to know the truth?"

Tyson nodded.

"This is all a dream."

Tyson studied Kevin's face. He blinked a few times, trying to comprehend.

>>> RUN EMOTIONAL BUFFERS/ALL
>>> ENABLE PERSONALITY MATCHING
>>> ENABLE NLP REVERSE PROGRAMMING
>>> TERMINATE MASK ALTKEVSESS2501
>>> ENABLE SESSION TRACKING

Kevin's personality and face subtly changed back. He smiled. "It's time for you to wake up." He deftly pulled a syringe from his coat pocket. Motioning like he was patting Tyson on the back, he plunged the needle deep into his back and depressed the plunger. Within a second, Tyson's eyes clouded. Kevin had used this serum before. Injecting it shut down the target's ability to talk and made them subservient to a certain host. In this case, Tyson became an unwilling follower of Kevin. "I can see you're ready to go home."

Tyson nodded.

"Good, don't worry. You won't remember this. You'll remember some, and not for long." Kevin stood from the barstool. "I'm going to leave now and wait for you in the alley to the side of this bar. You're going to wait exactly two minutes and then leave and meet me there."

Tyson nodded.

Kevin stood and walked out. Two minutes later, Tyson joined him in the alley. Kevin produced a key and opened a black, rusted door at the back of the alley, motioning Tyson inside. Kevin followed and closed the door behind him.

Kevin made sure that no one was around and could see Tyson and him in the small back room of what he guessed was a dry cleaner. He looked at Tyson's emotionally blank face.

A chat box opened in his peripherals.

/// IS THERE AN ISSUE 925387 ///

...

/// No issue ///

...

/// THEN COMPLETE ASSIGNED TASK 15 AND BEGIN OTHER TASKS ///

...

/// About to fix his mind code now ///

...

/// JUST TERMINATE THE ERRONEUS DREAM AND BEGIN OTHER TASKS ///

...

/// Programming solution will have fewer ripples ///

Kevin closed the chat box, ending the conversation. He wanted to shake his head in annoyance, but knew that management was watching. Opening the coding screen, Kevin began looking at the code that made up Tyson's current dream.

/// 925387 WHAT IS THE DELAY? ///

Kevin kept scanning the code, not even bothering to acknowledge management. He had done this enough times to see the programming that needed fixing. A few inserted commands later, and he closed the coding window. "It's okay, Tyson, ID 8923221. I can't delete your memory, but I corrupted the code well enough that it will all be a strange dream. A few weeks later, your mind will write over it and you won't remember this at all. Now, go to sleep."

Tyson nodded his head once and then let his head fall to his chest. Tyson disappeared as his code began running correctly, pulling him back to the century and location where he belonged.

>>> ENGAGE INVISIBILITY PROGRAM
>>> TRANSPORT CONCSIOUSNESS TRACKING 8923221

Kevin's consciousness jumped into a modern condo. Kevin looked at the tile floor he was standing on. His reflection was missing from the glossy polish. The invisibility protocol was doing its job. He turned and scanned the room. Tyson was lying in bed, on top of his covers. Tyson was back in his own apartment, in his own time. Kevin wanted to ensure the success of his programming. He looked at the flat-screen television mounted on the wall.

>>> TELEVISION DISPLAY ON, PROGRAMMING: DOCUMENTARY, TIME PERIOD: 1912, LOCATION: NEW YORK CITY, FOCUS: BAR SCENE

Kevin watched as a PBS broadcast began playing. The sun had already risen through the window, and the noises of outside were filtering through as well. Sounds of ambulances and construction loudly echoed above the din of traffic.

>>> ACTION: 8923221 WAKE UP

Tyson coughed and sat up in bed. Looking around with bloodshot eyes, his gaze settled on the television. Staring for a moment, he searched for something, a memory he couldn't quite recall. Giving up, he shook his head and rubbed his face before reaching for the remote and turning off the television. Tyson walked out of the bedroom and into the bathroom.

>>> **ID 925387 TASK 15 COMPLETE**
>>> **ID 925387 LOAD ASSIGNED TASK LIST**

Okay, who's next? Kevin thought as he scanned the task list.

Over a thousand coding fixes and strange program instances later, Kevin was washing the blood off his hands in a wooden bucket. He sat on the ground outside a canvas tent in the 1800s. The glow of small fires barely held back the darkness of the night. Kevin admired the beauty of the code that dictated the waving of the flag of the Confederate States of America. He looked back inside the tent at the noise of a whimper. The man whose code Kevin had just finished reprogramming was an injured Union soldier whose death code had frozen, leaving him in a loop of agony. To not raise suspicion or cause other storyline issues, he had pretended to be a battlefield surgeon.

Poor bastard, Kevin thought. *I can't imagine having a loop that keeps you stuck in a near-death pain for three days. It's okay. It'll be over soon.*

>>> **ID 925387 TASK 1650 COMPLETE**
>>> **ID 925387 QUERY LOGIN TIME**
>>> **ID 925387 LOGIN TIME: 12 DAYS 3 HOURS 32 MINUTES**

Two days left.

>>> **ID 925387 LOAD ASSIGNED TASK LIST**
>>> **970 GRASS UNDER GROWING 983**
>>> **1390 VIEWS OF PAST 2190**
>>> **2000 INCORRECT STAR LAYOUT 1223**

Boring. "Grass Under Growing," really? That's a task for new programmers, not a high-level editor. I guess it's the end of my task list, so I can't be too upset about simple tasks. Three more and then I'll be freelance. Kevin cracked his neck. *I hate freelance. Management always watches so closely. Hmmm, I wonder.*

>>> **SHIFT AWARENESS TO DREAM 50%**

Kevin's eye opened to the world of the programming room. He scanned down the stairs, looking at the management center. A manager occupied every one of the twenty programming pods. *Shift change.* Now was his chance.

>>> **DISABLE SESSION TRACKING**
>>> **RUN MASK ALTKEVSESS2501**
>>> **RUN TRACKSUBROUTDREAMRECENT_X5_HI95.0ALP**
>>>ID>>>
>>>925387
>>>........>>>>

Kevin closely watched the management pod. *As long as the pods are full, they should be in their end-of-shift meeting.* He glanced at the code running across the screen, still running the sub-routine he had created and hidden deep in the Dream States mainframes. *Come on. Let's go.* As if to answer his thoughts, the screen populated with a result.

>>> **ID 925387 DREAM, LAST FOUND** >>>
>>> **DISPLAY OBITUARY**

A text-only obituary, written as a celebration of life by someone dreaming as Phillip Welsh's family, filled his view window. Kevin quickly scanned the text, glancing every few seconds at the management pod. As Kevin finished reading the life summary of his most recent dream, he couldn't believe his life had been so... normal. *A rug salesman? How could I only have been a simple small-business owner with a family, "full of love," and reached the eightieth percentile? That doesn't make sense.* Motion drew his attention. Half of the management pods were opening their doors. The meeting was over.

>>> **TERMINATE TRACKSUBROUTDREAMRECE NT_X5_HI95.0ALP**

The code screen went blank.

>>> **TERMINATE MASK ALTKEVSESS2501**
>>> **ENABLE SESSION TRACKING**
>>> **SHIFT AWARENESS TO DREAM 100%**

Kevin's eye closed as his mind shifted back to the Dream States simulation.

>>>**OPEN TASK 970: ID 925387**

Kevin's consciousness transported to a grassy hill in the middle of England. A thick fog rose in the valley below to his north, covering the lowland in a dense pinkish haze, colored by the early morning light. A bird flew overhead, calling to the morning sky with a loud caw. Kevin watched the bird soar high above. He spun in a circle, searching for any other sign of life. There was only the chirping of a cricket coming from the tree line to the west. Looking down at his feet, he understood why he was there. The grass was not just growing slower than coded; it was growing fractal. The "blades" had taken the shape of small square blocks and were circling out in a ring nearly thirty feet wide.

Weird, Kevin thought as he reached down and plucked a chain of the small-block grass from the ground. *How could this have happened? This shouldn't even be possible. Then again, a carpet salesman who did nothing of historical mark or discovery with his life shouldn't be a level 80 dreamer. I shouldn't be increasing in rank with such a normal life, or maybe that's the key? Maybe every other dreamer is terrible. No, that can't be right. Why me, then? What makes me so special?*

CHAPTER 3

DREAM STATE 8

What makes me so special? The thought had stuck with Kevin for the last two days of this work shift. It had haunted his mind as he fixed coding errors. It had been on his mind as he logged out and changed from the programming suit back to his regular clothes.

What makes me so special? The question consumed Kevin all the way until he reached his car in the lonely parking lot. He sat in the car and finally, because of mental exhaustion, replaced the confused sentiment with another, one of desire to escape. *I don't want to think about it anymore. Get me to Dream State 8.*

The drive flew by, a blur of landscape as Kevin made his way back to the promised relaxation of The Dream States. He could feel the excitement building in him. An hour left of driving and he would arrive at the entrance for Dream State 8. He had switched the car to manual after Dream State 6. The auto-driver was too slow. Now he was flying down the highway with the accelerator handle squeezed to the max. The electric motors whined as Kevin soared down the interstate.

Kevin had turned the one-hour drive into thirty-seven minutes. The miles raced by as fast as his heart beat in his chest. As Kevin took the exit, turning to the entrance of Dream State 8, his eyes widened with anticipation. A short drive later, he could see the gate. A large, white stucco wall over thirty feet wide stood on either side of an ebony gate. On the left side, bright-white neon spelled out the word "Dream." On the right, the bright neon spelled "State 8."

It shined bright and beautiful in contrast to the darkness of the artificially covered sky. "This is so cool!" Kevin couldn't contain his intrigue inside his body any longer.

As he drove the Mustang up to the gate, a short man in an all-white guard's uniform stepped out. The man had black slicked-back hair and a clean-shaven face. "Welcome to Dream State 8. Home of your next life. Please make your ID scannable, sir," he said with a level of professionalism that had clearly become second nature. Kevin pulled back his sleeve and held his arm out the window of the car. The guard slid a white plastic cylinder around Kevin's forearm. It cinched down, securing itself.

Kevin flinched visibly as it scanned his arm, activating his mind chip in the process. "You bio-scan here?"

"Yes, sir. Is this your first time in Dream State 8?"

"Yes," Kevin flinched as the cylinder pulled the deepest code from his mind chip to verify his identity.

The cylinder chimed, and a green light illuminated on the side of it. "Welcome," the guard said while removing the now-unlatched scanner. "What you're going to do is drive straight down this road," he said as he pointed past the gate and into the Dream State. "When you hit the neon sign two miles in, you're going to go to the right. It will lead you first through the metal forest. That's quite an amazing sight. Then you'll drive onto the river bridge and follow the road around the curve, and it will take you straight to the main lobby of our Dream State."

"River bridge?"

"Yes,"—the guard paused for a moment—"I think it will be better for you to find out on your own. Enjoy your stay. Oh, and just park the car out front if the greeter isn't there."

"Greeter? Wait, do others drive here?"

"Sir, there is no train into our Dream State. Most of our dreamers are driven here by their drivers." The guard winked as he stepped back into the gatehouse. He pressed his hand on a bio-scanner.

In front of Kevin, the two massive ebony gate doors creaked softly as they opened inward. Kevin smiled as he saw the long, straight road ahead of him light up. Flood-lights three feet off the ground, mounted on rounded arms, lit the way. Kevin took a deep breath, attempting to calm his mind, and sped up. Kevin didn't look back to watch the ebony doors swing shut; his focus stayed forward. In the distance, a white glow pierced the night. Kevin drove slowly along the road, enjoying the experience of this new Dream State too much to rush. After ten minutes, he found himself at a stop sign, staring at the neon sign the guard had told him about.

We live in our dreams.

The white letters were mounted on the front of a dark, rectangular wooden sign. The letters filled most of the fifty-foot-wide and nearly fifteen-foot-tall sign. It was truly beautiful. A smile crept onto the left corner of his face. *If this is just the sign, I can't imagine what the rest of this place will be like.* He exhaled a clearing of energetic breath. *Alright, let's do this.*

Kevin turned the car to the right and headed into the metal forest. He looked back and forth from his windshield to his side windows, admiring the steel palm trees that lined the one-lane road. Each stood twenty feet tall and had five metal leaves and three plastic coconuts that all glowed a soft pink. A quarter mile later, he hit the begin-ning of the bridge. *"Forest" is a bit of an overstatement. That was cool, though.*

Kevin felt the car jostle slightly as it drove over a small dip, leaving the mainland and transitioning onto the bridge. He glanced from the pavement to the short, white-stone railings. They were solid but short enough that Kevin could see the black water reflecting the light from his car. It was rushing past the bridge. *Must be the river,* Kevin thought. A large splash of water spurted into the air. He watched it crash onto a rock in the stream. It was then that Kevin suddenly realized he hadn't been looking at where he was going. He looked forward just in time. Kevin straightened out his car just before he would have run into the left side of the railing. He shook his head, steeling himself. *Don't die before you get to go back to the Dream States.* He finished the short traverse across the river and felt the car jostle again. *Back on land.* Kevin turned the car around a sharp curve, which navigated past a large rock formation. As he rounded the bend, Kevin passed under an archway of metal built between two massive boulders. On its girders, white neon spelled out a greeting: *Welcome!*

As Kevin passed under it, he saw Dream State 8 for the first time. The road passed a vista overlooking a massive complex. Over a thousand buildings, each traced with white lines of neon along their walls and roofs, lit the entire area. Kevin could see roads running in a complex maze of patterns between the buildings. In the distance, a pair of tall towers stood at the far end of the complex. On each of their walls, bright white lights spelled DS8. Kevin soon arrived at the main lobby.

The lobby was a large building, adorned with several wide domes, each rimmed with neon and glowing bright in the black. As he pulled up to the building, he looked around but couldn't find any parking lots. *Park out front if the greeter isn't there. Don't know if I trust that.* Kevin stepped from his Mustang under a polished-steel canopy in front of the lobby building. A warm, dry breeze greeted him. He took a deep breath, smelling the freshness of the air.

Before he could exit the vehicle, a woman wearing the same uniform as the guard stepped out of the main lobby's glass door. She made her way down the white-tile steps to greet Kevin.

"Welcome, sir," the woman said as she stepped around the front of the car.

"Hi. How are you?"

The woman looked at him, confused.

"Um," the woman stammered for a second, but then became extremely serious. "Welcome, sir. Please check in inside to begin your dream. Your vehicle will be waiting for you when you are finished."

"Okay." Kevin handed her the key to the car, gave her a slight bow. "Thank you."

The girl furrowed her brow, studying Kevin's face. Reluctant to accept whatever answer she arrived at, she asked in a serious tone, "Sir, may I ask you a question?"

"Yeah, of course."

"Is this your first time dreaming in Dream State 8?"

"Yes, actually."

"It isn't wise to use terms like 'thank you' or other words of emotionality here."

"Okay."

"You will check in right through the glass door at the top of the stairs."

"Thank—" Kevin caught himself. "Okay."

The woman nodded.

Kevin had a strange feeling as he stepped up the stairs and opened the door into the main lobby of Dream State 8. That feeling washed away in an instant as the smell of lavender filled his nose.

"Welcome to Dream State 8."

Kevin turned to his left. The voice had come from a motion-sensor video board that stood six feet tall.

"Dream State 8 is designed not just for the best dreaming experience but also for your personal comfort. You may have already noticed the smell."

Hard to miss, Kevin thought, taking another relaxing inhale.

"That scent is a mixture of lavender and white-fir essential oils diffused through our air filtration system. It's just part of one of the many things we do to make sure that your sleep is as relaxing, enjoyable and deep as possible. There are several à la carte options you may also add to your dream experience. These can all be discussed with your concierge, who will be with you shortly. Don't concern yourself with finding them—they will come to you. We are here to serve you in any way you desire. If you have questions, please ask. While you wait to be greeted, I recommend having a seat at the main bar on the mezzanine.

Just follow the lighted signs and begin your experience with a drink or snack." The girl vanished from the screen, and a large green arrow with the caption *MEZZANINE* on the screen pointed into the lobby.

Kevin turned on the tile floor and faced the main lobby. His head was on a swivel as he walked along the wide main aisle. To his left, after twenty feet, the hallway opened into a massive open room. Three stairs fanned out into a twisting maze of nicely appointed round couches and tables. The light-blue leather of the couches shined, lit only by a dimmed light hanging from the excessively tall ceiling. On each small silver-metal and glass table sat a pitcher of water and several glasses. Kevin knew the layout. On his last work shift, there was a ghost at a Las Vegas club he had been tasked with fixing. Each of these couches was a private booth that gave guests checking in some privacy. As he continued pacing down the main path, Kevin scanned to the other side. It was a mirror image, stairs fanning out into twisting-off private sitting areas.

Kevin smiled. *It's empty now, but imagine how packed this place can get. Thank God all those people aren't here now. That would be mayhem. Well, maybe not. Maybe they have enough people to help you check in here. Dream State 7 definitely didn't.*

Kevin's mind and feet had kept moving him through the open entryway of Dream State 8, and after a short walk, he reached the main stairs. He half jogged up them, skipping steps to reach the top. He barely glanced at the neon sign pointing up the stairs. His short ascent ended as he arrived at the mezzanine. As his eyes laid sight on the round, brass, polished-steel and glass bar, and the matching pastel-blue leather barstools, he had a strange thought. *I can't remember the last time I actually ate or drank anything. Everything I've eaten or drunk for I don't know how long has been intravenous. I wonder what it will be like. Do I even remember how?* Kevin started laughing at himself.

His pace quickened as he crossed the distance to the bar in a power walk. He sat down on the closest barstool.

The leather felt welcoming as he sank into the cushion. A whirring noise emanated from behind the wall of colorful bottles that formed the center of an island inside the full-circle bar. On each side of the bottle wall were two rotating cylinders filled with various foods. Kevin was eyeing a sandwich as the robotic bartender came around to his side of the round bar. Its small engine whirred as it rolled along its track, stopping in front of Kevin. The robot, a faceless metal body wearing a black bow tie, had an LCD screen for a head which lit up, turning from a solid silver to a bright-neon overlay. A girl's face appeared.

"I see you made it," she said with a smile on her video-broadcast face.

"Yeah, I guess you gave me good directions." Kevin shrugged and smiled.

"This robot will..." the girl continued without acknowledgment.

Kevin's smile lessened. *Guess it's not AI. Not really worth talking to. They got you, Kevin. They got you. Dumb.*

"Would you like something to drink? Maybe something to eat?" the robot asked Kevin.

"Uh, yeah, sure, but I don't know—"

"Please make a selection using the touch screen here." The robot's arm pointed to the bar top where Kevin sat. A menu displayed on the glass surface.

Kevin looked at the menu, overwhelmed by the number of choices. He used his finger to select a purple drink that looked interesting.

"An excellent choice. Would you like anything else?"

Kevin thought for a moment. "Yes." He paged through the menu until he found the sandwich that had caught his attention earlier.

"An excellent choice. Would you like anything else?"

"Wait, how much does this cost?"

The robot paused for a moment, its mechanical brain searching a database. "Mr. Altair, it appears this is your first trip to Dream State 8, which means your first concession trip of one drink and one food selection is free." The robot made a double-pointing gesture, attempting to make the inclusion a fun bonus.

"Thanks." Kevin was more unnerved than entertained.

The robot turned, reached for bottles, and poured them into a mixing cup. As it worked, Kevin surveyed the room. Along the outline were a few of the circular couches that he had passed on the way in and three sets of double doors. The first set of doors to his left had golden letters over its frame that read, **DREAM HALL ASSIGNMENT.** The set to his right read, **DREAM STATE OUT-PROCESSING.** Kevin leaned to his side in order to see around the rotating food cylinder. The far set of double doors read **PRIVATE.** *Hmmm. Wonder what that's about.*

"Your selections are ready." The robot with the woman's video face had finished its tasks. Kevin sat straight again and looked down at the drink and sandwich. His mouth watered. "If you require further assistance, please say, 'Robot Wake.' Until then, I will go into power-saving mode. Enjoy." The video screen that made the robot's face turned off. Kevin looked up at the metal husk that now stood lifeless in front of him. He had the strangest feeling. The thing didn't even have a face, but it felt like it was watching him. Kevin picked up his drink and sandwich. He turned to walk away from the bar, almost running face-first into the concierge. "Oh!" Kevin jolted as he turned from the blank robot and was suddenly face-to-face with a young woman. In his sudden panic, he dropped his sandwich onto the floor. Son of a—

"Sir, I'm so sorry. Would you like another sandwich?" the young woman asked with concern in her voice.

Kevin looked at the woman standing five feet tall. Her face was soft and caring, her blonde hair pulled back in a tight ponytail. She wore a light-purple pantsuit that conveyed professionalism. Kevin looked at the ground, at the lettuce, bread, cheese and meat spread across the floor, a hint of mayonnaise sticking to the tile. "No. No, it's okay." He straightened up, trying to move on from the disappointment. "I've still got my drink, at least."

"At least you won't have to have the stomach cleanse now."

"Cleanse?"

"If you have food before you can dream, you must go through a digestive cleanse."

"Oh. What about the drink?"

The young woman smiled. "You're alright."

"Good." Kevin smiled back and took a sip. The lavender water tasted fantastic.

"Please follow me. We will get your check-in process underway." The young woman turned and walked toward one of the circular couches.

"Don't we..." Kevin didn't finish his question before a small robotic cleaner rolled out of the bar bottom and began working on sweeping up the sandwich pieces. "Never mind." Kevin took another sip of his drink and joined the woman on the couch.

"So, 925387,"—the young woman was looking at a tablet scrolling through a list of code—"this is your first time to DS 8. You're a newly upgraded dreamer, it appears."

"Yes."

"Great. Well, I'm here to help you set up your dream. My goal is to ensure you have the deepest and most immersive dream possible, and to make sure your stay here in Dream State 8 is as comfortable as possible. We can provide special sedatives and better conductive serums. We also offer massages and physical treatments more to keep your physical body in good shape. They are much better than traditional electrical stimulation."

"Okay." Kevin nodded. "What's your name, by the way?"

"We don't do that here," the girl said with a professional grin. She turned her attention to the tablet again and navigated through menus.

"You don't have a name?" Kevin leaned forward on the couch, toward his attendant.

"I do," she said without looking up. "But we don't share them with clients."

"Why not?"

"Well, the goal is to be nameless so you can go into the dream as uninfluenced as possible. It helps you get into a deep dream state faster."

"Huh." Kevin tilted his head. "I guess that makes sense. It still feels weird."

The concierge looked up from her tablet. "I don't mean to be out of place, but frankly, does it matter? The burn takes your memory of ever meeting me away. You won't even remember this conversation."

"The burn takes away memories other than the dream?"

"Yes. You didn't know that?" It was the concierge's turn to be confused. "All the Dream States do that, so every time you come back, you feel the sensation of awe and excitement while arriving, or a sense of it not being good enough if they want you to focus on progressing."

"I didn't know the burn could do that. Wait, no, that can't be right. I can still remember what the check-in at all the other Dream States was like."

"That's because they don't burn the memory if you upgrade. If you are moving up, then letting you remember the lower amenities of the previous Dream State enhances your experience. The opposite is true if you downgrade. They must erase that memory or you'll be unhappy with your circumstances. It's all done for your good."

Kevin sat back, not okay with the revelation. "I didn't know the burn took memories outside of the dream away."

Sensing Kevin's discomfort, the concierge leaned in close. She whispered low, ensuring no one else could hear. "My name is Katy."

Kevin looked at her in time to see the faint smile she let appear before regaining her professional disposition. He smiled faintly himself.

"So what I was saying," Katy continued, "is that we have many add-ons here in Dream State 8. Let's first discuss your dream medication options."

"I'm going to stop you right there. I don't want any bonuses or add-ons."

"Sir—"

"I know that all the à la carte options can improve my dream, make the transition after dreaming easier, and maybe even move me up in ranking faster. And I'm sure that you have a quota to meet for extra sales, but I'm sorry, it's something I'm not interested in."

"Okay, although our bonuses are better than any Dream State you've been in before, and you don't even know what you're missing. But I'm here to serve your desires, so if you want nothing special, I'll accept it."

Kevin smiled big. "It's a way of belief at this point."

"No add-ons, then..." Katy turned the tablet off and winked at Kevin. "... this time. Are you ready to see Dream State 8?"

Kevin took a big swig of his lavender water, finishing the glass. "Absolutely."

The young woman stood. "Follow me."

Kevin rose and walked behind her as she strode through the double doors with the **DREAM HALL ASSIGN-MENT** signage. He looked over at the private doors as he walked. As they entered a long hall that led to a golden elevator door, Kevin asked her, "What's behind the private doors?"

"Mr. Altair, in Dream State 8, we have some clientele who require unique care."

"What does that mean?"

"Maybe someday you'll find out. Until then, that's all I can say about that area." The young woman reached the elevator doors and pressed the call button. The bell rang immediately.

As Kevin stepped inside the elevator, he forgot his train of thought. He was looking out through a glass wall, over an amazing scene.

The valley below was aglow with white light. The massive complex of buildings he had seen earlier from the road was alive. Small carts darted down the roads, neatly packed between the square buildings. Each structure was five stories tall and laid out in perfect squares, a mosaic of structures in a perfect pattern. The neon lining of each of

them shined brightly into the dark night. Its pale lumines-
cence cast a wash of daylight over the entire area. It was
almost too bright. Kevin squinted to take in all the details.

"Beautiful, isn't it?" Katy said while pushing a button on
the elevator's control panel. The doors closed, and the lift
began moving.

"Yeah, it really is."

"It's pretty amazing how well designed everything is. At
the center of each square building complex is a central hub
that houses the computing power. So each building has a
backup server linked to the major network, just for their
unit. This guarantees uninterrupted and less-error-filled
dreams."

Kevin was looking into the distance at the towers. "Am I
wrong or are the complexes closer to the towers brighter?"

"Very astute. They are brighter. The closer you are to our
two large hydroelectric towers, the more power your unit
gets."

The elevator's view disappeared as the lift descended
the final few feet to the bottom floor, obstructed by a tall
hedgerow.

"More power?"

"Yes, some bonuses, which you chose not to hear about
this go around, require additional power."

"Hmm."

"Actually, many of them do, meaning the more bonuses
you purchase, the closer you get to the towers. I'm sure you
noticed the small cars?" Katy asked as the elevator door
opened and she stepped outside.

"Yeah."

"Well, you won't need them this time." Katy led Kevin
around the end of the hedgerow. She took a sharp left turn
toward the closest building, which stood only a few feet
away from the elevator. "Here we are."

"Here?" Kevin asked as they walked up to a frosted-glass
door on the outside of a brick building.

"You're the one who chose no upgrades. Unless you'd
like to change that choice?"

"No, it's alright."

"Great." Katy swiped a key card across a reader. A soft hiss came from the door as it opened out. "Follow me."

"Welcome to your dream room," Katy said as she stepped to the side, allowing Kevin to enter.

Inside the small ten-foot by ten-foot room was a well-appointed bed with lavender-colored linens that draped over the side to a wooden floor.

"This is your doctor." Katy pointed to the other person in the room, whom Kevin had somehow glanced over.

Kevin turned and faced the tall black woman who stood in a lab coat next to a standing desk. Her strong cheekbones framed a slender face. A pair of red glasses sat over her nose and disappeared into her well-fluffed afro.

"Hello," Kevin said.

"It's a pleasure to meet you," the doctor spoke professionally but also matter-of-factly. She turned to Katy, "If you'll excuse us now."

"Yes, doctor." Katy nodded and left the room.

"Bye," Kevin said as Katy closed the door behind her.

"Please remove your clothing, put on the gown provided and lie on the bed."

Kevin disrobed and pulled himself under the sheet.

The doctor walked to the side of the bed. "This isn't your first dream, so you know the procedure. We use a more powerful sedative here, so the IV needle may sting more than you're used to. Understand?"

Kevin nodded.

The doctor held Kevin's arm firmly but not too tightly and pressed a large needle into his vein. Kevin let out a small grunt as she taped it in place. She reached behind her and hooked Kevin into the IV drip system. Next, she hooked a cord into Kevin's mind chip. She moved to the other side of the stand-up desk and typed a few commands into the computer. "Okay, in a few moments, the drip system will activate and begin your dream. One last step. In Dream State 8, you choose your own first name. What would you like to be known as in your next life?"

"I get to choose a name?"

"Yes."

Kevin thought for a moment. "I always liked the name..."

Thairn pushed the large wooden door open as he confidently stepped into the large office. He walked across the twenty feet of open space, stepping over the metal numbers inlaid in the marble tiles. He glanced at the golden hue of the brass spelling out *150*. Thairn walked to the far end of the room. He stood in front of a dark-ebony wood desk that contrasted against the man sitting on the other side. He wore a tight-fitting white-latex shirt and matching pair of pants. His skin was stark pale, making his entire look even more bleached.

"Sir. I'm pleased to report that we are moving forward with 925387."

"Did they make contact?"

"It won't be long now. We put him under the care of a sympathetic and are ready to trigger an awakening."

"I'm still not sure about this plan."

"It's going to work, sir."

"If it doesn't."

"He has reached Dream State 8 and checked in. We made sure he upgraded, no matter his performance metrics. Now he's high enough in rank that he's a target for them."

"And a danger to us."

"We're tracking him. He has just started his new dream. We instructed the concierge to include a free name customization on his account, to make it easier to watch him as well. Kevin Altair's new name is Jaared, Jaared Johns."

CHAPTER 4

WAKING UP EARLY

*R*ing . . . Ring . . . Ring . . .

"I'm up," Jaared grunted as he threw his legs over the side of his bed. He reached over and turned the alarm clock off. He slogged across his bedroom floor, heading for the bathroom. His feet barely left the ground as he shuffled to the shower. Turning on the water, he jumped, the cold water catching his hand and wetting the sleeve of the shirt he was still wearing. Jaared stood in front of the open door of the large shower, testing the temperature with his hand until it reached skin-scorching hot. He adjusted the water temperature, quickly stripped and jumped into the life-giving warmth. It took twenty minutes for it to fully heat his stiff body. When he stepped out of the shower and toweled off, he looked at his reflection in the mirror.

His skin was red from the hot water of the shower, and steam was emanating from his silhouette. Although the heat in his apartment was keeping the temperature at a comfortable sixty-eight degrees, winter mornings seemed to always feel cold. Jaared looked at the beard he had been growing for the last two months for that exact reason. *Could use a trim,* he thought as he rubbed it. His gaze drifted upward and noticed his dark-brown hair, which having just been dried with the towel, now looked fluffy and overgrown. *Not the only thing that could use a trim. I hate shaving or getting my hair cut when it's so cold though. It makes it so much worse. Then again,* Jaared looked at his clean-shaven chest. *Maybe after the meeting today. For now, though,* he reached down and grabbed his extra-hold product. Jaared quickly squeezed an oversized portion of the hair gel into his hand and worked it through the mop that was his overgrown hair. A few tweaks and it looked passable. He shrugged his shoulders, *good enough,* and walked out of the bathroom. He quickly slipped into a pair of dress pants and a button-up shirt and made his way to the kitchen.

Jaared unenthusiastically poured himself a bowl of cereal and ate it standing at the counter. He just finished slurping down the color-stained milk left over from his Froot Loops before the alarm on his phone began ringing again. Jaared put his bowl and spoon in the dishwasher and threw on his coat. As he opened the door to start his short walk from his apartment door to his Jeep parked outside, he found the exterior hallway had turned into a wind tunnel of icy air. The cold bit into his face and froze his still-damp hair. That's when the headache started. The migraine crept into his brain. Every second of his twenty-minute drive to work, it grew worse. By the time he had reached his office, all Jaared wanted to do was lock himself in a dark room and cry. Instead, he opened the door into the basement meeting room and was assaulted by light.

The conference space was forty feet wide by forty feet long, with one wall all glass, looking out onto a small garden area. In the spring and summer, this area was lush green, its bushes and shrubbery soaking in the sun. Now, though, the winter snow had blanketed everything. Its icy surface reflected the sunshine into a white blast of light. Jaared closed his eyes and rubbed the bridge of his nose. The searing pain that shot through his head sent a tingle through his whole body, causing him to shudder. He forced his eyes open. It hurt so bad his stomach churned; the pain causing him to feel nauseous.

"Jaared!"

Jaared looked to the front of the room, closest to the bright windows. His mother was waving her hand in the air. She pointed at the empty seat next to her. *Shit,* Jaared thought. *I was going to find a seat in the darkest corner and just survive this meeting.* He made his way to the front of the room and sat down in the seat his mother had saved.

"Morning!"

Jaared's mother's high-pitched, cheery tone irritated his migraine, causing him to half close his right eye. "Good morning." He eked out through the pain.

"Hey, how about we go on tour together after the meeting?"

"I don't know."

"Come on, it will be fun. You can drive us both, get me a coffee along the way, and we can see some of the new houses for sale. I have a few that I have to see, and the company would be fun."

"I don't know if I'm going on the home tour today," Jaared was rubbing both of his temples, trying to find relief. "I'm not feeling too good."

His mom's face turned from enthusiastic to judgmental, as did her tone. "Maybe if you didn't stay up so late..."

"I wasn't up late."

"Of course you were. You always are."

"No, I wasn't."

"You know you need to stop being so lazy. You know, they always say the most important thing is to show up!"

"I'm here, aren't I?"

"I don't mean just showing up for the meeting. I mean, showing up for the whole day and working hard. You know, when I first started, I worked eighty hours a week. I had to grind and put in the work. It didn't matter if I didn't feel well—I still showed up. I didn't go home."

Jaared had heard that story a hundred times. If he had more energy, he may have protested more, but the migraine was stealing his desire to talk, let alone argue. "Okay," he murmured.

"Good morning!" the office manager said, starting the meeting.

The next thirty minutes went by as a painful blur for Jaared. With every new home sales pitch and charity drive announcement, his brain was melting. The second the meeting ended with a group clap, Jaared made a beeline for his car.

He pulled out of the parking lot and turned to head home, clipping the curb. His depth perception was not exactly what it should be. The snow melting on the ground had turned the road into a bright reflection that would cause eye strain for a normal person, but for Jaared, it was torturous. A few minutes into his drive, his phone rang through the car speakers. He glanced at the display on the dashboard and saw it was his brother calling. Jaared pressed the phone button on his steering wheel, answering the call.

"Hey," Jaared said.

"What's up, bro?" Justin's upbeat yet low sounding voice came through the speakers.

"I'm dying."

"What?" Justin laughed at his Jaared's response.

"I have such a bad migraine right now. I'm driving home to take some ibuprofen and crash out."

"Sorry. Is it just a migraine, or are you hungover? Fun night last night?"

"No, just a migraine."

"You're twenty-four years old, you're supposed to be healthy. You get migraines a lot."

"I think the cold combined with the sun shining off the snow caused it."

"Ooh yeah, that brightness can be killer."

"Is it bright there?"

"Well, it's night here now. Germany is eight hours ahead of you, and the sun sets early."

"Oh. Right."

"It is cold as balls, though."

Jaared laughed. "Ha ha. Oh, ow. Laughing makes my head hurt worse."

His brother laughed this time. "Ha ha. It's that bad?"

"Yeah. I'm about to get home, though. Did you need something?"

"No, I was just calling to say hi. I miss you, man."

"I miss you too," Jaared said as he turned into his apartment complex's parking lot. "I'm home now, though."

"Alright, feel better."

"Thanks, man. Have a good night."

"Bye."

Jaared pressed the phone button, hanging up the call. He pulled into a parking spot and practically fell out of the Jeep. Stumbling from the pain in his skull, he made his way down the windy hallway to his door. Using all the focus he could muster, he lined his key up with the door lock and opened it. He shut the door, turned the bolt lock in place and dropped his briefcase where he stood. Kicking his shoes off in random directions, he stumbled into the kitchen and grabbed some ibuprofen. *Should I take more than usual? Or maybe take the extra-strength migraine medicine?* Jaared thought for a moment. *I'll start with the basic. It usually works.*

Jaared took four pills and swallowed them. Not even thinking about finding a glass, he turned the faucet on and swallowed water straight from the tap. After turning the water off, he shuffled down the hallway to his bed and buried his head in the pillow.

Light shone through the blinds covering the sliding glass door in Jaared's apartment. It was a strange configuration having a ground-floor unit with a sliding glass door to the patio off of the master bedroom. In most cases, it didn't matter, but today was different. The flimsy sliding blinds barely kept the sun from blasting into the room at this hour. It felt like the sun itself was trying to barge its way in. Jaared had been rolling around in bed, trying in vain to bury his head in pillows and blankets. The migraine was ripping through his skull, splitting him in two. The light was not just making it worse; it was slowly yet surely killing him.

"Why?" he asked his pillow. Jaared was in good health, but occasional migraines were something that cursed him. Usually they were short-lived and went away with an enormous glass of water and a little extra sleep. Today's headache was different. It had already been thirty minutes since he got home, and there was no sign of relief. Jaared tossed and turned, pulling pillows tightly to his face. He receded deep under the covers, assuming the fetal position, trying his best to imitate an ostrich, shoving his head forcefully into the mattress. Nothing helped. With a whine, he threw blankets off himself and walked with one eye closed to the kitchen down the hall.

Before Jaared even made it the fifteen feet to the kitchen, the pain overwhelmed his insides. He felt his stomach churn and bubble, angry at the long-lasting and never-ending headache. Jaared ducked into the bathroom and fell to his hands and knees at the toilet. Not a moment too soon. White vomit leaked from his mouth as his back arched and his body wretched. The burning pain in his head had caused him to puke. That was too much.

Jaared flushed the toilet and shuffled to the kitchen, not even bothering to wipe the stomach bile from his lips. He reached into the cabinet and pulled out a bottle of migraine medicine. The instructions recommended two. Jaared was in no mood for recommended doses. He shook the bottle, and four white tablets fell into his hand. *Close enough.* With a swift motion, he swallowed them, ducked his head under the sink and drank from the faucet.

God, please let them work quickly, he thought as he turned the water off.

Jaared grabbed his sleeping bag from the closet and dragged it and himself into the bathroom he had just left. This bathroom was truly massive. Not only did it have enough room for a double sink, a separate shower and tub, and a water closet, but it even had a small linen closet. Considering the meager size of the apartment, it was strange the builder had put a third of the square footage in the bathroom.

Jaared laid the sleeping bag down on a rug that covered the main open space of the bathroom. He turned back and shut the door. Pitch black overtook the room. The only light fighting against the darkness was a thin line of sun shining from under the doorframe.

Finally, some relief.

Jaared pulled himself inside the mummy sleeping bag and zipped it shut. A few minutes later, he felt himself sweating. The sleeping bag had a minus twenty degrees Fahrenheit rating and it was seventy inside the house. Jaared didn't care. As the sweat accumulated, he tasted the humidity of his breath, and felt his heart racing, an effect of the coupling of the body heat with the large dose of medicine.

I don't care. Sweat away, body. Pump away, heart. Just let this headache go away.

Jaared felt his eyes grow heavy as the sleep he had been trying to find for the last half hour finally beckoned.

Beep . . . Beep . . . Beep . . .

Jaared fought to open his eyes against what felt like a thousand pounds of sand. Fractured and glossy light blurred his vision.

"Paging Dr. Flo. Dr. Flo, ID 925387 is waking up."

As Jaared's vision cleared, he could see the inside of a light-purple, striped-wallpaper room. He watched in a dazed confusion as a lady in a white lab coat walked in. Her hair was in a large afro, and her skin was stark black. She reminded him of the woman you would see in a vintage disco video from the 1970s. She walked to his side and reached for something. Her hands found the flow controller on an IV drip.

"Don't worry. Go back to sleep. I'll take care of you."

Before Jaared could say anything, everything turned black. He found himself lost in blackness for an undeterminable and tortuous amount of time.

At the sound of a whip cracking or a mouse trap spring-ing, Jaared shot up, wide awake, panting and sweating on his bathroom floor.

"What the hell was that?" Jaared had always had strange dreams, but something about that felt different. That moment had felt so real. He sat on his bathroom floor, thinking.

Was that a dream? I mean, it had to be, right? It didn't feel like a dream, but what else could it be? That had to be a dream. But I know it wasn't. What was that?

This train of thought repeated in his mind, time after time, for half an hour. Needing respite from his confu-sion, Jaared decided to go for a drive. His headache was gone, and he needed to go back to the office, anyway. Might as well use that time to clear his thoughts.

He dressed in a pair of golf slacks, a polo shirt, and a thick coat, and headed out the door. It was a beautiful day outside. The sun was shining and brought a little heat to the cold winter. As he walked to his Jeep, Jaared still couldn't shake the feeling that something about that dream was real. There was something about it that was so... unforgettable.

As he rounded the corner of his apartment building and made his way through the parking lot, his head was down, watching the cracks of the sidewalk more than his surroundings. He walked like that the whole way to his Jeep. He climbed inside and turned the key. The engine came to life with a quiet rumble. Jaared turned his head, preparing to back out of the spot. What he saw almost made him slam the gas down by accident as an instinct reaction. The billboard looking over the lot, which had for his entire life advertised the local sports bar, had painted on it in bold red letters: **WAKE UP!!!**

What the hell!? Jaared thought to himself as his heart rate skyrocketed. *That's just weird. That sign wasn't painted like that last night. Was it this morning?*

He turned his head forward for a second and looked back. The writing was gone. *What the—Am I going crazy?*

Jaared turned the Jeep off and sat in silence. He didn't even have the capacity to think. That made what happened next freak him out even worse.

A loud pop shot out of the speakers in the car. It was like a recorded gunshot sounded from the speakers at full blast. Jaared grabbed his ears, trying to heal them from the sonic assault they had just received. His hands muffled the voices that came from the speakers next, but he still heard them clearly enough to make out.

"We have less than two minutes. Hurry and get that out of his arm!" A man's loud, commanding voice resounded through the speakers.

"It's time to wake up." Another voice now came through his car stereo. It was a woman's, but it also sounded like a mixture of hard and soft. He could hear the strength in her tone yet feel her compassion.

Jaared pulled his hands from his ears, feeling somewhat recovered from the initial speaker shock. He looked around as the world seemed to close in on him. Black dots soon showed up in his vision. Bit by bit, they grew and multiplied until, soon, blackness was all he could see. Then, from the void, he heard that woman's strong, calming voice again.

"Come on, wake up, we have to go."

His mind followed that voice, and light punctured the hard shell of black that had just engulfed him. Soon the light was all he could see. Then, piece by piece, the fog that surrounded him faded. His eyes settled on a masked face, staring through goggles at him.

"Welcome back. I need you to shake it off. We need to go." The mystery woman wore a ski mask, making it impossible to see the details of her face, but her piercing brown eyes were all that Kevin could look at in that moment. She stood up and walked to the door, the simple black jumpsuit she wore clinging tightly to her thin figure. Leaning out, she yelled to an unseen person, "He's up. Give him thirty seconds and we're moving."

As he grew more clear, he realized he had seen this room before. He had just been here. This was the room from his dream. His mind understood. It wasn't just a dream. This was the room that he, Kevin Altair, had come to for his vacation. This was Dream State 8.

A man wearing a black ski mask and jumpsuit stepped through the door. He was larger, standing well over a foot above the woman, and built with a wide, muscular frame. "We don't have thirty seconds." The man took a few massive steps across the room. He stood imposing over Kevin, who still lay in the hospital bed. "Can you walk?"

"Uh..." Kevin stammered, still in shock from everything going on.

"Yes or no?" The man demanded an answer, his voice aggressive.

Kevin moved his legs, testing them, unsure in that moment if he could move anything, out of fear. He found the strength to nod yes.

"Good." The man grabbed Kevin's arm and forcibly tore out an IV plug.

Kevin reached for it in pain, but before he could soothe his aching arm, the man had hold of it and was dragging him out of bed. Kevin swung his feet under him and caught his balance, barely missing stepping on the hospital gown that was loosely tied around him. The man led the way, pulling Kevin by the arm, out the door and into the night. A camouflage-painted van with big off-road tires sat idling a few feet from the door. The woman Kevin had seen earlier ran to the van and opened the two back doors. Kevin hunched over as he pushed inside and onto a bare, steel trunk space. The inside of the van was completely empty. There were no seats or carpet in the back, just a ridged trunk space and cold metal. Kevin was looking out the windshield over two bucket seats that made up the front of the van when he heard the doors close behind him. He turned to find that the larger of his two assailants had joined him inside. Without a single word, the man grabbed Kevin and threw him to the ground. Kevin fought the man, trying to stand, but to no avail.

"Stop! Stop resisting!" the man yelled.

Kevin stopped trying to wrestle the man off, breathing hard from the exertion. "Okay. Okay."

"Good. We have to disable your tracker."

"My what?" Kevin barely finished the question before he felt a sharp pain in the back of his head. "Ow!" he yelled. The pain persisted, getting worse by the second. Kevin wanted so badly to reach for the back of his skull, but he was paralyzed somehow. He was stuck in pain, staring face-first at a metal floor in agony. A few terrible seconds later, he felt the pain dissolve, though his mobility was still gone. He let out a sigh.

"It's done. We should leave this plugged in, though, or he may try to fight us."

"No," the woman responded from the passenger seat at the front of the van. "He won't fight. Let him up. I'll sit back with him. You drive."

"Fine. Then you pull it out."

Kevin heard the man's massive figure open the rear doors and hop out of the back of the van, followed by the sound of a smaller set of boot steps entering and the doors slamming shut. Another door opened and closed, and the van shifted into gear. Kevin slid backward as the van sped up. His lip dragged up to his nose against the metal. He felt a tug at the back of his head, and a shock went through his body. Instinctively, he reached up and grabbed at his head. Feeling the source of the pain, Kevin realized he was touching his mind chip. As he pushed himself from the floor and turned to sit against the wall, the van hit a bump and almost sent him back to the ground. The masked woman caught his fall.

"Sit down against the wall. It's going to be a bumpy ride back here."

Still holding his head and mind chip, he braced himself against the wall of the van. "What did you just do to me? Why does my mind chip hurt?"

"Embedded into the code of your mind chip is a GPS tracker. It runs off your body's natural electrical production, so we can't just turn it off. So we injected a virus into the code itself to delete the commands that allow the GPS to work."

"You gave my mind chip a virus!" Kevin yelled in fear.

"Oh, don't worry, you'll be fine. It's not like you're the first person we've done this to," the girl said, waving her hand in a dismissing manner.

"What? Who are you people? What do you want from me?"

"We—" the girl started.

"Transition!" the driver yelled back.

The girl braced herself by shifting into a low squat position. A second later, Kevin understood why. The van jumped a curb and moved off the paved roads of Dream State 8 and onto a rough desert landscape. Kevin reached down, grabbing his tailbone, which had just connected with a rivet in the floor. "Oh, God."

"Ha ha," the girl laughed. "Sorry, I guess I should have warned you."

Kevin adjusted himself against the wall of the van and away from rivets as they bounced down an unpaved trail.

"We are the Awake."

"The terrorist group?"

"Is that what they call us now?" the driver shouted from the front seat.

"Yeah, you sabotage people's dreams."

"Really? How so?" the driver asked again.

"You break into the Dream States and hijack code, inserting terrible nightmares and diseases. All to ruin dreams for people. You vandalize Dream States to instill fear into incoming dreamers so they don't stay long. And..." Kevin paused, too nervous.

"And?" the woman asked.

"And you kill people."

"Do they say why we do all these things?" the driver asked, a small laugh escaping his lips.

"They say that you're the unlucky. The rare statistic group of people who can't dream. You're not able to connect to the network. So you have developed a twisted sense of morality that has led you to believe that dreaming is evil and that no one should be dreaming. That is your goal. To stop everyone from dreaming and destroy the Dream States."

"They make us sound like pathetic victims, don't they?" the driver said, not even trying to hide his laughter. "At least they're right about the killing."

"Is that really what they tell you?" the woman asked Kevin.

"Well, yeah."

"You have a lot to learn. Are we clear of the cameras yet?" she asked the driver.

"Yeah, we're clear, but this one sounds pretty sold. I don't know if it's smart to take off the masks."

"Suit yourself, but I hate this thing." The woman pulled the ski mask off, freeing her shoulder-length brown hair to fall to one side of her head.

Kevin stared, studying the no-longer-faceless woman in front of him. Her hair held a slight wave—an imprint left from the ski mask—that swooped over her forehead and down the cheek of her face. Her skin was tan, a glowing amber in the dim light of the van, a feature he hadn't seen outside the Dream States in some time. Plump pink lips did little to hide a slight smile framed by her narrow chin bones. Kevin found his eyes drawn up the length of her straight nose and into the magnetic grasp of her almond-shaped eyes. Her eyes drew Kevin in. It took him a second to realize they were staring back at him. Kevin averted his eyes, suddenly aware and shy.

"We aren't all that terrorizing, are we?" the girl asked.

"No. No, you're beautiful," The words escaped Kevin's lips before he could think about what he was saying. "Did I just say that?"

"Ha ha ha," the driver laughed.

"I'm, I'm so sorry," Kevin said.

"Why?" the girl asked, smiling.

"Because that's not something you say to someone."

"Why not?"

"Because it's just not."

"Maybe not in the world you're used to. Maybe it's a weird thing to say when you don't have friends or don't connect with anyone outside of the dream. But where I come from, it's a compliment."

Kevin nodded, somewhat calmed but still embarrassed. A long pause of awkward silence threatened to swallow him. He forced out, "I'm Kevin, by the way." He pushed his hand out to shake the woman's.

"Nice to meet you, Kevin." She reached out and shook his hand. "I'm Sarah."

Kevin held the handshake a second longer than he should have. Her soft, warm skin felt so welcoming. The driver broke the magic of the moment by yelling over his shoulder, "My name is Diehl. If anyone cares."

Kevin let go of Sarah's hand. "So, Sarah, where—" the van lurched, cutting Kevin off. The driver had not avoided a soft spot in the terrain, causing the back right tire to sink in a pothole. It threw Kevin off balance and sent him plummeting into Sarah. She wrapped her arms around him as they tumbled to the ground. They rolled, landing with Sarah on top of Kevin.

"My bad," Diehl said.

"Are you alright?" Sarah asked Kevin, pushing herself off of him.

"Yeah. You?"

"I'm fine," Sarah said, sitting against the opposite wall of the van.

"Sorry for tackling you."

Sarah winked at Kevin. "Just don't make a habit of it. Besides, if Diehl could drive, we would be fine," she yelled, making sure Diehl heard.

"You know it's hard driving in the dark over unmarked desert trails without lights!" he shouted back.

Sarah smiled, having fun ragging on Diehl. She stared at Kevin. He was sniffing the air with a strange look on his face. "Are you alright?"

"Do you smell that?"

Sarah smelled the air. She shrugged her shoulders, not smelling anything but the metal of the van.

Kevin kept smelling. He sniffed to his left. He sniffed to his right. Then he leaned forward, moving closer to Sarah, and sniffed again. "Are you wearing perfume?"

Sarah had a bewildered look on her face. "Yeah. It's—"

"It's peonies." The world turned black for a second, and Kevin transported into a different place, a different time.

"Jaared, understand?" Delia asked in her thick Russian accent.

"Y-yeah," Jaared answered back.

Delia crossed her arms in front of her. "Repeat."

Jaared looked at Delia Sartan. She was a five-foot-tall, stout woman who always wore a paisley-patterned dress. Her stern eyes glared through round-brimmed glasses that matched the circular wave of her jet-black hair. "Well, you said that this perfume, or eau de parfum because it's dissolved in alcohol rather than water, is a floral scent that many women will find light and fresh smelling. It has hints of vanilla and citrus, but the principal base of this scent is peony."

Delia nodded. "I rarely like to hire young men. Most nineteen-year-old boys don't focus on selling perfume, only men's cologne. If you can remember women's fragrances, you will have much better sales."

"I will."

"Remember," Delia said as she sprayed a tester card and handed it to Jaared, "this scent is peonies."

Jaared took a deep inhale. Peonies. As the fragrance filled his nose, he felt his mind pulled into the blackness again. As he emerged from the memory, Jaared was Kevin again, in the back of the van.

What the hell was that? Kevin thought to himself, scared and confused. *It's like, oh, God. I never went through the burn.* "Take me back!" he screamed. "You have to take me back! I have both memories!"

"Yeah right." Diehl yelled as he threw the van into a higher gear. Kevin and Sarah lurched as the old-model motor kicked and whined against the hard shift.

Sarah used her body weight to pin Kevin in a seated position against the side of the van. "There's no going back."

"You don't, you don't understand," Kevin said, panicked, trying to push the woman off of him.

"No, you don't understand. You can't go back."

"We saved your ass. If we take you back, you're dead!" Diehl yelled over his shoulder.

"What are you talking about?" Kevin asked.

"Look," Sarah said, "you woke up from your dream, right?"

Kevin thought for a moment, flashing back to the migraine that had pulled him from the dream. He nodded in answer.

"Then we saved you," she continued. "You're dangerous to them now."

"Dangerous to who? What are you talking about?" Kevin yelled his last question, emotions running high.

"Shut him up!" Diehl shouted while turning the van abruptly. Sarah lost her balance, falling shoulder first into Kevin's face.

His nose started bleeding as tears filled his eyes. "What the..."

She leveraged her body and grabbed hold of Kevin's arms. Sarah reached into the breast pocket of her jumpsuit and pulled out a syringe.

Kevin saw the needle through his blurry vision too late. He felt the syringe push into his neck and let out a scream. "Argh!" He fought to free his arms from the woman; however, the injection was stealing his strength. A few moments of struggle later, he could barely keep his eyes open.

Sarah relaxed her grip on Kevin, feeling his fight leaving. "Don't worry. It's going to be okay. You're going to like your new home."

But, Kevin thought, *the burn... I can remember. I can still... I can... the burn... peonies...* The drug took its full effect on Kevin. Blackness overtook him.

"Bro! Wake up!"

Jaared rubbed his eyes and sat up straight in the leather passenger seat of the 2001 Ford Escape. His legs squeaked as they unstuck from the seat's material. "I'm, I'm awake," he said as he rubbed his eyes. A quick glance out the windshield helped Jaared remember where he was. "Well, Utah is boring." He watched a brown, water-starved landscape pass by the window in a blur.

"Yeah, it is," his brother, Justin, said as he changed lanes to pass a semi-truck. "But you're the navigator and DJ.

You're riding up front, and your job is to keep the driver up and attentive. You're not allowed to fall asleep. That's the number-one rule of road tripping."

Jaared unstuck his leg again. "It's so hot. Why are we running the heat again? It's like ninety-five outside. I'm sweating like crazy right now."

Justin let out a small laugh. "Me too, bro, but that's half the fun."

Jaared turned away from the desert landscape he had been staring aimlessly at and looked at his brother. His brother was smiling widely, his aviators rising on his cheeks as his grin pressed to the side of his face. Justin's dark-brown hair matted to his head with a flop-sweat from the heat. The gray tank top that loosely fit his wire-thin sixteen-year-old frame was hanging low, heavy from the dark spots of sweat that had changed the color of the front of his top. Jaared let out a small laugh. "Why are we doing this again?"

Justin reached and turned the heat dial to the highest level. "Just embrace it. Just let it happen."

"Pffft."

Justin and Jaared both glanced to the back seat of the SUV, their attention grabbed by the loud fart. Their dad tossed a little as he napped across the bench seat. Although they could only see his back, the sweat had changed the color of his shirt as well.

The two brothers looked at each other, sharing a jovial glance, and laughed in unison. "Ha ha ha ha."

"How long has he been sleeping now?" Jaared asked.

"About ten minutes. He was mumbling earlier, talking in his sleep."

"Really? What was he saying?"

"Nothing in particular, just random words and mumbles. Must be having a weird dream."

Weird dream? Weird dream. "I had a weird dream," Jaared said.

"Really? You weren't even asleep that long."

"Yeah." Jaared thought for a moment. "I don't remember much of it."

"Was there a hot girl in it?" Justin asked, letting out a boyish chuckle.

Jaared thought for another moment, letting his mind travel back. "There was a girl, and she was hot, but, but she was..." Before the words "kidnapping me" could come out of his mouth, blackness overtook his mind.

As his consciousness came back to him, he could feel the metal floor of the van and smell the stale air. He tried to look around but couldn't see anything but black.

"Relax," a calming female voice said. Kevin recognized Sarah's tone. "We had to cover your head," she continued, "but you're okay. We're almost there."

"Where?" Kevin asked.

"Home."

A few minutes later, the van stopped. Kevin couldn't see anything but a faint light leaking in from the bottom of the bag, covering his head. The sweet peony perfume Sarah wore came faintly through the material of his head covering.

"That was a long drive," Diehl said from the front seat.

Kevin heard a door open and slam shut, presumably Diehl exiting the van. Kevin's ears and mind followed the sound of footsteps outside as they rounded to the back of the van. With a click and a creak, the back doors opened. Kevin felt the warmth of sunlight.

"You think that was long for you?" Sarah said. "Try riding on that metal floor."

"I told you to just sit on him. He was sleeping anyway."

"Yeah, right, I would have broken his ribs. I swear you hit every bump on purpose."

"Not every bump." Diehl laughed. "Is he still out?"

"No. He's up."

"Ready to get out of that van?" Diehl asked Kevin, slapping him on the leg.

"Ready to get my ass off this metal." Kevin surprised himself with his snarky answer.

Diehl laughed. "Okay, help me out here. Don't fight or try to run away. Deal?"

Kevin nodded his head. "Okay."

Diehl grabbed Kevin by the arm and half dragged, half led him out of the van, helping Kevin get his legs underneath him.

Kevin let out an audible groan as he straightened up after being laid out for such a long period of time. His feet felt the ground. Grass and dirt, surprisingly soft. Kevin strained to look down through the slim gap of air between the bag and his body.

"How'd it go?" An unknown male voice called out from a distance.

Kevin turned, attempting to zero in on where the voice was coming from.

The man must have seen Kevin clearer. "Head bag, huh? Is he a biter?"

"No," Sarah responded.

Kevin turned his head toward her voice.

"He was just a little shaken. We had to pull him out of the middle of the dream roughly after the doc had put him back in."

"And he didn't break?" the unknown man asked.

Diehl laughed and slapped Kevin on the shoulder. "This guy not only didn't break, but even had the balls to flirt with Sarah on the drive back."

"Well, at least we know he's not crazy," the man said, complimenting Sarah.

"Thank you, Harmon."

"It was funny," Diehl said.

"I'll take the new awakening from here," Harmon said. "Diehl, park the van. Mei saved you some dinner. Sarah, he wants to see you."

Diehl clapped his hands in anticipation of the meal. "Sounds good to me."

Sarah lightly squeezed Kevin's arm for a moment, reassuringly. "See you later."

Kevin felt Harmon's hand grab his arm and pull him, leading him in a direction away from the van. Harmon's hand was rough, full of calluses. As Kevin was led away, his ears pricked, trying to pick up any clue where he was, and where he was being taken. That clue never came to his ears, but his nose picked up the smell of hay. A few seconds later, his feet felt the soft grass give way to hard-packed dirt and then loose straw.

Harmon half pulled him along. "Come on, keep walking. We're almost there."

"Where is 'there'?"

"Here," Harmon said, forcing Kevin to stop. He pushed Kevin down onto a wooden chair. Kevin let out a gasp, surprised by the sudden shove.

"Okay, where is 'here'?"

"Welcome to the Ranch," Harmon said as he walked around to the back of Kevin. "The Ranch of the Awake."

Kevin felt a rope loop around his chest and arms, followed by a cinching as Harmon tied it tight. Kevin strained to turn his head to follow the source of the voice. "What do you want with me?"

"What do you know about the dream world? What do you know about its purpose?"

"What? What do you mean?"

"What do you know about the dream world?" Harmon asked again, sterner this time.

"It's a vacation. It's where we truly live."

"I'll ask you one more time," Harmon shouted. "What do you know about the dream world and its purpose?"

Kevin writhed in his chair, in fear. "What do you want from me? It's a vacation. I told you."

Harmon ripped the head bag off. The sudden explosion of light burned Kevin's eyes, causing him to squint and fight the pain. Harmon stepped in front of him, put a .45 caliber gun in Kevin's face and cocked the hammer back. *Click.* "Why are you here?"

Kevin struggled to think for a second, staring at the barrel of the gun pointed at him. He couldn't think or even focus on anything but that muzzle.

"Why are you here?"

The outburst of violent speech broke the dam that was holding Kevin's mind at bay. "I don't know! I was just dreaming, and the next thing I know, I'm being dragged out of my bed, thrown into a van, without having my memories burned, getting stabbed in the neck by the girl with the great-smelling perfume, and now I'm here, prisoner of a terrorist group, tied to a chair." Kevin let out a gasp as he had spoken his response without breathing.

Harmon leaned in close, pressing the barrel of the gun against Kevin's forehead. "Should I kill you?"

"No," Kevin squeaked out. "Please."

"Please what?"

"Please. Please don't kill me. I don't know anything."

Harmon stared at Kevin for a long moment. "Look at me. Look at me in the eyes."

Kevin looked up, staring straight into Harmon's hazel eyes, for the first time looking at the man who threatened his life rather than the barrel of the .45. Harmon's eyes squinted, and a serious tension in his face spread wrinkles across his bony-structured cheeks and up his large forehead. The wrinkles stopped when they reached where Harmon's hairline would have been, had he not shaved his entire head. The hair he lacked on top of his head had apparently migrated to his chin. A two-inch-long beard of light-brown hair grew from ear to ear. Harmon wore a simple plaid shirt and a pair of tan pants that hung loosely on his lithe frame. His skin was tan from working in the sun, day in and day out.

"Do you feel that?" Harmon asked. "Do you feel that rush? Your heart beating out of your chest, a strange heat covering your body as your hands sweat and your lungs make it hard to breathe. Do you feel it?"

Kevin only shook his head in acknowledgment.

Harmon pulled the gun from Kevin's forehead and smiled from ear to ear. "Now you're awake!"

"What?" Kevin asked as he let out a gasp.

"Breathe deep. You're awake now. Now you know what it really feels like to be human. To experience it. Not just dream it."

"So you're not going to kill me?"

Harmon laughed, shook his head, and untied Kevin's restraints. He gave Kevin a hearty slap on the shoulder. "Come on. Let me show you your new home. I have to say, I'm impressed. Most new awakenings, myself included, bawl their eyes out, but you didn't even shed a tear."

"I can't," Kevin said, rubbing his arms.

"You can't what?"

"I can't cry."

"Lucky you," Harmon said as he offered Kevin his hand to help him up from the wooden seat. Kevin nervously took his hand. Harmon pulled him up with an energetic zeal that took Kevin by surprise. "This,"—Harmon waved his left hand in an arc, showcasing the room in front of them—"this is the barn. It actually is a barn, which used to house a whole stable of horses, but we not anymore. It has stables on each side of the main open area here and has a large door at the front and back. The ladders you see scattered about lead to the storage areas that used to house hay and all kinds of farm equipment. But now we use those spots for extra living areas and food storage. As you can see ahead of you in the main open area, there are some picnic tables laid out side-by-side, Oktoberfest style." Harmon paused. "Did you ever go to Oktoberfest in the dream they pulled you out of?"

"No, umm," Kevin stammered for a second, remembering a memory from a life that was not his own but still felt all too real. "But my brother did and sent me a lot of pictures."

"Too bad. That's one of my favorite memories from my last dream."

"They pulled you out too?"

"Yeah, most of us here were. You'll meet the others later. They are all busy running missions or doing farm work at the moment. This community is all Dream States rescues except, of course, the Master and his daughter."

"The Master and his daughter?"

"Yeah, the Master is the man who started the whole Awake movement. He's the OG. His daughter, Sarah, is who pulled you out of Dream State 8, along with Diehl. That guy is huge, right?"

Kevin nodded in agreement.

"Well, anyway, the way they build a barn is, they—"

"Uh, you can skip that," Kevin interjected. "I, well I guess not me but the last dream identity I was, grew up in Colorado, so I have experience with barns. Actually, one year, my friend's parents did a live Nativity scene in their barn, and I played a shepherd." Kevin smiled as he reminisced. "We were supposed to act in awe of the baby Jesus as people came in and made donations for their church, but I got the hiccups, and not the gentle kind. I couldn't go more than a minute without hiccupping so loud that I would make the other actors jump and startle. That triggered uncontainable laughter for me. I just couldn't stop, so I had to just leave. After that day, though, Nativity scenes always put a smile on my face." Kevin was smiling big, his mind in a happier place and time. His smile faded. "I guess that isn't real."

Harmon patted him on the shoulder. "That's good. You can still remember the cheerful things. Even if they aren't real. Well, let's show you to your room," Harmon said. Together, they walked to the back of the barn. Harmon slid open a large wooden door mounted on a track above. "We have converted each stall into a room. To get your own private room, you usually have to be one of the top dogs. You're in luck. This room just opened up. We are going to use this as your holding cell until you've met with the Master."

"Holding cell? So I'm a prisoner here."

"It's for our protection, not yours. Don't worry though, you'll get to keep the room after you meet with him."

"You said it just opened up?" Kevin looked at an empty stall. It was wood walled, with a simple wooden floor covered sparsely in hay. A stool, metal bucket and blanket sat on the ground in the corner.

"Yeah, poor Milton," Harmon said, with sadness in his tone.

"Milton?"

"This used to be his room."

"What happened to him?"

"Well, he broke his leg. So we had to shoot him."

"What?" Kevin asked, stunned at the nonchalance of Harmon's answer.

"It's just mercy to put him out of his misery. Even if he had survived, what kind of life would he have?"

"Is that how the Awake treat their own? They slow you down, so you just kill them?"

"Milton was our last horse."

"Oh," Kevin let out.

"Yeah. He was a good horse. Anyway, we'll get you a bed soon. Uh, let's see, what else? Well, the bucket is for what you think it is for, and the blanket, well, if I have to explain that, you're in trouble. The picnic tables I pointed out are where we eat breakfast, lunch, and dinner. The food here is good. All natural and cooked by the best free chef in the land, me." Harmon smiled at his self-appreciation.

"What do you people want with me? Why am I here?"

"You're here because we, the Awake, saved you. You needed us. Now you're going to help."

"Help with what?"

"Help us fight the system."

"What fight?"

"Wow, you really are a newbie. When you meet with the Master tomorrow, he will explain it all."

"Take me to him now. I want to know what's going on."

Harmon shook his head. "I can't. He's busy, and I've got work to get to too."

"So, what, I'm supposed to just sit here and wait?"

"Not exactly," Harmon said as pulled a syringe out of his back pants pocket. "We can't trust you yet."

"No. You don't need to do that. Come on."

"It's okay. Besides, this injection will also cleanse the chemicals from your last dream out of your system."

"Really, you don't have to."

"I really do." Harmon advanced on Kevin. Kevin tried to fight him off, but Harmon overpowered him easily, his lithe frame hiding his strength. The needle burned as it sank into Kevin's neck. "Relax. You're going to drift off to sleep in a second. When you wake up, you'll get some of your answers."

Kevin felt his fight give out as the chemicals absorbed through his body. He disconnected from his physical self for a few minutes. He couldn't feel the hay or the hard floor as Harmon laid him down in the stall. The blanket that Harmon pulled over him and the latching of the stall door affected none of his senses. He was completely numb. It was that complete lack of feeling that he was trapped in as sleep overtook Kevin's mind.

The frozen top layer of snow crunched under Jaared's hiking boots as he trudged up the gentle slope. It was late June, but at twelve thousand feet, the cold still maintained control over the forest. Ice and snow covered the rivers, and there remained a frost on the pine needles. Jaared stopped and pulled out his phone to take a picture of the view ahead of him. An alpine lake nestled high in the Colorado mountains, between two steep rocky slopes, glistened diamonds on its frigid surface in the early afternoon sun. Thunder Lake in Rocky Mountain National Park had been a favorite place of Jaared's ever since he had spent a weekend in college, camping there with his best friends and his brother. The hike was long and challenging, but the view was worth it every time.

Today had been extra difficult. The trail being covered in snow was an obstacle Jaared hadn't expected to have to tackle, since below timberline it was over seventy degrees. He had only packed his light jacket and enough water and food for the hike. What he didn't pack was a GPS. That would have come in handy once the path under his feet turned to frozen snow. Others had to have hiked Thunder Lake already this year, but the snow was so hard that the only footprints Jaared could follow were hoofprints. Jaared had wrongfully assumed they belonged to the park ranger's llamas.

Jaared, now looking at the view he had set out to see that day, laughed to himself. *The tracks must have been deer or elk,* he thought. They had led him to the other side of a large hill and far from his intended target. He had made his way up and over the hill, jogging through the snow, fighting for footing and praying he didn't step in a deep snowbank. His recent dedication to endurance training had paid off. He had made it, and now he stood staring at Thunder Lake. Jaared slid his backpack off and set it on the hard snow. Reaching inside, he pulled out a protein bar and his water bottle. He ate the bar and drank some of his water. *Just drink half. Save some for the hike back down.*

Jaared stood and surveyed the view for a few minutes more. He had planned to relax and let the mountains soak into his soul; however, his unintended detour had taken too much time. He put his backpack back on and turned to head down the mountain. In front of him stood the end of the trail, clear to see. *Let's see if I can't stay on it this time.*

Thirty minutes later, the trail had disappeared, hidden under the remaining blanket of winter. Jaared was walking in a direction that, to the best of his knowledge, seemed like the right way to go. He pulled the trail map out of his pocket and looked at it. *Well, that's not much help.* The map only showed the trail and a few lakes and rivers on brown background. No topography, no identifying features. Just 2D lakes and rivers, and a dotted line labelled 'Trail.'

Well, if I head downhill and listen for some water, I should be able to find a river. Then this map may actually help. He turned around and listened as the wind blew through the nearby pine forest. *That will not be easy. I wonder.* Jaared pulled his cell phone out of his pocket. He read the words at the top left of the screen: *No Service. Not low enough yet.* Putting his phone away, he surveyed the area he stood in. Trees surrounded him, the ground was covered in frozen snow and dead pine needles. *I guess that way?*

It took twenty minutes of arduous hiking downhill before Jaared finally picked up the unmistakable sound of water. He quickened his pace and turned in its direction. Soon he could hear the water clearly. The sound of the river rushing and bubbling over rocks and trees filled the air and Jaared's ears. He stopped and listened to it. It seemed to be all around him. *Where is it?* He thought as he spun in a full circle, unable to spot the source of the noise.

CRACK! CRACK! THUMP!

The sound of ice breaking and falling into the river caused Jaared's heart to skip a beat. It was directly under his feet. Not even a second later, the ice bridge he had unknowingly walked onto gave way. Jaared dropped without resistance. The sudden fall and shock of the frigid rushing water stole the air from his lungs. Cold water penetrated every ounce of clothing he had on. All the warmth that had built up in his body from the physical exertion of hiking disappeared in an instant. The only feeling he could experience now was the cold. He scrambled and fought to breathe, swallowing cold water, as he was dragged downstream under a sheet of ice by freezing water.

"Cauuglh." Jaared coughed and gargled as he attempted to fight for breath. His lungs couldn't grasp air. The cold penetrated his soul. His heart raced as fear overtook him.

It was in this exact moment that the sound of a loud latch being drawn pulled Jaared out of the dream and back into his body and mind as Kevin Altair. The newly abducted member of "The Awake." The door to his stall swung open with a loud creak, its rusty hinges complaining from the sudden use. Kevin shot up to a seated position on the hay floor, the blanket that had been laid over him falling to his waist.

"Well, good morning," Sarah said with a small laugh. "I don't think I've ever seen someone pop up quite like that."

Kevin blinked his eyes a few times, still emotionally caught in the feeling of drowning in a frozen river.

"Are you alright?" Sarah asked, squatting down so her face was on the same level as Kevin's. "I know some people we rescue take some time to get used to sleeping again."

"I slept?"

"Yeah, the injection that Harmon gave you didn't just knock you out, but also cleared your system out. Since you were a kid, they have kept you up to date on injections and medicines to keep you awake or asleep, back and forth. We just hit the reset button."

"That wasn't right," Kevin said, his mind still dwelling on the dream.

"We've done this before. You'll be fine."

"No, you don't understand. It was wrong."

"What was?"

"I, I had a memory pop up when I was out. A memory from the dream you pulled me out of. I was lost in the woods when I was hiking, but I found my way out with no issues, but this time, I dreamt it differently."

"How so?"

"I fell in the river."

"Dreams are dreams. They don't always make sense."

"Now I have two memories of the same event, though. How do I make sure I don't confuse what actually happened?"

"Well, you'll remember your dream for a little while, but you'll forget it. I can't tell you what I dreamed about last night, but when I first woke up, it was vivid."

"You forget dreams without a burn?"

"Yeah, real dreams, at least. I mean, they just kind of fade away."

"Even if you have a mind chip?"

Sarah pursed her lips, thinking. "I don't know. I assume so, but I'm,"—Sarah pointed at her head, behind her ear—"I'm not plugged in, so I have no reference, but I know someone you can ask."

"Who?"

"My father." Sarah stood and turned to reach out of the stall. She picked up a small pile of clothes and turned to hand them to Kevin. "Here, put these on."

Kevin grabbed the clothes, suddenly overly aware that he was still wearing the hospital gown and nothing else. "Thanks. I think hay is in places hay shouldn't be."

Sarah smiled. "Get dressed. Then come out." She turned to leave, but stopped in the doorway. "My father, or as other people call him, 'The Master,' will decide your fate today. We've rescued people who turned against us, so he's going to need to know your story. Word of advice, don't hold back. If he thinks you're lying, then we will have to hack your mind chip. It's painful but effective. So please, just tell the truth, and all of it."

Kevin nodded. "Thanks."

Sarah nodded back and left.

Kevin shook his head, dislodging a negative thought that was forming but hadn't taken root. He stood and pulled the clothes on. The boxers fit well, but nothing else did. He was drowning in an old gray T-shirt and worn jeans, held on by a belt he had to tie in a knot to keep cinched. The slip-on shoes were a tad tight, squeezing his toes, but would keep his feet dry. He took a deep breath to steel his nerves and stepped out of the stall that they had deposited him in last night. As he stepped out of his small enclosure, he found himself engulfed by the tantalizing smell of breakfast. The toasting tortillas, cooking scrambled eggs and sizzling potatoes all reached his nose and overpowered even the smell of hay and musk of the wooden architecture of the barn.

Ten sets of eyes turned to look at Kevin from the picnic tables in the center of the barn. Blue, brown and green glared at him, boring into his soul. He felt like he was being led to the firing line. He glanced in their direction but didn't make out a single face. Kevin looked away, watching his feet tread along as he passed the eating area.

"You'll get breakfast after talking with my father," Sarah said. She stopped him as they reached the door of the barn. She grabbed a canvas bag from the wall. "Don't resist or I'll have to hurt you."

"Resist what?"

Sarah answered by pulling the canvas bag over his head.

An awkward, stumbling walk across uneven ground ended with Sarah helping Kevin up a set of wooden steps. A door creaked as she pulled him inside some building. Kevin felt Sarah's hand grab the bottom of the head bag. She removed it with a quick pull.

Kevin blinked as his sight readjusted to the light. It was dimmer than he had expected. Kevin turned his head, surveying the room. The room was so different from everything he had experienced on the farm up to this point. He was sitting in a traditional living room out of the American 1970s. Ornate wallpaper covered every wall, and the carpet was a lush red shag. Two fabric loveseats, each a paisley design, sat facing each other, separated by a small coffee table. Sarah ushered to one of these, where he sat down. He was looking at a collection of porcelain angels in a glass armoire when the Master walked down the hall leading from the back of the house.

"Hello, Kevin," the old man with snow-white hair said.

Kevin swallowed, nervous. "Hello."

The Master stepped to the opposite couch and sat down with considerable effort. "Would you like some tea?" the Master asked with a kind smile.

Kevin looked at this smiling old man. His overalls and plaid shirt made the man look more like a farmer than the leader of an insurgent group. "Are you the Master?" Kevin asked, his doubt clear from his tone.

"Yes," the older man said, sitting forward and smiling bigger now. "Not what you expected."

"Not exactly."

Sarah, standing guard by the door, let out a slight laugh.

"It's funny. Every time we rescue someone, I get to have a discussion with them. Sometimes I tire of answering the same questions over and over, but I never tire of that shock at seeing me." The old man chuckled to himself and sat back against the cushions. "I imagine you have a lot of questions. But first let me introduce myself. I'm the Master. Sarah is my daughter. And my organization focuses on rescuing those members of mankind who outgrow the Dream States. We save people like you."

"Everyone keeps telling me you saved me. Saved me from what? You grabbed me in my sleep, threw me in a van, and then locked me in a barn. Doesn't exactly feel like you're the good guys."

"Let me guess. You've been told we are a terrorist group, right?"

"Well, yes."

"No."

"No?"

"No," the old man said, smiling.

Kevin looked at Sarah. She shook her head, smiling as well.

"You are the Awake, right?"

The old man nodded in acknowledgment.

"And you attack Dream States and deface property to scare people away from dreaming."

"More or less," the Master answered.

"That makes you terrorists," Kevin said, connecting dots that seemed clear to him. "Not to mention you have killed people in your attacks."

"It's all a matter of perspective. We fight for something that upsets the status quo, and that scares the leadership. But fear is not our goal. We are not bent on world destruction or murder." The Master studied Kevin's face. "I can see you don't believe me. The Awake are not crazy terrorists. We are those who learned the truth and escaped. The people on this farm are those who have survived the consequences of leaving the dream system, and they are the rare ones. You are now one of the rare ones."

"What are you talking about?"

"Let me summarize what the Dream States are to you, okay? Stop me if I'm off track or wrong." The Master sat forward on the couch. "You have been told and taught and shown the basics of how this entire system came to be and what its purpose is, right?"

Kevin nodded.

"You believe that the Dream States are the key to our prosperity. They are the foundation of our ability to live nigh eternal, and the reason for our peaceful existence. That they are where we all get to be free and experience the wonder and creativity that is only available to us in our minds. Our world directly results from their success."

"Yeah," Kevin said, somewhat confused how the Master word-for-word recited how he would have said it.

"They tell you of the time before the Dream States," the Master continued. "How we lived in twenty-four-hour cycles and how this pattern made us sick, full of mental health issues and unhappy with our lives. Then, like saviors coming to set us free, Eli and Anders invented 'sustained dreaming,' allowing mankind to heal and grow. Soon after, the government got involved and helped the dream network grow. They instituted the Karma and Overall Rank system to ensure fairness and appropriated land and resources for Dream State development, all of which brought us to the world we live in now. A peaceful planet of doing your job and dreaming well. Does that sound right?"

"Well yeah," Kevin said. "That's the history of the Dream States. Are you telling me that's not the truth?"

"It's partial truth," Sarah said.

"Partial truth?"

"Yes," the Master said. "While the major events happened, how they happened is a different story altogether. When the Dream States began, our country and our planet needed help. We fought over almost every issue of political or social importance. People were stockpiling weapons and resources, preparing for the worst. The government had to step in, bringing martial law to the streets. This led to uprisings of militias and protests. We were in a battle with our brothers on the sociopolitical and socioeconomic front. It forced the wealthy of the time to hire small forces of armed men just to keep themselves safe. While all this was increasing in fervor, fed by the power-hungry politicians, the average citizen who wanted only to work, live safely, and enjoy moments of recreation scrambled just to avoid the turmoil. Soon, to deal with it all, they recalled all Armed forces from foreign posts, which led to an exponential rise in terrorism. The threat of annihilation hung over everyone. The political climate during the time of the Dream States' creation was one of corruption, power mongering and fear.

"All this pressure led to the need for an escape, a reason not to despair. Everyday people had lost trust in the system. The Dream States became a way to let off steam and keep from snapping."

"At first, even with all the promised freedom and escape, dream centers had difficulty gaining traction. They struggled to stay open, because of the cost of using high levels of electricity, and inflated taxes in an attempt to appear to be saving the earth from climate change. At the brink of failing, Eli and Anders used their clients in a way that some would view as wrong, but in the end, it was for the greater good."

"Using the mind chip, they began implanting code and harvesting information. Eli and Anders found the triggers that had caused their clients to come in the first place and began targeting their marketing better. Combined with the word-of-mouth marketing success that came from the implanted burning desire to tell others of sustained dreaming, the Dream States began their astronomical climb."

"The mind chip can do that?"

"Quite well, actually. They use that function now to implant thoughts and quell dissension among the entire population. They have fed you beliefs since you were a baby."

Kevin scrunched his face, both doubting the Master and fearing the implication.

"Think about it. How else would you know half of the stuff you do? The mind chip reteaches you, right? Well, they teach you a few extra things each time to help you fill the role they need to keep the system going. It's as simple as that."

Kevin was feeling a little disturbed.

"Using that implantation was the next step for the rise of the Dream States," the Master continued. "Eli and Anders took two lower-level politicians and promised them that if they would just dream once, they would guarantee them a rise in power. As this was the only desire of these particular politicians, they took the deal. Eli and Anders implanted ideas of how to use the government to increase the power of dreaming into these politicians' minds and then used a "your first dream free" sales campaign to implant the desire to vote for those candidates. They each won by a landslide. A few elections later, the Dream States were insulated from legislative punishment. A few years later, dreaming became required, used for school and work training. The government disbanded soon after, yielding to the system we have today."

Kevin shook his head. "No. This can't be."

"It's the full truth," Sarah said, chiming in.

"Why? Why would they do something like that? I suppose you'll tell me Eli and Anders were just evil?"

"No," the Master answered. "They weren't at all. They just believed in a different moral code. Every line they crossed was under the belief that it was best for the good of all."

"Was it?"

"In some ways, yes. Thanks to the Dream States, mankind has solved overpopulation by removing the desire to reproduce from our minds, and we have been making progress in solving climate change, and almost completely solved other issues, like drug use and crime."

"I guess without you, they would solve soon all the problems."

"No," the Master said, smiling at the accusation, "because there is one major problem that the Dream States themselves created. Remember, dreaming became a government mandate. Well, there were free radicals who arose. People who couldn't dream and those who woke up from dreams, unable to be plugged in again."

"Which is where you came in?"

"Yes and no," the Master answered. "They classify non-dreamers into three categories. The first category is those who are just unable to sustain dream. Their genetics make it so they can't connect to the system. Those in control eradicated that population, blaming the inability to dream on a viral outbreak. A quarantine and extermination solved the issue."

Kevin's eyes grew large, not at the idea, but by how nonchalant the Master sounded saying it.

"The second category," he continued, "are the mental-rejection dreamers, or the early wakers, as we call them. Which is what you are."

"No, you're wrong."

"You woke up from your dream, right?"

"Yeah, because your people yanked me out of the bed and dragged me here."

"No." The Master waved his hands in front of him. "No, you woke up first on your own. Your doctor contacted us so we could get there before the others could get you."

"The others? There are others now?"

"Yes. Don't you see? You are a threat to their system. If you wake up from your dream, your mind is rejecting the program. If you can't dream, they can't control you. There is only one option then: eliminate you."

"You are crazy."

"I wish I was," the Master said. "But I've seen it. I've experienced it. You and I aren't all that different. When I was a young boy, I woke up early. I was one of the youngest ever to wake up. People didn't know what to do. Something caused me to reject the programming. They first tried to just use the burn to reset me, but my mind rejected the wipe. My memories stayed."

"You rejected the burn? How is that possible?"

"They postulated that the issue came from my mind being so empty it would search and find pieces of information and reconstruct the memories, so they moved on to implantation."

"Implantation?"

"When you delete something in a computer or brain format, it's still there until you write another piece of information over it," the Master said. "So they used the mind chip to put other memories inside my brain. It didn't work. My mind fought the implanted code. They studied the timetable, locked me in a room, and observed me. For years, they tested new dream realms, different drug cocktails and programming. I was a zoo animal. They even tested whether my 'situation' could spread. They brought in other people as test subjects, had us become friends. Then they reprogrammed them. Time after time, my best friends forgot me. I thought I'd be alone forever. I had little hope. So I joined them. I went to work to solve the issues that someone like me would cause in the dream network. I learned the code and made a name for myself. Soon I was known as Kenneth Ulbert, the genius non-dreaming kid, working to save the thing he couldn't access himself. I was a hero. When I unveiled my 'kill code,' I was celebrated. My work had created a simple way to solve the problem of other early wakers crashing their dream networks. My code, it sends out a command to the shared dream, which kills the memory of the dreamer's disappearance and replaces it with a memory of a tragic death. It's still used today. If you ever had a friend die under tragic or unexpected circumstances, they most likely woke early and my code covered it. This process solved the issue for the Dream States. The network keeps running, the problem entity identified and the non-dreamers can be pulled out of the population without issue."

"Those people can't dream again?"

The Master shook his head. "No, their minds will reject the dream from that moment forward."

"Then what happens to them?"

"They are culled after the fact, ending the issue."

"Culled?"

"Exterminated," Sarah clarified.

Kevin wasn't buying it. "You're saying they are just killed?"

"Yes," the Master continued. "It's for the greater good. What does the death of a few people matter when we're saving the planet, saving billions?"

"Hmmm." Kevin pondered the idea.

"You understand that?" Sarah said, bewildered.

"Well, kind of, yeah," Kevin said.

The Master held his hand up toward his daughter, calming her. "It's okay. Please tell me, why do you think you feel that would be an okay sacrifice?"

"Well," Kevin said, "it's just a numbers thing, and if eliminating a few people, cursed with the inability to dream, saves billions who can dream, it kind of makes sense."

The Master nodded. "I lived with that belief for years too, until a nurse helped me realize something. It wasn't a curse. Those who couldn't dream, including me, are blessed. We are the free ones. I am the master of my mind.

No one could overwrite it and change my thoughts or beliefs ever again. So I dropped the moniker of Ulbert and changed my name to 'The Master' to remind myself of that fact."

"A nurse made you think that?"

"She didn't make me think it. No one can make me think anything. She helped me accept who I was, and she showed me what life was about. She and I fell in love, real love. Sarah, my daughter, is the product of that love. I thought I'd felt love before, but when Sarah came into this world, I knew I'd never be the same, and I haven't." The Master paused, tears coming to his eyes while he looked at his daughter.

"Where is she now, this nurse?"

"I was eight when they came," Sarah said. "Woken up by the sound of yelling and loud pops outside my window. I didn't know the sound of gunfire."

"Who's 'they'?" Kevin asked.

"The government, Kevin," the Master answered. "Sarah's mother and I had started something. It was something secret, something of great importance."

"The Awake?" Kevin interjected.

"The last lie of the Dream States I helped cultivate was that of a common enemy. There are few things as unifying and quelling of dissent as a singular enemy everyone can disdain and, sometimes, fear. History is littered with examples of this, from nations coming together for retribution after a terrorist attack to entire civilizations becoming one people after the unjust decree of a dictator attempting to expand his control. Human nature to rebel. We strive and yearn for freedom. So we started a fake resistance movement, a false-flag organization who could be blamed as the reason for removing free radicals and eliminating them."

"The Awake is fake?"

"It started that way, but then something happened. Sarah's mother and I we felt actual love, and soon, Sarah was born. The first natural birth in over a century. We,

Sarah's mother and I, kept Sarah a secret and executed the commands of the government. But we knew that the world we were living in wouldn't accept and allow our daughter to survive. So something had to be done. This false flag became a false, false flag."

"What?" Kevin asked in disbelief.

"We started saving people and helping them escape. The heads of the corporation didn't like that. So they started trying to track us down. Of course, I had disabled our GPS tracking, but they still found us, time and time again. So we started going after them."

"So you are saying to believe you're not just the part of the system that you... were?" Kevin's brow scrunched in a strange twist.

"Yes, the first of the true resistance to the Dream States. The problem was that when I felt genuine love, true non-programmed love, I became the most dangerous person in the world. They coudn't program me, they couldn't erase my mind and now they knew I knew the simulation was inadequate, and I had the proof."

"What proof?"

"Me," Sarah replied.

The Master nodded. "Sarah is the product of true love. Her life, her existence, is evidence that love and life outside the Dream States is not only possible, but it's more real. That's a dangerous notion."

"I don't get it. This nurse who helped you, why? Why would she risk herself for you?"

"That's what you don't get?" Sarah asked more aggressively than intended.

The Master held his hand up in a calming motion. "Sarah." The Master turned toward Kevin. "My wife was an amazing nurse. She was one of the top ranked in her district. That meant she both had a gift for caring for the afflicted and was dream exempt. This made her the least reprogrammed and most actual human person I'd ever met. She risked everything for what she knew was right. For me, a stranger she grew to care for, she gave everything. That's life. That's actual emotion. I'm not surprised you have trouble grasping that concept. It's put in your head that connection is a waste. Sacrifice is a squandering of your potential. Let me ask you a question. Have you ever felt so strongly about someone that you would die for them?"

Kevin thought for a moment and then shook his head.

"No. How could you? You don't remember anyone for more than a few weeks."

"I remember people."

"You remember personalities, but can you tell me a story of a memory that you and another share?" The Master let his question sink in for a moment.

Kevin's furrowed brow gave him the answer he expected.

"The Dream States are turning the world into a population of zombies, machines that don't show emotions, but over time..." The Master pointed at Kevin.

"Me?"

"No matter how much you or the system try to suppress emotions, they come back. When that happens, your subconscious rejects the dream. It's true humanity, overcoming."

"If that were true, then everyone would wake up."

"Everyone does."

"So why aren't there more people not dreaming, then?" Kevin asked, with a hint of an accusatory tone.

"Not everyone has a Dr. Flo," Sarah said.

"What my daughter is saying," continued the Master, "is that when most people wake up, it's the end for them."

"The end?" Kevin asked.

"Yes, ninety-nine percent of people wake up somewhere around their fortieth birthday. When that occurs, they become what the people running the Dream States fear most, free radicals. Without a culling of those uncontrollable minds, the entire system would die. Non-dreamers are like a cancer."

"What?"

"Think of all the people you remember, not from your last dream, but from the real world. How many senior citizens have you seen?"

"I... I... they're just not around my work. They rank higher, or retire."

"Permanently." Sarah said.

"No." Kevin shook his head. "You're wrong."

"Occasionally, someone wakes up early. How old are you, Kevin?" The Master asked.

"Twenty-four, if my memory is right, which, if I believed you, isn't."

"Weirdly enough, they don't mess with age. It's a way to ensure your tracking code isn't affected. Twenty-four is extremely early. Everyone wakes up. They make some into the managers who run the Z-Banks or the Dream States themselves. They kill the rest. But when someone wakes up that much before their forties, they pose a greater threat to the system. Your mind is more powerful and able to overcome implantation better than most. Let me ask you, how did you wake up?"

"How? I don't know."

"Did you do something specific in the dream? Drugs? Meditation?"

"No, I just had a terrible headache, and then I was in a hospital bed, and some lady told me to relax and adjusted the flow on the IV thing. Then I started seeing the words 'WAKE UP,' and your daughter grabbed me."

"A headache?"

"Yeah, just a bad migraine."

"Hmmm. That's interesting." The Master rubbed his hands together.

"What? What is it?"

"You saw the words 'WAKE UP'?"

"Yeah, uh, a billboard changed for a moment."

"That means you're even more lucky Dr. Flo is a sympathizer to our cause. She contacted us, and we came and got you before they reported your sleep disruption to the higher-ups. You're alive because of her. If you were projecting messages in the dream network, that means you're the third category of non-dreamers. You're a lucid dreamer."

"A what?"

"When your mind realized you were in a dream, and was pushed back inside, instead of just kicking you out again, it took control and started changing code."

"That's possible?"

"Everyone holds this ability to an extent, and many even use it. They spread knowledge of it through the dream to encourage cooperative building. Most dreamers know this as the law of attraction or manifesting, but in reality, they are coding. But some can do this at a higher level. As children, these people do this unknowingly, but there have been a few occasions where older, more understanding lucid dreamers have been documented," the Master said. "These special lucid dreamers can destabilize the entire dream network, causing major crashes, or even implanting ideas into people's minds. This means you can even use the dream network's own code to change anything at will."

"Am I supposed to believe any of this?" Kevin asked.

"What does your heart tell you?"

"My heart?"

"Yes, look, the dream has power over the mind, and we could trick you mentally, but no one has power over your heart. You can feel the truth better than you can understand it."

Kevin looked at Sarah and her father. "Why?"

"Why?" the Master asked back at Kevin.

"Why tell me? Why would you admit to being part of the government?"

"We need your help," the Master said. "And before you agree to help, I believe it's only right for you to know everything. I spent most of my life lying. Not anymore."

"What do you need me for?"

"I want to end this," the Master said, looking at his daughter while speaking to Kevin.

Kevin glanced between the two again. "End this? You want to end the Dream States? That's impossible."

"Nothing's impossible, but that's not what I mean. I want to end this." The Master said, waving his arms in a big circle. "I don't want my daughter to live in hiding, in constant fear that the Dream States are coming for her. I want her to have freedom."

"If I'm to believe what you've told me so far, then that can't happen."

"The only way it will happen is if we never existed," the Master said, smiling a sly grin.

Kevin's mind understood, but couldn't grasp the idea. "The kill code?"

"Yes, it's been used to keep the dream running smoothly, but it can also erase all records of us."

"We disappear," Sarah said.

Kevin looked at her for a second and then back to the Master. "That's not possible. There is no way you can just erase everyone's mind like that."

"Not only is it possible, but I have already written the protocols for it. We need you to learn them so you can put them in the dream network."

"Me?"

"Yes, I can't dream anymore. My mind rejects the network," the Master said. "Yours will too after a time, but for now, you're still early in your awakening period. Combine this with your coding training and you're ready to learn how to code free in the network."

"How do you know about my coding job?"

"We've been watching you for a while, Kevin," the Master said. "We've tracked your dream lives, your Karma actions, and your job assignments. You were on our watch list. So when Dr. Flo called, we rushed to get you out."

"So what do you say, Kevin?" Sarah asked.

"No."

"No?" Sarah almost yelled.

"No."

"I'm going to be clear with you," the Master said. "You're a danger to their system, meaning if you went back to the Dream States, they'd kill you. You don't trust us, and I understand. Trust takes time. What you need to understand is that we don't trust you either. You're a danger to us as well. So I'm going to give you a week to learn more about the real Awake movement. Over the next seven days, I want you to meet the members here. Learn their stories and experience what life is like. Then we'll have this talk again."

"And if I still feel the same way, you'll kill me?"

"I can't risk this base. I won't risk her safety." The Master pointed at Sarah. "I've told you already that I would die to save her. Believe me, I have killed to save her already and will do so again if needed."

"So, death. Not much of a choice."

"We aren't murderers, Kevin, despite what you may have heard."

"Memory wipe," Sarah said. "Primitive burn."

Kevin thought for a moment. "You said the burn won't work on me."

"Even with non-dreamers, chemical lobotomies are still effective at scrambling the mind." The Master said.

"You're serious?" Kevin asked.

"Yes," the Master answered. "In one week, we'll have this discussion again."

Sarah stepped toward Kevin with the bag held out. "Want to put it on yourself this time?"

"Fine," he said, grabbing the bag and pulling it over his head in protest.

The Dream State 8 control room was dark, the only light coming from a large computer screen that two men huddled over. All the other screens in the room were off, the chairs that sat twenty other controllers empty. This room had been cleared because of the sensitive nature of the situation.

"Show me the abduction again," Thairn said.

"Yes, sir." The technician typed a few commands, and a security video popped up.

Thairn leaned in close, watching as the two masked assailants pulled Kevin Altair from his Dream State 8 bed. "Now show me the dream view of this again, but synched up with the abduction."

"Sir, what's this about?" the technician asked as he typed in commands. "You've watched these videos at least twenty times now."

Thairn put his hand on the technician's shoulder and squeezed forcefully.

The young man shuddered at his aggressive touch. The message was clear. Don't ask questions. "Here you go, sir."

Thairn released his grasp on the young man and pulled out his phone. He pressed a button that dialed a preset number.

The young man rubbed his shoulder and listened to Thairn's side of the conversation, trying to understand what was going on.

"Yes, sir. The Awake took him. Yes, sir, the migraine trigger worked perfect. Yes, sir. They will be cleaned. Yes, sir." Thairn hung up his call. "So," Thairn said as he addressed the young man, "can you pull up your work profile and the rest of the controllers, as well as everyone who aided ID 925387 in his checking-in process and care?"

"Okay." The young man did as asked.

Thairn pointed at the results on the screen. "Are these start-of-shift times accurate?"

"Yeah."

"Great, I need to see everyone on this list immediately, except for... Dr. Flo."

"Sir, what for?"

Thairn looked at the young man. "Send the assembly message."

The young man typed a message into the system and sent it out. As soon as the message finished being sent, Thairn slammed the man's face into the desk. He struggled under the force of the assault, but Thairn held him down.

Thairn spoke into his ear, angry. "Everyone else is going to have their mind set back to the start of their work shift. All this will be a memory that disappears. But you. You. Well, do you have a terrorist attack if you don't have a casualty?"

Blood and brain matter spattered over the keyboard as the bullet from Thairn's handgun ripped through the young man's skull.

CHAPTER 5

THE RANCH

K evin sat in his stall. He reached and picked a piece of canvas from his hair, the last remnant of the sweaty head bag. Sarah had escorted him back to his room following his conversation with the Master.

"Breakfast," Sarah said, handing Kevin a plate piled high with eggs covered in salsa, and a corn tortilla.

"Thanks," he said, taking the plate.

"I know this a lot to absorb," Sarah said. "Understanding the enemy is important in winning the war. Besides, it's the truth."

Kevin tore a piece of tortilla and piled on a small portion of eggs and salsa. "If you say so." He took a big bite of his breakfast.

Sarah handed him a canteen.

He took it and swallowed the water to help him finish his overzealous bite. "If everything I've learned is untrue or has been hiding the truth, why?"

"After this next week, you'll understand. The dream is not real, Kevin."

"I know that, but at the same time -"

"No, you understand, but you don't know. That makes you dangerous, so we have to be careful." Sarah said, her smile turning to a tight-lipped expression.

"People keep saying that," Kevin said, his annoyance and frustration over the last day leaking past playful.

"It's true." Sarah's face showed a hint of sadness. "We've made mistakes trusting new awakenings before."

"What happened?"

Sarah's jaw hardened as a memory from the past came to mind. "Stay here," she said, turning and closing the stall door behind her with a loud bang.

Kevin stared at the door for a second. *Okay.* He finished his breakfast and lay down to sleep for a few more minutes. A few hours later, after falling back asleep for longer than intended, Kevin found himself woken by a visitor.

"Knock, knock."

Kevin looked up to find Harmon standing in the open stall door, wearing an apron and carrying another. "Hey."

"Hey." Kevin sat up and rubbed his eyes.

"Long morning?" Harmon asked.

"Yeah," Kevin said. "Talking with the Master can be... confusing."

"Confusing?"

"Yeah."

"Well, how about a mental break? Want to help me in the kitchen?"

"Uh."

"I need some help with the potatoes. I kind of cut myself." Harmon showed Kevin his bandaged hand. A small streak of red leaked through the wrapping. "I can't chop the rest well, and if I don't get it done fast, then dinner might not happen tonight. I don't want to deal with everyone here angry."

Kevin stammered, "Sarah said to stay here."

"As long as you stay in the barn, you're good, right? I've got an extra apron." Harmon held the apron out toward Kevin. "Please."

"Yeah, sorry, I'll help," Kevin said, standing up. "Chopping potatoes, huh? You couldn't need help to taste cheesecake?" Kevin smiled, happy with his off-the-cuff comment.

"That was yesterday," Harmon answered back, equally coy. He handed Kevin the apron, turned, and let him out of his stall. A short walk later, they were in the barn's kitchen. The Awake had pieced together a large assortment of appliances and tools, forming a well-stocked kitchen. "The potatoes are in the sink there. You're lucky. I already peeled and rinsed them. Just need to finish the mise en place."

"The what?" Kevin asked as he made his way over to the sink full of potatoes.

"It's what you call it when you get everything portioned out that you're going to use to cook with before doing anything else. For example,"—Harmon used his uninjured hand to point at three large bowls that sat on a counter on the other side of the room—"I filled each of those with either chopped carrots, onions or herbs. Everything but the potatoes is ready for the stew tonight."

"Stew, huh?"

"Hey, it's a good thing my mother taught me everything about cooking before they pulled me out of the dream," Harmon said. "A lesser man couldn't do what I can with so few ingredients to work with."

"Alright. Uh, well, do you have a knife?"

"Right, sorry." Harmon turned in a whirl and took a chef's knife out of a bucket of soapy water that sat on the counter to his right. "Here you are, freshly cleaned."

"Thanks," Kevin said, taking the knife. "So, expert chef, you remember your last dream too?"

"Yeah. I was H. Hewitt Clancy, a young, wild teenager who was trying to get his life back on track after a stint with drugs." Harmon shook his head, laughing. "One relapse and my mind overloaded in the dream and I slipped out of the network. A few days later, I'm brought here and realize all my trips had nothing on how messed up the truth could be."

"Drugs woke you up?"

"Yeah, at least that was the trigger." Harmon motioned to the potatoes. "Chop and talk or we're not going to get this done."

"Right." Kevin turned and started chopping the potatoes.

"A little smaller than that," Harmon corrected him.

"Okay." Kevin nodded, taking instruction and trying to chop as consistently as possible. "So, H. Hewitt Clancy. The 'H' stands for 'Harmon,' I'm guessing?"

"Howard." Harmon laughed.

Kevin looked at him with a smiling glance. "So why Harmon?"

"It's a reminder." Harmon sat on a stool and leaned against the wall. "When I woke up from my last dream, I was in love in it at the time. She was the reason I was turning my life around. Harmony Thomas was, she was an angel. She was my everything. When I got here, I cried for days. I knew I'd never see her again, and that whoever was dreaming as her would forget me. The woman I loved was gone, just ripped out of existence,"—Harmon snapped his fingers—"like that. So to keep that memory and her alive, I changed my name."

"I'm sorry," Kevin said as he continued to chop. "Were you in love when you woke up?"

"No, no, I was... I was pretty alone. My brother, who was my best friend, he had left. I was living in a one-bedroom condo by myself, working a career I didn't enjoy and just waiting for something to inspire me to greater. I don't know," Kevin said.

"How old were you?" Harmon asked. "In the dream, that is."

"Twenty-four."

"You're so lucky."

"How's that?" Kevin asked, grabbing a new potato, having just finished with one.

"Let me guess, you have the strange dreams?"

Kevin stopped mid-chop, the knife hovering over the potato. "Yeah."

"I'm thirty-two years old, Kevin. When I woke up from the dream, I was a nineteen-year-old. Imagine, in those dreams or memories or whatever, that you were a teenager. Two different maturity-levels and hormone-production states in your head at the same time. And your heart is breaking because the woman you love is gone."

"Hmmm."

A few minutes of silence followed as Kevin continued to chop and Harmon stared at the ground, lost in a train of thought.

"All done," Kevin said, putting down the knife.

"Great. That would have taken me forever with one hand. Now help me put everything in the big pot."

Kevin gathered his diced potatoes and the other ingredients and put them all in a large pot. "What next?"

"Now we add some water. Get the hose from over there and fill the pot here until you reach that nick on the side."

Kevin got the thin hose, kinked it, and turned the water on. He walked over and started filling the pot. The flow was slow. As the level rose, Kevin said, "Harmon, I'm sorry about you losing the girl you love."

"Thanks. You know, most people here don't care about what happened in the dream. They just want to ignore it. It's kind of nice to talk about it."

"Can I ask you a question?"

"Yeah, shoot."

"How long do the dreams last?"

"Uh," Harmon stammered, "the dreams are your mind healing itself, I think. I don't think they'll ever stop, but they get less intense," Harmon said. "Oh, that's enough water."

"Oh, right." Kevin kinked the hose, stopping the flow. He stepped to the spigot and turned it off.

"What the hell is this?" Sarah almost yelled as she stepped into the kitchen.

"I'm helping Harmon," Kevin said.

"I cut myself and needed an extra hand."

"Then you come find me! You don't have the new guy, whom we haven't cleared yet, handle our food! Are you crazy?" Sarah more yelled than asked.

"I just was helping," Kevin said.

"Get back to your stall," Sarah said, pointing out the kitchen door.

"Relax," Kevin said.

"Sarah, it's really not that big a deal," Harmon said.

Sarah turned on a heel and glared at Harmon for a second, silencing him. She turned back to Kevin. "Get back to your stall now!"

"Okay," Kevin said, putting his hands up in surrender. "See ya later, Harmon." He side shuffled past Sarah and out the kitchen door.

"Sarah, he didn't do anything but help me finish chopping some potatoes," Harmon said.

Sarah looked at Harmon in disbelief. "You gave a new awakening a knife. Do I really need to explain how bad an idea that is to you?"

Harmon shook his head, submitting to Sarah.

Sarah took a deep breath, calming her emotions. "Do you need any other help with dinner?"

Harmon shook his head no.

"Good." Sarah turned and walked out of the kitchen.

"I was just helping him get dinner ready. No need to freak out like that," Kevin said to Sarah as she escorted him to his stall.

Sarah cut him off. "I'll tell you what's a big deal and what's not. For now, you stay in this stall." Sarah slammed the stall door shut, latched it, and locked Kevin inside before stomping off.

Kevin shook his head, feeling unjustly chastised. After an hour of pacing his stall, he cracked a kink in his neck. *I need to do something. I'm so bored.* He tried the stall door, only to find it locked. *Shit.* Surveying the room, he noticed for the first time a metal pipe that hung parallel to the ceiling. He jumped up and caught hold of the pipe. Pulling himself up with great effort, he felt his shoulder pop a little, protesting against the sudden exertion. He dropped off the pipe and shook it out. No injury, just a noise. A few minutes later, Kevin was sweating as he did a workout his mind remembered from his life as Jaared. He paused, catching his breath. He nodded as he thought, *Okay, work out. That, I can do.*

Dinnertime came quickly as Kevin spent the day exercising.

"I'm sorry about you getting chewed out," Harmon said as he handed Kevin a bowl of potato stew.

Kevin looked at it for a moment, but decided to set the bowl to the side for now. "It's alright."

"She's right though," Harmon said. "I shouldn't have given you a knife like that. If Sarah had walked in and seen you holding it, she may have overreacted, and you could have gotten hurt. Not to mention, you could turn on us." Harmon smiled awkwardly.

"Why does everyone keep thinking I'm going to turn into a freak and killer? Am I putting off a ridiculous vibe or something?" Kevin asked, confused and frustrated at the same time.

"It's not your fault," Harmon said. "It's just that there have been some things in the past that have taught us to be careful with new awakenings."

"What happened?"

"I,"—Harmon paused—"it's not my place to tell. But Sarah told me you and the Master are going to have a picnic tomorrow morning. Ask him when you see him. He'll tell you. Anyway, enjoy your dinner. I've still got the dishes to do." Harmon turned away, leaving Kevin with his bowl of stew. Kevin took a tentative bite. Hmmm, pretty good. He gulped it down, coughing once because of how quickly he was spooning mouthfuls.

The physical exertion of his workout day, combined with a full stomach of potatoes, made Kevin's eyes grow heavy. He fell asleep curled in a ball on the hay floor.

<<<...01010110101 1010 1 101 010 10 1 010 10 10 10 1010 10 10010 0....ULTRA... 1 01010101010 0101010 0100000 0101010 010 0101 0 0101010 01 01 0 0101... TRACK.

.. 1010101010 1010101 0101 01010101 01010 10... MAS
K... 010101 10101 01001 01001 00101... RUN.... 101001
01010 100101 0101010 10101010 01010... EXECUTE.
.. 1010 10101 10101 01 01 01 010 10 1... DIRECT..
. 010010101 1010 1010 1001 1001 001 01010 01010110101
1010 1 101 010 10 1 010 10 10 10 1010 10 10010 0....IND
IE... 1 01010101010 0101010 0100000 0101010 010 0101
0 0101010 01 01 0 0101... UNDO... 1010101010 1010101
0101 01010101 01010 10... MODULE... 010101 10101 01001
01001 00101...MISSION.... 101001 01010 100101 0101010
10101010 01010... CANCEL... 1010 10101 10101 01 01 01
010 10 1... LOG... 010010101 1010 1010 1001 1001 001
01010 01010110101 1010 1 101 010 10 1 010 10 10 10
1010 10 10010 0... UNKNOWN... 1 01010101010 0101010
0100000 0101010 010 0101 0 0101010 01 01 0 0101...
PROGRAM... 1010101010 1010101 0101 01010101 01010
10... ANDER... 010101 10101 01001 01001 00101... FA
CE.... 101001 01010 100101 0101010 10101010 01010..
. TOG... 1010 10101 10101 01 01 01 010 10 1... NOW...
010010101 1010 1010 1001 1001 001 01010 01010110101
1010 1 101 010 10 1 010 10 10 10 1010 10 10010 0... LO
CK... 1 01010101010 0101010 0100000 0101010 010 0101
0 0101010 01 01 0 0101... AGENT... 1010101010 1010101
0101 01010101 01010 10... FORMAT... 010101 10101 01001
01001 00101... TRUNK.... 101001 01010 100101 0101010
10101010 01010... SENSITIVE... 1010 10101 10101 01 01
01 010 10 1... WATCHER... 010010101 1010 1010 1001
1001 001 01010 01010110101 1010 1 101 010 10 1 010 10
10 10 1010 10 10010 0... DEBUG... 1 01010101010 0101010
0100000 0101010 010 0101 0 0101010 01 01 0 0101...
RUNTIME ... 1010101010 1010101 0101 01010101 01010 1
0... TRY ... 010101 10101 01001 01001 00101... IF.... 101001
01010 100101 0101010 10101010 01010... QUERY... 1010
10101 10101 01 01 01 010 10 1... MULTIPLE... 010010101
1010 1010 1001 1001 001 01010 >>>

>>>

>>>

ERROR: 43522123493

"Good morning, Mr. Altair," the Master said.

Kevin shot up, instantly awake. He blinked his eyes twice, trying to clear the stream of numbers and words from his consciousness. "What was that?" he asked the air.

The Master leaned in toward Kevin, closer. "What was what?"

Kevin rubbed his eyes and shook his head. "Uh. Nothing. Good morning."

"Hmm," the Master said. "Get up. We're going for a picnic."

Kevin stood up and dusted himself off.

"Follow me," the Master instructed.

A long walk later, Kevin sat on a checkered blanket overlooking a field of wild grass swaying in the wind, with a small assortment of breads and jams spread out in front of him. He took some strawberry and spread it on a piece of bread that looked like French but tasted saltier. The Master took some of a darker-colored jam, Kevin assumed blackberry, and spread it across two halves of a roll he had torn in two. The Master took a bite of one half and handed the other to Sarah, who stood guard a few feet away. Kevin looked at her for just a second. His eyes glanced at the handgun strapped to her right leg. He couldn't have looked at it for more than a second before Sarah caught him staring. She answered his stare by putting her hand on the hilt and popping free the clasp that held it in the holster. Kevin quickly looked elsewhere.

"So tell me," the Master said, "what are you currently thinking about our discussion yesterday?"

"Honestly?"

The Master nodded.

"It makes no sense."

"I'm sure they taught you the history of the ancient times. Romans, Greeks, Colonization?"

"Of course."

"Where do you think we get that history from?"

"Well, I assume it's from the archeologists who studied them."

"Yes, we got some information from dig sites that scientists excavated. But most of what we know about those civilizations and times came from the writing that was found preserved. Now imagine that you could travel back to those times. Do you think the world you'd find yourself in would look like what you expect? I'd say probably not. The unfortunate truth is, the writings we have most often come from the richest class of people. Their writing made their country and lifestyle look as good as possible. It's romanticized, and even false at times." The Master finished his last sentence by gesturing with his hands.

Kevin felt he was supposed to understand something. He didn't. "Okay," Kevin said.

The Master stopped gesturing and spoke in a plain tone. "So how do you know the history they taught you isn't the same fabrication?"

"I guess I can't. Is that what you want to hear?"

"What I want to hear?"

"Yeah. Is that what you need me to say so everyone stops threatening to kill me?" Kevin shot a glance at Sarah, whose hand still rested on the hilt of her gun.

The Master touched Kevin's shoulder, bringing his attention back to him. "I don't want to hear anything, and I don't want to kill you. Any threat of violence comes from a need for self-preservation."

"Self-preservation? You and your group, you're the ones who are threatening me. You've abducted me and said it was for my own good. Then you lock me in a horse stall, with a bucket to use as a toilet, which, by the way, I think should be emptied at least once in a while. Even your daughter is sitting there with a gun, just hoping to blast my brains all over this picnic."

The Master turned a glare at his daughter. "Locked in the stall?"

She shrugged. "Better safe than sorry. Besides, it's not like he didn't get food and water, and privacy."

"He needs to socialize with the others. That's the only way he can become free of the programming. You know that."

"Socialize? He's a machine. It'd be like trying to make a toaster connect with others."

"Hey." Kevin jumped in, turning his palms up, giving the universal sign of offense.

"Oh, sorry," Sarah said sarcastically. "Do you want to be friends?"

"I, I," Kevin stammered, "I don't know if I have any friends."

The Master smiled as he watched Kevin struggle with the thought. "Kevin," he said, "you weren't supposed to be locked in the stall. I'm sorry, that wasn't supposed to happen. She's just protective. We've been through a lot, and she just wants to make sure nothing bad happens again. From this point on, though, I promise you won't find your stall locked."

"So I can leave?" Kevin asked, almost more confused than asking for permission.

"Well no," the Master answered. "You will need to stay with us for the time being. For your protection and ours."

"Everyone keeps saying that. What happened?"

The Master took a deep breath, preparing to talk.

"Dad, don't."

The Master put a hand up to calm his daughter. "It's a sore spot for us. We had an issue with an early waker, like you, before. He, too, woke up from a dream early, and we saved him. He became part of the group and started going on missions. We attempted a mission that threatened the fabric of the Dream States. It was then that the truth came out." The Master paused, his mind going to a painful place.

"Please, if you're going to keep threatening me with this you have to tell me what happened."

"We were farther south, near a corner of Zone 3, in an area that used to be called Louisiana. Klay, that's what he told us his name was, was an undercover agent. When he turned on us, his betrayal brought us near destruction. He almost single-handedly ended the Awake. We, well, we used to be a lot larger group. Sarah and I escaped, and by sheer blind luck, we reunited with a few others and reached a safe zone. Now the Awake, the real Awake, has been rebuilt. We operate in loosely affiliated splinter cells, staying small and more widespread so that if one of us goes down, the movement doesn't die."

"So this guy, Klay—" Kevin started.

"Stop saying that name!" Sarah commanded.

"Um, okay." Kevin put his hands up in surrender. "So this other early waking-up guy. He was like a spy?"

"Yes," the Master said. "The worst kind. The kind who don't know they are. The government has tried to shut down this movement many times. Most of their tactics are easy to discover and root out. But that was a new line to cross. What they did was take an agent and wipe his mind, clean slate. No government espionage training, or combat skills, nothing that would make us suspicious. They put him in a simple job, in his case, cleaning the solar tiles. When he woke early, he looked like the perfect candidate for us to save, and he was. He was a lost soul with no purpose, whose mind rejected the dream. What we didn't know was, they hid pieces of code deep in his mind chip. When he reached a certain level of security hacking, a switch flipped and,"—the Master snapped his fingers—"he was an agent again. He didn't know it until that moment. Then he's trying to kill us."

Kevin's eyes had grown three sizes larger. "They can do that? Hide an identity in your mind chip."

"Yes."

"Then how can you know who I am? How can I know who I am? No. That can't be right."

"It's right," the Master said.

"So that's why everyone says they can't trust me. I could be a ticking time bomb, just waiting to go off at the right moment."

"We just have to be careful. Sarah may take it too far, but it's better we are safe than sorry."

"How can... is there a way to know for sure that I'm not? I mean, you're saying he didn't know before, so doesn't that mean...?"

"Are you a spy?" the Master asked.

"No. Or at least I don't think so. I don't feel like one."

"I can tell you one thing for sure," the Master said, smiling. "You're not like him."

"How can you tell?"

"There is something different about you, something that the system would have trained out of you. I spent my early life around the government and their zealots and spies. Hell, I used to be one of them. I know what their training does to a person, beyond just the mind. I can see it on people, and you're not like them."

"But you didn't know last time. How can you say you could tell for sure?" The Master sat in a guilty silence. Kevin read his face and the look that his features contorted into. Looking at Sarah and seeing a similar demeanor, Kevin understood. "You knew."

"Yes. I spotted the telltale signs right away. There are small things that no manner of training or reprogramming can hide. But I thought I could turn him. I was one of them at one point, and I changed, so he should have been able to as well. I thought I could change him and make him understand. It didn't work. When his hidden code activated, all the memories of his past, his training, his mission all came flooding back. I failed, and we almost lost everything, but that's my fault. I approached it the wrong way. Because I came at it with logic, the second the mind chip activated and the brain triggered, it was all wiped clean."

"Why? Why didn't you just kill him?"

"We needed him. We needed the government clearance code hidden deep in his mind chip. His code was necessary to allow us to steal something."

"Did he know? That you were using him for that?"

"No. I kept that to myself," the Master said. "Another error, but I was afraid that telling him about it would trigger his code and we'd lose our opportunity."

"Was it worth it?"

"The cost of that opportunity was higher than I was ready to bear at the time, but yes, the mission was a success." The Master nodded to Sarah.

She took her hand off the handgun and walked to a bag she had set down by a tree when they first arrived. She pulled a small flash drive from it and brought it to her father.

"This was the mission," the Master said.

"A memory stick?"

"This drive contains information that, if used correctly, can be a weapon against this whole Dream States lie." The Master looked at the small memory stick, his fingers trembling. "People have literally died to bring it to this point."

Kevin instinctively reached for it.

"Not yet," the Master said, pulling it back. "I need you to understand. We have lost loved ones over this. That pain is more than you could comprehend. The knowledge it contains is dangerous. It's the reason you're here."

"Why me?"

"Most of the people we rescue are mechanics, farmers, solar-panel cleaners or security. Something about doing hard work or having guilt over your actions makes the brain reject the dream faster. But you, you're special. You have programming training, and you're a lucid dreamer. Your brain can program and dream at the same time."

"I guess maybe my half-awake, half-dreaming editing could have trained my subconscious."

"Half-awake, half-dreaming editing?" Sarah asked.

"I'm an editor. I fix dream errors. Or I guess I did. Well, when I had the chance, I would look into my dreaming history to see echoes of my past life. Management wouldn't like that, so I would wait until they were briefing shift changes to look at them. I would keep one eye open to watch their meeting progress."

"Interesting," the Master said. "Most people wouldn't do something so rebellious. Why did you?"

"I wanted to know. Something about me didn't feel right."

"What do you mean?" the Master pressed Kevin.

"I don't know. I just felt something was wrong," Kevin said.

Sarah looked at her dad. The Master smiled back at her.

Kevin watched them, feeling a little awkward being the subject of an unspoken conversation. "So you weren't sending me 'WAKE UP' as messages?"

The Master shook his head. "No. I wish I could say we were, but we can't inject code into the dream network like that. We've tried, and failed, but never succeeded at inputting a single line. The dream rejects and deletes any-thing we put in."

Kevin sat looking at them for a second. "So what's your plan?"

"We'll get to that later," the Master said. "We'll see if you still want to be a part of what we're doing. Then we'll go from there." The Master turned his attention to his daughter. "No more locking him in the stall."

"Fine. But if you get out of line," Sarah said to Kevin.

The Master smiled. "She's so much like her mother. A lot of love, a bit of angry."

"I think you may have that reversed," Kevin said.

The Master laughed a hearty belly chuckle. "She's only like that with you."

"Lucky me."

"She'll take you back to the barn now. I look forward to seeing you again soon, Kevin." The Master stood and extended Kevin a hand to help him stand. He took it, surprised by the strength the old man exerted in pulling him up. "If you have questions or want to talk, you can find me in the house or the bunker most days."

"Sounds good. Wait. The bunker?"

"Oh, that's right, someone locked you in a cell," the Master said, turning to Sarah. "Why don't you give Kevin here a tour of the Ranch on your way back to the barn?"

"Come on," Sarah said to Kevin.

"Do you want us to help you clean up the picnic?" Kevin asked the Master.

"Thank you, no. I'm going to enjoy it a little longer."

"Okay, see you later."

The Master waved as Kevin and Sarah started the walk back to the barn.

Sarah led Kevin through a field of wild grass, constantly changing direction.

"Why are we walking all over the place?" Kevin asked.

"To avoid making any obvious tracks," Sarah responded. "It takes time, but we can't leave evidence for the drones to see us."

"Drones?"

"There is a system of aircraft searching for our splinter cells at all times. We have to be careful not to leave any clues for them." Sarah's answer was short and to the point.

"Why don't you like me?"

Sarah stopped walking and faced Kevin directly. "One, you could be the enemy. Two, you aren't one of us yet, so I don't know if I can trust you."

"I won't hurt you."

"We'll see." Sarah turned and led Kevin forward on their twisting walk.

Kevin spotted the farmhouse and barn to his left getting farther away as they walked. He felt like asking where they were going, but sensed it was better to follow without question at this point. After fifteen more minutes of zig-ging and zagging through the field, Kevin spotted a small dome-shaped hill twenty feet away, covered in dirt and grass. He may have missed it if he hadn't been on the ground. As he and Sarah got closer, he could see a small brown door.

"This is the bunker," Sarah said. "Inside are a bunch of computers. You'll see that later, but for now, just know where it is."

"Can we go inside?"

"I have a lot to do today, so let's just get the lay of the land to start. If everything goes according to plan, you'll spend a lot of time in there soon. Over this way are the greenhouses."

Kevin squinted as he struggled to spot them. "Where?"

"You see those?" Sarah said, pointing at two hills, one hundred feet away, that each covered a significant part of the horizon.

"Yeah," Kevin said.

"Those are canopies that cover our farms."

"Really?"

"Yep, just massive tarps that are painted damn near perfect for camouflage. One of our members used to be an artist before waking up. I'll show you the first one."

As Kevin and Sarah walked closer to the tent structure, it became much easier to see. The ruse of the paint job was well done, but as they got closer, its rudimentary camouflage became visible. Sarah led them to the far side of the large tarp, where an opening the size of a garage door let Kevin see inside. Neatly packed rows of corn grew under lights, each shining the bright white of UV grow bulbs. A man and woman, each wearing overalls, waved to them as they picked corn. Sarah waved back. Kevin half raised his hand to wave, suddenly feeling that the gesture of welcome wasn't meant for him.

Sarah's wrist watch beeped a chime of three tones. She looked down at it. "Come on, quick." Sarah pulled Kevin inside the undercover field.

The workers in the field also must have had watch alarms trigger, as they both looked at their wrists too. Kevin watched one of them reach into his pocket and pull out a small device. A few seconds later, the grow lights turned dark. "What's going on?" Kevin whispered to Sarah, instinctively quiet.

"Drones," she said, looking at the watch on her wrist. Its display had changed to a satellite image. Three small dots moved slowly across it. After five minutes, the red dots had disappeared, and Sarah's watch beeped once. She took a step toward the opening. "Come on, it's safe now."

Sarah and Kevin walked past the second covered field. Kevin didn't get a good look inside, but from the potatoes and eggs they had eaten earlier, he guessed that the other field doubled as a chicken coop and more farming. Soon they passed a barn that was in shambles, walls stained and pieces of the roof falling in.

"This is the vehicle garage," Sarah said. "It looks like a dump, but the bottom level of the barn is in good shape and just tall enough for us to hide our van, a pair of OHVs, a tractor and two dirt bikes."

Kevin nodded in understanding.

Sarah walked Kevin to the barn where he had been living the last few days. "You know this barn pretty well, and you've seen the farmhouse. That's it."

"Where is... um..." Kevin asked.

"Where's what?"

"Where is everyone else?" Kevin asked. "When I got here that first morning, I saw a bunch of people eating in the barn. I figured they were staying elsewhere. But if this is it, where are they?"

"My father sent them away after you talked with him in the farmhouse."

"Why?"

"I don't know." She shook her head. "But he was adamant about them moving to a different location, so I'm sure he had his reasons. When he's really serious about stuff like that, I know I have to trust him. It's the only way we'll have a chance in this fight," Sarah said.

"Why do you guys do all this?"

Sarah looked at him, half puzzled and half angered. "Did you not listen to anything we've said? Our story, the corruption of the government?"

"No, no, I did. I mean, why organize all this and fight the government? You could do all this and just hide and live happy. Why fight them?"

"You think they'd leave us alone?"

"Well, why not? If you're not attacking them, there is no reason they should think you're a threat, right?"

"You're stupid or just naïve."

Kevin smiled, trying more to de-escalate the moment than anything.

Sarah didn't smile back. "Goodbye, Kevin."

Kevin swallowed a lump of saliva that had gotten caught in his throat. He turned and stepped into the barn. It was empty inside, just the stray bugs flitting through the beams of light that penetrated through the cracks in the wooden walls.

A noise from the kitchen drew his attention. Pots clambered as they fell from the shelf. Kevin walked to the doorway. "Harmon? You okay?"

Harmon was standing on one leg, trying to keep even more pots from falling. "Help."

Kevin ran in and grabbed the two pots that were most in danger of falling.

"Thanks," Harmon said.

"Need help again today? Sarah's busy, so she's won't yell at us."

"Ha ha," Harmon laughed. "Yeah, I could."

Kevin pushed his sleeves up. "What's on the menu tonight?"

"Potatoes. And guess who gets to peel, and chop them this time."

"I can do that. If you trust me with a knife."

Harmon let out a little laugh and handed him the blade. "This time, you stick around long enough to help with dishes, too."

Kevin smiled.

"You're late."

Thairn winced at the comment, wanting to snap back, but knowing that his boss wouldn't take kindly to any disobedience. "Yes, sir."

"Do you know why I've had you flown here?"

Thairn studied the man dressed in an off-white suit. The man, whom Thairn only knew as "the boss," stood over six feet tall, with gray hair scattered through his finely kept beard and hair. They stood on a cliff overlooking the ocean. A breeze blowing kept the warm air from being too hot. The sound of the helicopter whose engine had just finished winding down still rang in Thairn's ears. "I figure you had good reason."

"You know, every day I plug in and sync with the dream network, to monitor the important happenings. Imagine my surprise when I learn the Awake has taken one of our editors. Imagine the shock I had when I didn't learn this from the reports that are supposed to be filed, but from one of my personal sources." The boss glared at Thairn, reading his face.

Thairn matched the boss's glare, understanding this was a test he must pass. "The plan, sir."

"Yes the plan. As part of that plan, tell me if I'm wrong, but I was led to understand that everything would be reported timely."

Thairn stood silent, unsure if saying anything at all would be the right move.

The boss stared Thairn down, reading his expressions. "So what's next?"

"We wait. It won't be long until they try to use him. When they do, his chip will do the rest."

Kevin sucked the tip of his finger, tasting a drop of blood. He had spent the better part of the past few hours peeling potatoes, chopping them and scrubbing burned-on grime off pots. He had nicked his fingers more than a few times, but one cut seemed to keep bleeding.

A bowl that held the leftover skin of a baked potato sat in the corner of his stall. Kevin smiled, looking at it, the last unclean dish. Who knew a plain potato could taste so good? He felt a yawn spread across his face. Kevin shook his head, trying to shed the tiredness he felt. The sleep won. He fell asleep with a smile on his face. The sun set, and the night passed as Kevin slept a dreamless slumber.

"Kevin!" Sarah yelled.

Kevin jolted awake. His breathing labored from the sudden startle.

"How do you do that?" Sarah asked.

"Wha... What?" Kevin asked, rubbing his eyes.

"How do you fall asleep sitting up? I always lay down before I pass out."

"I don't know," Kevin said, still rubbing his eyes. "Although, I wish I had laid down. I think my eyes were still open when I was sleeping, too."

"That's creepy. Come on, let's eat."

"Eat?"

"Yeah, it's time for breakfast."

Kevin and Sarah took a seat at a table in the center of the barn. Harmon brought them each over a plate of eggs, corn, and mashed potatoes. "Thanks, Harmon," Kevin said as he dropped them off.

"You're welcome," Harmon said, smiling. He turned and addressed Sarah, only giving her a nod before walking away.

"That was weird," Kevin said.

"He's still hurt about me yelling at you two the other day."

Kevin and Sarah ate their breakfast as they talked.

"So, how's the socializing going?" Sarah asked.

"Uh, well, I pretty much just hung with Harmon so far."

"Okay, well, today you should meet Mei. Her story is pretty sad. I'll have her come talk to you."

"Thanks. Hey, can I ask you something?"

"Yeah."

"All this twisted history you keep telling me about. What does it mean if I kind of, well, understand it?"

"You understand it?"

"I, in my last dream, the one I was in before you pulled me out, everyone was so at odds with each other over everything. People hated their own family members because they didn't recycle or eat only plant-based food. I just can see where they came from, I guess." Kevin saw the disapproving look on Sarah's face and backpedaled. "I mean, I can see how they were twisted into believing they were doing good. They weren't, but I'm just saying I can empathize with them."

"You feel sorry for them?"

"No, no, not sympathize, empathize. Understand, I guess."

"You understand mass murder and mind control?"

"No, but I get the feeling of being powerless, and what you'd do if you could actually change people's minds," Kevin said, feeling like he was just digging himself a deeper hole. "Look, can we talk about something else?"

"No. I think I'm going to take my breakfast to go." Sarah stood from the table. "Talk to Mei if you still feel that way. Then we'll have something to talk about." Sarah left Kevin staring at an empty barn.

"What just happened?" Kevin said to the air, not expecting anyone to respond.

Harmon had heard Sarah leave and stepped out of the kitchen. "It's not about you."

Kevin looked at him.

"She'll never fit with us, not fully. She's never dreamed, so she can't understand."

"Understand what?" Kevin asked, frustrated at the situation.

"You know," Harmon said, clearly reaching.

Kevin shook his head.

"Never mind," Harmon said, leaving Kevin alone to finish his meal.

Kevin ate it with little enjoyment and then returned to his stall, determined to work out and clear his mind.

It was a little before noon when Mei knocked on Kevin's stall door. "Hey. I don't want to interrupt."

Kevin got up from his plank position. "Oh, it's all good. I was just finishing."

"Okay, well, Sarah asked me to come talk to you."

"Yeah," Kevin said, brushing some hay from his pants. "Let's go sit out at the tables."

"Okay." Mei walked to the closest table and sat down on a bench. She shifted her lithe frame, allowing herself to cross one leg over the other. Her jeans protested a little, sending dust from working in the field into a puff cloud in the air.

Kevin sat on the other side and for a moment just looked at the small Asian woman, dressed in a plaid button-up shirt with her hair tied in a messy bun, sitting across from him. "So," he said, "I guess I'm supposed to socialize and learn people's stories or something."

"Sarah told me. She said that you're either ignorant or an ass."

Kevin smiled an awkward grin.

"Do you want to hear my story? Or are you just doing this to save your own neck?"

"Uh," Kevin stammered. "Honestly, kind of both. I have always liked the infinite possibilities of the dream, and everyone's story is so different. So I do want to hear about yours, but, yeah, I don't want to die either."

"Dream story?" Mei more said than asked. "You don't know?"

"Know what?"

"They did not save me from the Dream States like most of the people here. The Master saved me from a breeding center."

"A breeding center?"

"For five years."

"What, what..." Kevin stammered.

"What is it? What was it like?" Mei helped Kevin finish his thought. "It's hell. Did you know you can't dream while pregnant?"

Kevin shook his head. "Never really thought about it, I guess. I don't think I ever actually thought about babies or pregnancy, just in the Dream States, maybe."

"Well, you can't. So they keep you healthy, keep you active, and keep your baby growing right on schedule. You feel life grow inside you, your hormones change, and your heart and soul connect with a living thing like never before. Then, one day, you are rushed to a room where you endure the worst pain you have ever felt, more than you can ever imagine. Yet at the same time, you feel joy. You are bringing life into the world, and you can feel it." Mei's eyes grew watery. "The first time you hear your baby cry is... it's magic. Then, for a few weeks, your child feeds from your own breast. It's just you and them."

"Sounds nice."

"It is... until they come for your child. It's not yours, they say. This child belongs to the corporation. After ripping your heart out, they take you to a burn room and erase all your memories. All those magic moments, they just take. You come to from the darkness in that burn chair. You're in pain, still healing from giving birth, with tears on your face from the emotional trauma you underwent, but don't remember a thing. But they can't erase the emotions and that spiritual connection you have with your child. You can't remember any of it, but deep down inside, a piece of you is missing." Tears were running down Mei's face now as she spoke. "I can't tell you how many children they stole from me. But at some point, I felt like an empty shell of who I was. After my last birth, I think they knew. So instead of taking me to the burn room, they led me to an execution chamber. When the needle went into my arm, I didn't care. I was ready to end it all." Mei wiped her tears from her face. "I woke up in the back of a van. The Master had infiltrated the facility and switched the needle. Instead of killing me, it just put me to sleep for a while."

"I didn't know."

"No one does. But that's what the system is about. Lies and pain. The dream network, the government and their agents, all they deserve, is to die. A bullet to the head and an end to their power."

"How do you?"

"How do I carry on?" Mei said. "When I first got here, I was a complete mess. I just felt like a broken person shattered into a bunch of pieces. I didn't know how or if I was going to pull it together. Then Cassidy came to me and gave me this." Mei pulled a small glass disc the size of a quarter from her breast pocket. It looked like a small section of stained glass when the light shone through it. "Cassidy made it using small pieces of glass that he had collected over the time he's been out of the Dream States. Each piece was a broken shard from something else, but through some work and patience, he joined them together. When he gave it to me, he said that I was like this glass disc. Right now I may feel like I'm broken and scattered, but after time and some practice, I can put myself back together into something new. Sure, you'll always see the cracks, but I can keep going and become something whole again."

"I'm sorry."

"You're a victim in this system too. You don't remember everything they did to you either, but tell me, do you feel like something is missing? Do you feel like there is something deep inside you that's... lost?"

Kevin thought for a moment, his mind searching for an answer where none existed.

Mei nodded in understanding. "It was nice to meet you, Kevin," she said, standing and walking out of the barn, leaving Kevin to his contemplation.

The next few hours passed by in a fog of thought. Kevin sat at a table in the barn, eating an early dinner and staring off into the distance, not thinking, just mentally blank.

"Hey, man, how are you doing?" Harmon asked, taking a seat across from Kevin.

Kevin was staring through Harmon, still lost in the void. Kevin shrugged his shoulders.

"Are you alright?"

Kevin blinked a few times and looked at his food, pushing a piece of corn around the plate with his fork. "I'm alright, or I'll be alright."

"I can spit in Sarah's dinner if that would help," Harmon said, smiling.

"Ha ha." Kevin felt the laugh escape him. A smile crept to his face. "Thanks, but it's not her. It's..."

"It's the talk you had with Mei?"

"Yeah."

"Well, look, you're tired. Go to bed early tonight and rest up. Take a break from trying to understand this madhouse."

Kevin nodded. "That's a good idea."

"Don't sound so surprised."

"Do you mind cleaning this up for me?" Kevin pointed at his half-full plate.

"No problem."

"Thanks," Kevin said. He walked to the stall, closed the door, and wrapped himself in the blanket. After adjusting his pillow a few times, he found a comfortable position and fell asleep.

Another place. Another time. Another life. Level 150.

Kevin stepped into the office through the large wooden double doors. He walked over to the desk where Thairn and a man in a white latex suit stood sipping whiskey. Kevin knew him as Alexander, but to most others, he was simply "the boss."

"Hello, gentlemen," Kevin said in a confident tone. "Thank you for meeting us." Kevin looked at Alexander. "I know we have felt the pressure from recent events, and I'm here to tell you I have a plan."

Alexander nodded. "So what's this plan?"

"Those years ago, our agent came close, but we all made one mistake," Thairn said.

Kevin stepped to Thairn's side. "We didn't make the bait enticing enough."

Kevin woke up to find a piece of straw sticking deep into his nostril. He coughed and pulled it out, feeling the plant deep in his sinus. He looked around the stall. It was dark out, either early or late. He couldn't tell. Unsettled by the means of his awakening, he sneezed and adjusted his position. He couldn't fall asleep, the feeling of his plant lobotomy stuck in his mind. Giving up on sleep, he stretched the kink in his neck out. He had been up and stretching for twenty minutes when Sarah came to his door.

"Hey," Sarah said. "Didn't expect you to be up yet."

"Yeah, well, I guess I couldn't sleep."

"Talks with Mei will do that. Come on. Let's go watch the sunrise. The drones just passed over, so we'll be in the clear for a while. The view from the roof is awesome."

"Sounds good."

Sarah led the way up a ladder on the side of the barn. After reaching the top, she turned around and helped Kevin make the last step onto the tin metal roof. They sat staring at the horizon in the fading darkness, waiting for the fast-approaching sunrise.

"Judging by your reaction, I'm guessing Mei told you her story."

"The main bits, yeah."

"Do you feel different about what you said yesterday? Or do you still think what the Dream States did is right?"

"I never said I believed what they did was right, still don't. I was saying that I could understand how they could believe what they were doing was right," Kevin said. "I wouldn't ever be okay with the choices they made, but I'm not shocked that some people made those decisions. It doesn't surprise me people will go that far to save themselves."

"Yeah, not much surprises me with them. Why didn't you say it like that the first time?"

"You didn't give me much of a chance."

Sarah smiled. "I guess I didn't, did I?"

Kevin smiled back. "No."

They sat in silence. Neither said a word, but still enjoyed the company for the next hour as they watched the sun come up over the crest of a hill in the distance. The brightness flooded the landscape with a pink hue. Kevin stared as long as he could before the sun's light burned his eyes. He looked at Sarah, who was still staring at the sunrise. She was giggling.

"What? What's so funny?"

"I don't know why, but this sunrise made me think of when we first rescued Harmon." Sarah smiled and let out a little chuckle. "Harmon had been cooking for us for a week or something like that. He tells us he is making some special Spanish potato dish for breakfast. Diehl was in a mood that day or something. So he rags on Harmon about it and just making jokes about the 'potato pie.' Well Harmon got upset, and they ended up making a bet. Diehl had to eat a whole plate of it and still run a mile sub seven minutes. It was so stupid, but Diehl does it and wins the bet. Then he just pukes his guts out. Harmon just starts laughing so hard. I mean, he's crying because his laughter is so over the top." Sarah started laughing while telling her story. "Turns out, ha ha, Harmon had found, ha ha, some tobacco leaves and put them in Diehl's food, ha ha. So Diehl is trying to chase him down and beat on him, ha ha, but he can't stop throwing up every three steps. Harmon just keeps yelling, 'Don't mess with people who make your food!'"

Kevin was smiling as Sarah laughed wholeheartedly.

Sarah exhaled the last bit of her laughter. "With all that goes on, those two are playing jokes on each other. It just helped me remember the truth about it all."

"The truth?"

"Everyone we save from the dream is stuck in gray. They never feel actual pain, but they also never experience genuine happiness. The joy in a little prank or the feeling of belonging. That's why the Awake exists. It's that authentic emotion, the thing the dream can't simulate for all it's worth."

Kevin thought for a moment. "You really saved my life, huh?"

"You're welcome," Sarah said, smiling.

"Thanks."

"Kev," Sarah said, "I don't know if any amount of socializing can convince you to join us. But I hope that somehow, whether with us or in another life, you get to feel happiness. I couldn't imagine not living life in full color."

Kev. I like that. Kevin studied Sarah's face, tinted a pink hue in the early morning sun. There was something so alive about her. A glow emanated from her skin, an aura of existence. He could feel it. There was something about her he couldn't understand that called to him. Inside, he felt something he had never experienced. A spark lit in a dark room that promised the possibility of a raging fire. "I don't need to wait until the end of the week," he said. "I want to talk with your father now."

"Yeah?"

"Yeah."

"Okay."

A short walk later, Kevin, Sarah and the Master stood in the living room of the farmhouse.

"So, Kevin, will you being joining us? Will you set us free?" the Master asked.

Kevin looked at Sarah. He found himself unable to tear his eyes off her. "I'll do it. I'll help." Sarah smiled at Kevin. Kevin found it too much for him. He looked at his boots for a second before shaking his head of the cobwebs that had just taken root. "But if I feel you're lying to me, I'm out."

"I wouldn't have it any other way," the Master said. "Welcome to the Awake." The Master extended his hand, and Kevin shook it. "Come on, it's time for us to celebrate."

"Celebrate?" Kevin asked.

"Yeah, we always celebrate when a new member joins, but for you, we have something special planned."

Smoke rose to the top of the dome that covered the cornfields. Kevin watched a piece of ash float past his face. He closed his eyes and took a deep breath, smelling the smoke. It reminded him of a camping memory that he couldn't place from his last dream. He could feel the memory pulling on his mind, almost dragging him back into it.

"Eer's yer girlled swee' corn."

Kevin opened his eyes to find a man wearing overalls and a flannel button-up shirt holding a grilled ear of corn in a towel. Kevin had just met Cassidy, who spoke in a

thick Southern accent. He was currently working the "barbecue," a metal grid held over an open fire. Kevin had
seen Cassidy from afar during his tour with Sarah, but
now, having met the man, he immediately liked his simple
kindness. "Thanks," Kevin said.

"Thank ya. Always love a gud reason to girl swee' corn,"
Cassidy said, winking at Kevin.

"Attention, everyone!" the Master said, shouting to be
heard. "Can you all huddle around me?"

"C'mon on, Kev," Cassidy said.

"You know that the Southern-accent thing is probably
just left over from your last dream, right?" Kevin said as
they walked over to the Master.

"Yeah, I know. I,"—Cassidy cleared his throat— "I can
actually stop it whenever I want, and speak with perfect
diction, but I prefer the accent. Plus, Mei likes it." Cassidy
winked at Kevin.

Kevin let out a laugh, smiling.

"Today we welcome a new member," the Master said.
"But first let me say thank you to Cassidy and Mei for
the delicious corn. Oh, and a thank you to Diehl, who
is currently on guard duty watching over the farm so we
can have this little festivity. I know it has been a lot more
work on everyone with most of our members elsewhere,
so thank you all for the work you've put in. Kevin." The
Master waved Kevin over.

Kevin went and stood next to the Master, somewhat uncomfortable standing in front of Cassidy, Mei, and Sarah.

The Master spoke to the small group. "Today, Kevin
joins our little resistance. Kevin, do you promise to help in
any way you can to save those who wake, keep the other
members of the Awake safe and, most important, not do
anything to jeopardize the movement?"

"I do."

"Then welcome. As a token of our welcoming to you, we
give you your watch."

Sarah stepped forward. "Hold your arm out." Kevin followed the instruction. She put the smart watch on his

wrist for him. "This watch will alert if drones are coming overhead, and tell time," Sarah said, smiling.

"Thanks." Kevin smiled back.

The Master started clapping. Cassidy, Mei, and Sarah joined in. Kevin grinned awkwardly, feeling welcome and shy at the same time.

"Now"—the Master turned and reached into a case he had brought with him—"for a little celebration." He pulled free a guitar and played a tune. Kevin recognized the twangs of a country beat he had heard before.

"C'mon, Mei," Cassidy said, grabbing her hand.

"Cass, the corn is going to burn," she said.

"Let it burn," Cassidy said. "I love blackened corn anyhow."

Cassidy and Mei started to two-step in the dusty field.

Kevin and Sarah both laughed, watching them. Sarah turned to Kevin. "Do you know how to dance?"

Kevin thought for a second. "You know, for the first time since I've been here, I'm glad I woke up in the dream I did."

"Okay?"

Kevin extended his hand, smiling. Sarah took it and followed his lead. They two-stepped and country-swing danced, sharing the open space with Cassidy and Mei, laughing the whole time. As the Master's song ended, Kevin and Sarah finished with a hug and a glance, both held too long, both promising something unsaid, unanswered, and completely unyielding.

CHAPTER 6

BODY AND MIND

*B*eep . . . *Beep* . . . *Beep* . . .

Kevin scrambled to turn the alarm on his watch off. The glow in the dark stall was blinding. He finally, after much struggle, found the button. *Stupid watch.* He rolled over to get comfortable again. Kevin had just gotten to a perfect spot when the stall door opened with a slam. "What the—" Before he could finish his sentence, the light above turned on, blinding him. "Oh!"

"Wake up! It's time to get your ass in gear!" Diehl shouted, relishing the moment.

"What?" Kevin stammered, shielding his eyes from the light.

"You're a member of the Awake now, and the Master tasked me with getting you in shape and mission ready. That means morning training sessions to turn your dream-depleted body into the picture of health. Now get up!" Diehl yanked the blanket off Kevin.

"Come on, man," Kevin said, more whiny than anything.

"Let's go! Today, we've got a run and some bodyweight training to work on. We need to move it to make sure we finish before breakfast."

"Can we do this later?"

"Nope," Diehl said. "If you need me to, I can get cold water to help you get up."

"Okay," Kevin said, forcing himself up. "Okay, I'm up."

"Good, now let's go," Diehl said, taking a step toward the door.

Kevin didn't immediately follow. He was too busy rubbing his eyes, attempting to rid himself of the last pieces of sleep. Diehl grabbed him and dragged him out of the stall.

"Stick with me!" Diehl shouted back at Kevin as they jogged along a creek bank.

Kevin's face was flush red. His throat and lungs struggled to keep up with his exertion as he chased the spry, muscle-bound man. They had been jogging for over fifteen minutes, and Kevin's heart threatened to climb out of his chest. He stopped, hunched over, and put his hands on his knees.

Diehl circled back around, jogging in place next to Kevin. "You alright?"

Kevin stayed hunched over, speaking between giant huffs of air. "How... are you... so fast... you freak?"

"It's called being physically fit. Prepared for anything that could be thrown at you," Diehl answered, still bouncing as he jogged in place.

Kevin's air came back enough for him to stand upright. His face contorted in disgust as he forced air in and sweated at a ridiculous volume. "I, I thought I was fit."

"That's the product of the dream," Diehl said, finally just standing and no longer jogging in place. "You may have been fit there, so your mind thinks you're in shape. But really, you've been laying down your whole life. You're starting over from scratch."

"That makes sense," Kevin said, catching his breath.

"Come on, we've got half-a-mile left. Then we're gonna work on bodyweight exercises to get your muscles working."

"They aren't working already?"

Diehl smiled an evil grin.

Kevin saw it. "No."

"Hey, look," Diehl said, "just think of it this way. The more you train, the better your body will look, and maybe Sarah will want to see you naked."

"What?" Kevin said in shock at Diehl's candid statement.

"You're a guy. She's a girl. You've been flirting with her since we grabbed you from DS 8. Don't tell me you haven't thought of it."

"I haven't, I, I mean," Kevin stammered.

"Come on," Diehl said, pulling on Kevin's shirt to start their jog again.

"Oh, oh, oh." Kevin let out gasps of pain as he lowered himself onto the bench seat of the table in the barn.

Harmon walked over with a plate of eggs and potatoes. "You okay?"

"I think Diehl killed me," Kevin said, adjusting himself and shifting his seating position.

"Here, this should help," Harmon said, placing the plate down in front of him. "Hey, sorry I missed your welcome barbecue."

"Thanks, and that's okay," Kevin said, accepting the breakfast. He took a bite of the potatoes.

"No, it's not," Harmon said, sitting down on the other side of the table, across from Kevin. "You're the only person here who seems to care about my dream. Everyone else just doesn't want to hear it, but you listen. Last night, I was getting ready to head over to the celebration and, well, emotion took me."

"Took you?" Kevin asked through a mouthful of his breakfast.

"When they saved me, I didn't wake up like you did," Harmon said. "Your doctor called, and they pulled you out fast. My doctor tried to keep me under with an extra-powerful sedative. A nurse saw what he was doing, and she is the reason I made it out. You know how we talked about the dreams?"

Kevin nodded.

"Well, the sedative did something more to me. It riddled my mind. So sometimes I find myself pulled back into my... my demons from that last dream. Last night, I had that happen. I was in the kitchen, but mentally I was somewhere else. The Master has helped me learn to control the urges I feel, but I had to stay put and regain myself."

"Demons?"

"The drug world had a... lasting effect on me. I did things I'm not proud of. I just want you to know I would have been there if I could."

"Thanks."

"So," Harmon said, "Diehl is whipping your butt, huh?"

"Yeah," Kevin said and took another bite. "I think he loves pain." He smiled.

"I think you're probably right."

"I've got to meet him later for combat training too," Kevin said, shaking his head. "And before that, I have to meet the Master to train other stuff."

"Sounds like you've got a busy day."

"Yeah, but"—Kevin shoved another oversized bite into his mouth—"I've got enough time for a nap. Thanks for breakfast." Kevin stood, straightening his back slowly and painfully.

"You're welcome," Harmon said. "Good night."

"Good night." Kevin waved and headed to his stall. His nap lasted only an hour before his watch beeped. It was time for training with the Master. He dragged himself out of the barn and to the bunker, where he found the Master waiting.

"Welcome, Kevin! You're right on time," the Master said as Kevin shut the doors to the bunker behind him.

"The watch works," Kevin said.

"So, how was your first training session with Diehl?"

"I think every muscle in my body is crying right now," Kevin said as he walked over to the Master.

The Master laughed. "Well, hopefully that gets easier soon. Are you ready for our training?"

Kevin took a seat on a stool. "Sure. I don't know what we're training, but it can't be as painful as what Diehl and I did this morning."

"No, it won't be. You're going to enjoy this," the Master said. "Bring that stool closer. Let me show you something."

The Master and Kevin sat close, looking at a computer screen. It had a simple terminal window open.

"You've seen the code of the Dream States, right?" the Master asked.

Kevin nodded.

"Well, this basic terminal was used to make all of it. It's hard to believe since, today, by using the brains of everyone plugged in, the code takes on an almost 3D appearance, but it all started here," the Master said.

"I've seen something similar before. In my split dreaming as an editor, we'd see a terminal like this."

"Yes, you'd see something like this, but that was still an interface coded on this. This is the bottom building block. Do you understand?"

"Yeah."

"Good. So, today, our first coding lesson will be learning how to use this basic language. When you connect to the dream network, this language is there, so you can siphon pieces of the code and construct a terminal like the one you saw when you were an editor. Once you've done that, you can start programming and editing the dream. Even logging in and bypassing security measures is possible, because they still build the security measures in this language." The Master pointed at the screen and talked with his hands. Kevin smiled at the old man's excitement.

"So, how do we do this?"

"Well, you're going to go over in the chair." The Master motioned to a lawn chair that sat a few feet away. "You'll plug in." The Master handed the end of a cord with the fitting for a mind chip to Kevin. "We'll start by downloading, or teaching you, the language. Then you'll build a terminal using the code. Then we'll practice, in increasing levels of complexity, pulling that code out of dreams."

"You're going to plug me into the network?"

"No, these are training dreams housed only here on these servers."

"Okay," Kevin said. He walked to the chair and plugged into his mind chip. "Let's do this."

The Master opened a small metal box and pulled a needle and a small bottle from it. "I'm going to give you a sedative injection. It will only last a few hours, but that will be good for this first time training."

Kevin nodded.

The Master carefully filled the needle and injected the serum into Kevin's arm. He turned back to the desk. "Here we go," the Master said, typing into the computer. "Now I'm only teaching you what you need to create the terminal for today. We'll keep working, adding more and more as we train."

Kevin felt his mind chip as it poured information into his brain. His eyes grew heavy as the serum worked on his body. Lines of code appeared against the black of his subconscious.

"Let's get started," the Master said, his voice coming from nowhere in particular.

For the next few hours, Kevin and the Master ran simulations and practiced building the terminal.

Kevin ducked, attempting to avoid Diehl's reach. His tired muscles moved too slowly. Diehl grabbed him by the shoulder, turned him and pushed him face-first into the dirt. Diehl put his knee in the middle of Kevin's back for added punishment. He held Kevin down for a few seconds before releasing him.

"You can't leave your back open like that." Diehl chastised Kevin as he stood up, wiping dirt from his cheek. "If you were up against Dream States' security right now, you'd be dead. Now let's try that again. Remember, I'm bigger than you, so you can't take me head-on. Move fast and attack my extremities."

Kevin and Diehl squared up to each other. Kevin moved to duck under Diehl's grasp and wrap his legs. This time, Diehl drove his knee square into Kevin's face, contacting his jaw just above his upper lip.

"Oh!" Kevin grabbed his face. "You son of a—"

Before he could finish, Diehl had lifted him off the ground and was driving him into the dirt on his back. Diehl straddled Kevin. "Cover your face!" Diehl shouted as he slapped Kevin.

Kevin flailed, attempting to avoid the attack.

Diehl stood up and walked away from Kevin. "Come on! Are you trying to lose?"

Kevin pulled himself up, licking blood from inside his lip off his teeth. "You cheated."

"Cheated? You telegraphed your takedown."

"We were practicing the takedown!" Kevin shouted at him.

"And we are practicing, not telegraphing it."

Kevin felt his anger grow, and something inside clicked.

"Again!" Diehl said, charging Kevin.

Out of an instinct buried deep inside, Kevin sidestepped Diehl. Kevin swung his legs around Diehl's neck, scissored and clamped hard as he threw the rest of his body into a spin. The move threw Diehl to the ground hard, and he tumbled a few feet.

Diehl coughed as he pulled to a knee. "Where'd you learn that?"

"I, I don't know," Kevin said, confused how his body had just moved like that.

"Well, it's good. It means you have some fighting knowledge trapped in your brain somewhere. Now we just need to practice more to unlock it," Diehl said.

"That can't be right. I didn't do any fighting in my last dream."

"Hey, man, the mind is a complicated thing. You could have some left over from your computer training, or just watched enough movies in your last dream. Who knows? Let's try something else." Diehl threw a punch at Kevin.

Kevin's hidden fighting skill didn't show up. Diehl's fist connected with his cheek. The hit sent Kevin stumbling on wobbling legs. He stayed up for a few steps before he fell, and his consciousness faded into a dreamless sleep.

Beep . . . Beep . . . Beep . . .

Kevin fumbled with his watch, this time finding the button to turn off the alarm easier, but still with some struggle. He sat up with a painful turn. He lifted his shirt to find a good side bruise forming on his ribs. Kevin moved his jaw with a shooting pain.

"How are you doing?" Diehl asked from the open stall door, his silhouette illuminated by the rising sun.

"I think I got hit by a truck."

"Sorry about that. I thought your instincts would kick in again. Guess we'll have to work on it."

Kevin adjusted his position to lean less on his bruised ribs. "I don't think I can work out today."

"I figured you'd be a little sore," Diehl said, laughing under his breath.

"I think I'm a little more than a little sore," Kevin said. "And my jaw might be broken."

"It's not," Diehl said. "You can still talk, but I let you sleep in so you could recover for today."

"You knocked me out. I don't think that counts as sleep."

"It does today," Diehl said, stepping forward and pulling Kevin to his feet.

Kevin's legs almost gave out in pain. "Diehl, I don't, I can't."

"Relax. Today is yoga, so we'll get some blood flow in those muscles."

"Diehl."

"Let's go." Diehl walked out of the stall. Kevin limped after him.

Diehl and Kevin did yoga in a small grassy field to the side of the barn for the better part of an hour. As much as Kevin struggled and complained, by the end of their session, he could walk upright with minimal pain.

"Well, that's it for today," Diehl said.

"You mean this morning?"

"No, no combat training for today, but the Master wants you to head over right away. I know we skipped breakfast, but he wants you to head over right away."

"Okay."

"I'll see you tomorrow morning." Diehl said.

"See you then," Kevin said.

Kevin walked tenderly over to the bunker.

"I heard you had a rough afternoon yesterday," the Master said as Kevin entered the bunker.

Kevin immediately went to the lawn chair, lowered himself, and reclined. "Yeah."

"Diehl is good at unharnessing hidden traits, but sometimes he can be overzealous," the Master said.

"You could say so," Kevin said. "So, what's the plan today? More coding?"

"Actually, today we are going to practice something different. You know how when you were editing, you split your consciousness?"

"Yeah, kind of both awake and plugged in."

"Exactly. Well, that was possible because you were under only a mild sedative. It allows you to still perceive the world around you while also plugged in. Now the important thing there is that you've never plugged in without a sedative. Your mind would have kicked you out of the dream long ago without it."

"Makes sense."

"Well, today we are going to practice dreaming without one. Dry dreaming is what I call it. Did you eat breakfast?"

"No. Diehl said that I had to come over here right away."

"Good. This could cause some nausea if you had a full stomach. Plug in."

Kevin plugged his mind chip into the cord that rested on the armrest of the lawn chair. "Nausea? Why?"

"Dreaming without a sedative and connecting through the mind chip can irritate the little bones in your ear that dictate equilibrium. Do you feel anything?"

"No, should I?"

"No, it's a learned skill. That's what we're here for today. Close your eyes."

Kevin closed his eyes and adjusted his seated position to get more comfortable.

"Now think of the codes we used yesterday. Search for them in your mind. Think of how the code looked, and how the phrases and characters linked. Try to picture it all. When you see them, follow them."

Kevin followed strings of code that started as thoughts and then turned into images. Piece by piece, he found himself standing on an urban street surrounded by gray brick buildings.

"Kevin!" the Master yelled.

Kevin snapped to attention back in the bunker, ripped out of the dream he had just been experiencing. "What?"

"Now close your eyes. Quick, do you still see the dream?"

Kevin searched his mind, but he only saw black. "No."

"Well, you accessed the dream without a sedative. That's a good start. Now we need to practice staying asleep. Even if you need to open your eyes, or do something, keeping a piece of your mind in the dream is something we need to work on. Ready to try again?"

Kevin nodded and closed his eyes.

Fourteen days of early mornings and coding challenges had passed as Kevin grew in his programming skill and fitness.

Kevin jogged in place while rolling his shoulders, loosening up his joints.

"You seem chipper today," Diehl said as he stretched his calf against the side of the barn.

"I feel good today. I'm finally not sore, and my bruises from your wrestling lessons aren't hurting too bad. I feel so good, in fact, that I think I may just beat you on the run today."

"You must have hit your head in your sleep," Diehl said.

"No, last night I finally slept all the way through. No random dream memories from my past lives, no twig where it shouldn't be. I even woke up before the alarm on my watch went off, so I didn't have to hear that beeping," Kevin said with a smile on his face.

"Lucky you. I had double nighttime guard shift last night since Cassidy and Harmon are both needed for the harvest."

"The harvest?"

"Yeah, the corn is ready to pick."

"Huh. I guess it's fall, then?"

"Yep." Diehl noted the look on Kevin's face. "Right. This is your first season actually experiencing the passage of time."

"I've seen the seasons before."

"Yeah, but only glimpses as you rode between work and dreaming. This,"—Diehl made a pointing motion in a circle in the air—"this will be the first time you get to experience the slow transition of it all. Trust me, it's better."

"I lived in Colorado in my last dream, and we definitely got to experience the seasons changing."

"Trust me," Diehl said, "it's different."

"How cold is it gonna get?"

"Oh, it gets pretty cold. Just wait until you experience your first snow," Diehl said. "I bet you cry like a little baby."

"You forget I can't cry."

"We'll see."

"I guess so. You're going to cry after I beat you today."

"Wanna bet?"

"What's the wager?"

"There's a wild apple tree that grows along the creek. No one else knows about it. If you win today, I'll give you an apple."

"And if you win?"

"You take my guard duty tonight," Diehl said, a happy menace in his tone.

"An apple versus not sleeping?" Kevin asked, not convinced.

"You'll never have an apple any other way."

"What're the rules?"

"First one to finish the run and touch the barn wins."

"You're on," Kevin said, turning and taking off.

"Oh, you son of—" Diehl took off after him.

Kevin skipped as he entered the bunker. *Crunch.* The apple in his mouth popped with juice as he bit into it.

"Where did you get that?" the Master asked.

Kevin spoke as he chewed the bite of apple in his mouth. "Diehl. I beat him in a race today, so he had to give me one of his apples."

"Diehl has apples?"

"Yep, he found some wild tree, I guess."

"He did, did he? I'm going to have to talk to him about that. Hurry and finish it. We have a lot of work to do."

Kevin took a rushed bite, the juice dripping down his chin, which he wiped with his sleeve.

"Save the core," the Master said. "You can plant the seeds and start growing us an orchard."

Kevin nodded, took one last bite and placed the core on top of the desk, careful not to let the juice stick to the surface. "Okay. What's the plan today?"

"Today we access our own small dream network. You and I will connect to the mainframe and share the dream together so I can show you some things."

"Wait, I thought you said you can't dream anymore?" Kevin asked.

"I could dream once more, but they have programmed the network to lock my mind in. The last time I connected, I almost couldn't get out. This dream we network through, the one we are going to share, is one of my creation. It's a special design to let me dream safely."

"Oh," Kevin said, sitting in the lawn chair and plugging in. He closed his eyes and let his mind go dark, searching for code remnants until his consciousness pulled into the dream.

"Welcome," the Master said, or at least the Master's voice said as it came out of the mouth of an early forties man wearing glasses and a small man bun tied behind his head.

"Thanks," Kevin said. He glanced at himself and back at the Master. "Why do you look so different and I look, well, like I do outside the dream?"

"Remember, it's all a dream. You can be whoever and whatever you want." The Master finished his sentence by turning into a young girl, maybe ten, in a Girl Scout uniform, her hair up in pigtails.

Kevin stared for a moment. "Why can't I remember you changing? I, it's like you just transformed completely and my mind just accepted it."

"It's the nature of dreaming. Things change that break the rules of logic, but because we are in the subconscious realm, our minds accept it," the Master said, now speaking from the mouth of what can be best described as a Muppet. "Now you try. Do something that breaks the laws of nature."

"Like what?"

"Hmmm." The Master looked like himself now. "Well, how long have you been able to breathe underwater?"

"What?"

The Master just spread his arms to pet a school of fish that were swimming around them.

"How did that happen?"

The Master asked, feeding a sea turtle a piece of kelp he had plucked from the sandy bottom.

Kevin looked at the surrounding dreamscape. "You're changing the code, right?"

"Uh-huh. Look close."

Kevin stared intently at the Master. He fought to ignore the world around him melting from the lava planet Mustafar to a schoolroom to a forest to a pirate ship.

"Do you see it?" the Master asked.

Simultaneously, with him asking, Kevin noticed a small flicker the size of a firefly. A small blink of unmistakable white light, commands and characters glowed next to the Master's head. "Yes. Yes! I see it," Kevin said. "But that's not code, is it? It's too small."

The Master changed their locale to a rolling green hill of grass overlooking the English moors. "All your coding to this point has been longhand. What I'm doing now is using call names to shortcut the coding process. I'm accessing subroutines that I have stored in my mind chip, allowing me to code seamlessly and carry hidden code with me. This allows me to access complex code and execute it quickly."

"The code that can bypass dream-network security?"

"And other things."

"Like what?"

"What would you say if I told you that you could protect hidden memories from the burn, allowing you to remember things you don't want to forget?"

"I'd ask how."

"Let's wake up and finish this conversation," the Master said, disappearing from the dream.

Kevin pulled his mind from the dream, bringing his attention back to the bunker.

"I can't stay in the dream long," the Master said. "This network helps, but my brain still throws me out. Over the years, it's getting better at waking me up. You're new to all this, so you can stay in for longer, much longer, years of dream life if needed. Which is good, because you're going to need to spend a lot of time in the dream to pre-build the coding sequences you'll need."

"Okay," Kevin said. "Can't you just plug your mind chip into mine and download them?"

"Unfortunately, no. While the code for the dream is pretty universal, the way the code organizes in your brain is unique to you. So what I've done for you is create dream worlds you can go into and pull the correct coding sequences out of. It will take time, a lot of time, but in the end..."

"In the end, I can change the dream network like you were doing?" Kevin asked.

"Yes," the Master said. "And you can put in code that will change things in the real world."

"How?"

"I'll explain that later. For now, it's time for you to build these subroutines."

"Okay."

"You'll go into the dream and search for the code that doesn't fit. As you pull the code and build subroutines, you'll find yourself starting to be able to point at the name of that data and shortcut actual coding. Oh, and for the next week, you come here right away. This will take a long time to pre-program enough code to be effective, and I have a feeling we are racing the clock. Don't worry about breakfast, lunch or dinner. I'll bring them. Okay?"

Kevin nodded.

"Let's get to work," the Master said.

Kevin sat back and let his mind slip into the dream.

"Hey, man!" Harmon said to Kevin as he shuffled through the barn, trying not to stub his toe or make too much noise in the darkness. Only the kitchen light illuminated the central passage. "Come talk to me while I clean up."

Kevin nodded his head. "Alright."

"Here, dry for me as I clean these bowls." Harmon handed a towel to Kevin.

Kevin took it and started drying the already-washed dishes.

"So how have you been, man? I haven't seen you much this last week, just coming and going."

"Good, just been busy. The Master has me doing a ton of programming learning."

"Programming? In the dream?"

"Yeah, I've been getting pretty good at it." Kevin smiled, putting a now-dry dish to the side and grabbing another. "It's pretty cool. I can change my appearance, change the scenery, make things appear and disappear. Heck, I can even become a superhero."

"Sounds fun, but I don't know if I'd want to go back in. I think it would be hard to dream again. I feel myself pulled into the dream from random memories already going back in. I'm not sure I wouldn't snap and trade this glorious life for the freedom there. My mind might crack."

"Yeah, I guess it's easier for me since my job at the Z-Bank was kind of dreaming too."

Harmon nodded. "Hey, I know you're busy and all, but if you ever feel like learning about farming, Mei and I would appreciate the extra hand. Being that we're shorthanded without Cassidy, we could use the extra help tilling the fields."

"Where's Cassidy?"

"You don't know?"

Kevin shrugged his shoulders while setting a dish aside. "Know what?"

"Last week, Cassidy made a batch of home-brewed whiskey from the extra corn. And well..."

"Well, what?"

"He's dead."

"What? From whiskey?"

"Yes, and no." Harmon stopped cleaning dishes to face Kevin. "Cassidy, much like me, woke from his dream because of a tragic moment that broke him. In his last dream, his brother had died, and Cassidy had turned to drinking. The grief broke his heart, and the whiskey broke his mind. Well, when he had it again here, the memories and the emotions all came flooding back. But here his mind can't break and force him to wake up, so in his distraught state, he, he ended it himself."

"He killed himself?"

"Mei heard the shot and found his body. She's, she's holding on, but it's been tough," Harmon said.

"Oh, wow, I didn't know. I've been so busy with coding, I just didn't..."

Harmon picked up another bowl and began scrubbing a stubbornly dried-on piece of potato. "Everyone here is so focused on the mission at hand and just surviving that they forget about each other sometimes. They forget that everyone here has a story, and it's usually not a happy one."

"You're right."

"What about you? Are the dreams still taking you back to your last life?"

"No. At least not for a while. Thank God."

"Don't wish for it too soon. I'd kill to have one of those dreams sometimes."

"Really? Why?"

"To see Harmony again." Harmon rinsed off a bowl and handed it to Kevin. "After losing Cassidy, I'd love to just see her face. Hear her laugh. Something to remember her as real again."

"If you could choose, what memory would you want to dream about?" Kevin asked, drying a bowl with the now-damp towel.

Harmon paused, looking nowhere in particular, thinking. A smile spread across his face. "I remember this one time when I was clean, and we were both so focused on our health. We—" Harmon let out a small laugh that interrupted his story.

Kevin smiled, seeing the happiness on Harmon's face.

"We were so focused on health that we tried eating vegan for two weeks. Ha ha. What they don't tell you when you go vegan is that your gut bacteria changes or something. Basically, you just get ridiculous gas. This one night, she and I are sitting in bed. Keep in mind, she had never farted around me at all. She was always shy about that. All day, she's been holding in her gas. Ha ha. Well, she's almost asleep, like going in and out of consciousness. Ha ha, and ha ha, and as she almost starts dreaming, her body relaxes, and she, ha ha, she farts so loud and just so ridiculous. The bed rumbled, and it actually woke her and me up. Ha ha, we stared at each other for a moment like we just heard a gunshot or something. Ha ha, and then in that moment of embarrassment, she smiled, and I smiled back, and we just started laughing. I mean, the kind of laughing where you're gasping for air and your sides hurt. Then, as we laughed, we farted more. We just couldn't hold it in."

Kevin laughed along with Harmon as they enjoyed a moment of happy memory. "Do you remember her face and laugh now?"

"Yeah," Harmon said, turning to face Kevin, a tear forming in his right eye. "I think you're the first person I've ever told that story to."

"Well, thanks for sharing it."

"Thanks for being a friend."

Kevin paused for a moment. "I've always wanted a friend. I mean, in the real world. I know I wasn't supposed to, but deep down, I knew I wanted one."

"Well, now you've got one."

Kevin smiled at Harmon, feeling grateful for the moment.

Harmon spoke up and broke the moment. "Now let's finish these dishes so you can get to bed. I'm guessing you're going to need your rest to keep your coding up."

"Tomorrow I'm back to the training with Diehl."

"Then we better finish even faster," Harmon said, a note of an ominous tone in his voice.

Kevin looked at him, suspicious.

"Diehl has been looking around for you a lot lately. It seems like he's eager to bring the pain."

"Probably because I beat him in a race and won his apple the day before I started coding training."

Harmon laughed. "You're so dead."

Kevin laughed, not nearly as enthusiastically, and swallowed hard.

Dirt and grass smeared across Kevin's cheek as his face slammed into the ground. Kevin felt the pain radiate as he slid face-first. His eyes grew moist and his face turned red when his nose hit a rock that was in the right spot on the ground.

Diehl laughed as he saw Kevin turn over with watery eyes. "Are you going to cry? I'm not surprised that your fitness dipped after the last couple of weeks in the bunker, but the Master said nothing about turning you into a little girl."

"If he had turned into a girl, your slow ass would have lost," Sarah said as she walked to Kevin and extended her hand. He grabbed it as she pulled him up. "You know, you're never going to learn to fight if you try to fight like him," Sarah said.

"Thanks," Kevin said, wiping the dirt and grass from himself. "Hit my nose."

"I know," Sarah said, smiling at Kevin.

"How cute. You two girls should go paint your nails next," Diehl said, interrupting the moment.

"The way to kick Diehl's ass is to use his strength against him," Sarah said to Kevin. She turned to Diehl. "His inflexible, steroid-looking muscles make him slow." She turned to Kevin for a second. "And maybe stupid."

Kevin smiled at her. Sarah's confidence was engaging.

"I'm not slow," Diehl said.

"Okay. I believe you," Sarah said.

Diehl and she stared at each other for a second, each knowing what was about to happen. Diehl charged her and attempted to grab her. Sarah crouched low, ducking beneath his reach. She spun around behind him, jumped on his back and sank her arms into a rear naked choke. Diehl attempted to reach overhead and grab her, but his enormous arms couldn't. Thinking fast, he jumped back, attempting to slam her into the ground. She deftly jumped off his back, letting him slam himself.

"Hack, haeaah, ehahd." Diehl let out a cacophony of strange noises as he struggled for air, having knocked the wind out of himself.

Sarah walked over to Kevin. "See, you use speed and better range of motion to beat an opponent that is greater in size but slower in both reaction time and intellect. My dad always says the smart will win out in the end every time."

"You," Diehl choked out of himself, "cheated."

Sarah smirked. "How's that?"

Diehl rolled himself onto his hands and knees. "We were practicing throws, not choke holds."

"I just made you throw yourself. That's not cheating. That's just smart."

"What are you even doing here?" Diehl asked Sarah, standing upright.

"The tractor broke down again. Harmon and Mei need you to help push it back to the barn."

"What about training the new guy?"

"I'll take it from here," Sarah said. "He'll have to learn how to throw me." She winked at Kevin, and he felt his heart skip a beat.

"Why not have him push the tractor? That sounds like a trainee thing."

"He's staying here with me so he can learn something besides just how to get beaten up by you. Now go put your slow muscles to use elsewhere."

"Fine," Diehl said, stomping off.

"So where were you and Diehl before I got here?" Sarah asked Kevin.

"He was showing how to perform a basic throw."

"Well, which one? There are a lot of different throws. I assume he was teaching you judo?"

"To be honest, he was kind of just teaching by example, not really using names or anything. I think I've got a couple of them down, though."

"Show me," Sarah said, taking off her holster and setting it on the ground.

"Okay," Kevin said. He started walking toward Sarah. She backed away in a defensive posture. "Um, Diehl was teaching me, starting in an engaged position."

"Did he show you how to close the gap?"

"He was going to do that after. He said before I learned how to get close, I should know what to do when I got there."

Kevin and Sarah grabbed each other's arms. "Okay, so." Kevin swept his leg around the back of Sarah's and pulled it across her body in front, turning and pulling her, throwing her to the ground to the side of him while he held one of her arms. He held just enough to slow her fall, but not hard enough to hurt her wrist.

"Good. Good form," Sarah said, standing back up. "But you need to pull me closer." She grabbed Kevin's arms, putting them back in the beginning position. "Now try not to fall."

Kevin nodded.

"If you pull too wide..." Sarah pulled Kevin, sweeping his leg as well but keeping distance.

Kevin instinctively spun around the arm Sarah held, still standing and now facing her in an advantageous position.

"See? Now let's do that again, slow, and I'll show you the difference."

Kevin and Sarah went back to the starting position. This time, she swept his leg and pulled him close to her. Their faces were almost touching as Sarah held Kevin against her, not throwing him yet, letting him feel the position. He felt his heart beating. "See how much more connection there is to your opponent when they're close?"

Kevin nodded.

Sarah pushed Kevin back to two feet and the starting position. "Now throw me again, but keep me close."

Kevin swept the leg and pulled Sarah close as he threw her, this time executing the move well. She hit the ground a little harder than he had intended. "Sorry."

"That's alright," Sarah said as she stood up. "You should put me on my back aggressively. That's what this is all about."

"Okay."

"What other throws do you know?"

"Well, I think I've got one other down."

They got back in the starting position, standing facing each other, holding each other's arms. Kevin pulled Sarah's hands down and pushed them back by her hips. He curled his left leg behind her, tripping her as he put his body weight into her. She fell backward, and he was pulled on top of her. She hit the ground, and Kevin landed his upper body on her chest with his legs to one side.

"Oomph." She let out a little air as she fell.

"You okay?" Kevin asked as he leaned back, taking his weight off her.

"Yeah. So what next?"

"Um."

"That was the throw. Now you've got me on the ground. What is your next move?"

"I don't, I don't know."

"Put your weight on me, on my chest."

Kevin followed her instructions, leaning into her chest. The smell of peonies reached Kevin's nose. He smelled it and got lost in the scent.

"Did you hear me?"

"Sorry, what?"

"Straddle me."

"What?"

"Swing your leg over and pin me down."

"Uh," Kevin stammered.

"Switch me spots."

They rolled, so that Kevin was on his back, and Sarah was leaning on him from the side. "See, I put my weight into your chest. I push with my arms here to take weight off my legs." Kevin felt her press into his chest. "Now I swing my leg over and straddle you." Sarah swung her leg over Kevin's body, now straddling him. "From here, I can hit at your face." Sarah mimicked some punches. "I can control your hips." She squeezed her legs around Kevin's waist. "And I can pull a weapon if I had one." Sarah pretended to pull a nonexistent gun and shoot Kevin. "Get it?"

"Yeah, I do," Kevin said. *I'm so glad you're showing me this and not Diehl*, he thought to himself.

"If you find yourself in the bottom of this position, like you are now, what you need to do, and fast, are two things." Sarah said, continuing her instruction. "First, you need to throw your hips up, hard. Okay? Do it."

Kevin pushed up with his hips, but not fast enough.

Sarah leaned back, using her legs to stay balanced. "Faster than that. Thrust me like a bronco bucking a rodeo cowboy. Really throw them. Like, try to hump me into the sky. Can you do that?"

Kevin was dying inside. He braced himself and this time threw his hips hard. She fell forward, out of balance, her face almost hitting Kevin's.

"Hold your hips up now," Sarah instructed. "See how close we are now?" Her nose was almost touching his. "And see how I reached out with my hands to break my fall? Now reach with your arms and wrap my neck or arm up, and roll to the side."

Kevin tried somehow wrapping around her neck perfectly, now having her in a choke hold, with them on their sides.

"Keep rolling until you're on top." Sarah pushed out through Kevin's loose hold.

Kevin kept rolling, now lying on top of Sarah, his arm wrapped around her neck and his body pressing her into the ground. The smell of peonies again filled his nose. He shook his head and let go of Sarah. He stood and adjusted himself before helping Sarah to her feet.

"Good," Sarah said, "real good. Remember to use your body to help you move between positions. Now let's work on getting close."

Kevin swallowed hard. "Sounds good to me."

Kevin watched the trees of the forest morph into clouds as he changed the landscape around him. He felt the air pass under his wings as he flew, his near-seven-foot wingspan catching an updraft from the warm sea below. He had been flying, as a condor, through some scenes as he practiced changing the code.

The air felt good as it passed over his feathers. He flew lower to feel the mist coming off the ocean waves. The warmth and moisture made him think of the heat and sweat that he and Sarah's bodies had shared earlier while practicing combat. He thought of the feeling of being thrown by her, how she had swept him with such momentum to the side.

A hurricane formed over the ocean and pulled on him. He focused on the landscape again, morphing it into a desert. The hurricane had changed into a mountain range, standing tall and steady. Kevin shook his head, amazed at what had just happened. Kevin changed back to himself, standing in the sand, barefoot. *That was weird.*

Where did that hurricane come from? I didn't make that. I was just thinking about Sarah and our training. His mind went to the feeling of Sarah sitting on him and pressing on his chest. Before he even comprehended what was happening, he was lying in the sand and sucked into it. *What? What!* He panicked. Blackness overtook him for a split second before he shot awake in the bunker.

"Whoa! Hee heee heeee." Kevin panted as he awoke from his sudden nightmare.

"What happened? Your code is broken all over the place. You have code coming in from your subconscious that is overruling your intentional programming! You were in a critical cascade. If I hadn't pulled the plug, you could have lost yourself in the dream," the Master said.

"Sorry, I was just..."

"What were you thinking about that was so strong you overwrote code unintentionally?" The Master was reading through an error message, trying to track the issue.

"Nothing, wait, what do you mean 'lose myself in the dream'?"

The Master didn't look up from the computer screen as he spoke. "Dreams will always be a place of the subconscious. If your subconscious becomes so attached to the dream in the awake dreaming state that you were in, your logical mind will lose that battle and your brain will get trapped in the computer."

"That's a possibility!"

"Yes, and that's why you need to focus. Ah, here we are." The Master had almost tracked down the break in the code.

"You have me in there for the last couple of weeks without telling me that?"

"Just...don't..." The Master stopped and turned to Kevin, looking away from his computer screen. "Just don't think about my daughter while you're in there and you'll be fine."

Kevin swallowed, uncomfortable. "What do you mean?" His voice cracked, giving away his understanding.

"I can see Sarah's name in the code. I can read your thoughts, literally."

"Oh my god," Kevin said. "I'm so sorry, I—"

The Master stopped him. "I see your emotions in the broken code, too."

Kevin didn't know what to say. "Okay," is all he could muster.

"All this"—the Master circled his finger over his head—"everything I'm doing is for her. I want her to be free. To live in a world where she's not being constantly hunted and hiding in fear of death. I could override logic and gain freedom from the control of the system because of my love, first for Sarah's mother. I know what that emotional code looks like. My code is full of my love for Sarah." The Master laughed for a moment. "You know, most fathers would have to ask the guys in their daughters' lives if what they say about their feelings is true. I know they are, in your case."

"What do you mean?"

The Master looked at him, a softness in his face Kevin hadn't seen before. "There is some code that is not created by your mind or the system. It appears from real deep emotion. You can't control it or get rid of it. It's too powerful. You have that code running through you. Your identity is filled with love for my daughter now. It hasn't fully built itself yet, but the pieces are there and they are growing."

"I don't know, I mean, I know, but."

"But you're not sure what you feel?"

"Yeah."

"Of course you're not. You couldn't be. The only connection you've felt up to this point has been programmed into your mind. Genuine emotions come from somewhere else."

"Where?"

"That's the age-old question. Some people believe it's your heart, others your soul."

"Well, my heart beats fast when she's around."

The Master stared at him.

"Sorry."

"Those feelings, let them motivate you. But don't get distracted here. The better you can focus, the better chance she has at a life. You want to help give her that, right?" the Master asked.

"Absolutely," Kevin said, nodding his head with a determined tempo.

"Good. Then let's try this again. This time, though, stay focused."

"Right."

Kevin checked his watch again. Diehl was late.

Where is he? He's never been late. Kevin was sitting on a tree stump, waiting for Diehl to show up for their morning run.

"Morning!" Sarah said as he bounded across the open space from the farmhouse to the barn.

Kevin jumped up from his perch. "Morning."

"Ready to run?" Sarah asked, jogging in place.

"Uh, where's Diehl?"

"Change of plans. You're training with me from now on."

"Oh, really? Did you make that decision?"

"No, my dad did." Sarah stopped jogging, now just standing. "Why? Do you not want to train with me?"

"No!" Kevin said, a little louder than he intended. "No, no, I would love to train with you. I'm excited to train with you, just surprised is all." Kevin smiled, forcing a joking tone out of himself, trying to backpedal. "Kinda figured the high point of Diehl's day was making me hurt."

"Well, now it gets to be the high point of my day," Sarah said, smiling.

"Lucky you."

"Oh yeah, by the time I'm done with you, you'll be on your back, sweating, out of breath, wondering what just happened," Sarah said. "Come on, let's go!" Sarah took off running.

Kevin put his hands together in a prayer pose and mouthed to the sky. *Thank you.*

"Come on!" Sarah shouted, already a hundred feet away.

"Coming!" Kevin shouted back, taking off to catch up.

"I'm so glad you and I finally got time alone," Sarah said as she brushed a hair from her face.

"Me too," Kevin said. "I've been wanting this so bad."

"Now that we're alone out here in the middle of this field, with no one around us, what are you going to do about your desires?" Sarah asked, a hint of something deeply enticing in her eye.

Kevin pulled her close and pressed his lips against hers. He felt the softness and warmth, tasted the sweetness of her, and smelled... nothing. Kevin broke the kiss.

"What's wrong?"

Kevin smelled her neck. There was nothing.

"What?"

"Peonies."

"What?"

"I don't smell peonies," Kevin said as realization dawned on him. "This is a dream."

Kevin opened his eyes in the barn stall. He looked around. He was alone, except for a cricket that sang his song from somewhere in the hay in the far corner. Kevin sat up and rubbed his eyes. *Wow, I've got to get myself under control. Come on, keep it together. It's not like she's the first girl you've ever met.* Kevin paused. *Wait, is she? It doesn't matter. Look, just get some sleep. Don't think about her. Just think about coding or something else. And no matter what*—Kevin thought about the dream he had just woken from—*don't think about peonies.*

Peonies.

The soft floral scent reached Kevin's nose, pulling him from his slumber. He breathed it in, smiling subtly as he filled his nostrils.

"Rise and shine," Sarah said in an upbeat but subdued tone, easing Kevin into the morning.

"Morning," Kevin said in an upbeat manner. He stared at her, the memory of last night's dream still burning in his mind. He studied her face, the smile that pinched her cheeks forming a slight dimple. She had tied her hair back in a ponytail, ready for the morning's run. Kevin imagined what it would feel like in his hands again.

"What?" Sarah asked, aware that Kevin was staring at her.

"Nothing. Just. Nothing."

"No. Come on. What? Do I have something on my face?"

"N-no," Kevin stammered. "No, you... you just look, um, yours is a better face to wake up to than Diehl's."

"Thanks. I think."

"Yeah."

"Okay, well get up. It's time to go running. Today we are doing a longer loop."

Kevin stood up and started stretching his body awake. "Longer than the two-mile creek loop?"

"Yeah, today we are running a five-mile trail that I found when I was a teenager." Sarah smiled. "You should feel lucky. I haven't taken anyone on this run before. It's kind of my secret, peaceful route."

"I do feel lucky."

"Well, get your shoes on, then."

"Right." Kevin tied his shoes snug, and he and Sarah took off.

For half an hour, he followed her, running through creek beds, jumping over tree roots and avoiding loose rocks. They were about to crest over a ridge when their watches beeped.

Beep . . .

Beep . . .

Beep . . .

Sarah grabbed Kevin's arm, "Quick! Duck under the out-cropping here."

She and Kevin squeezed into a small divot that had formed over an outcropping of rock. They had to hug close to each other and intertwine their legs to fit. Kevin felt his heartbeat as he watched the radar readout of the drone passing overhead. He fought to control his breath in fear of getting caught. As the red dot passed by, Kevin let out an exhale of relief. It was then he realized he was holding Sarah close, and she him.

He couldn't hear the breeze blowing outside. He couldn't feel the hard ground underneath him. He couldn't see the beetle crawling over his hand. In that moment, all he could sense was her. The feel of Sarah against him, the sound of her heartbeat and breath, the smell of her sweat mixing with the sweet peony perfume she wore. Some-where inside, code and emotion connected. The world turned on like a light. Color flooded in as he was pulled from a gray existence.

"That was close," he said, afraid more of ruining the moment than of the drone catching them.

"Yeah. Thank God this outcropping was here."

"Yeah. Thank God."

Sarah and Kevin stared into each other's eyes, faces close.

"We should go," he said, breaking the tension.

"Yeah," she said in a rushed and tense manner. She hopped up and dusted herself off. "Come on. We've still got a couple of miles left."

"Lead the way," Kevin said.

"Try to keep up," Sarah said, winking at Kevin as she turned and started jogging.

Kevin took a big breath, trying to calm his nerves. He blinked twice, shook his head, and took off after Sarah as she ran across the barren landscape.

"Is it that bad?" Harmon asked.

"What?" Kevin asked back, looking up at Harmon.

"The stew? Is it bad? I tried some new spices I've been growing." Harmon pointed at a full bowl that Kevin had been stirring for the last fifteen minutes.

"Oh, um, no, it's fine," Kevin said, adjusting his sitting position on the bench of the table in the center of the barn.

"Okay, well, if you want more, let me know," Harmon said, turning to head back to the kitchen.

"Harmon," Kevin said, wanting to say more but not knowing how to ask the question he wanted to know the answer to.

"Yeah?" Harmon said, turning and facing Kevin again.

"You, you were in love before, right?"

"Yeah. Still am."

"How do you know?"

"Well, it's not something you can describe. It's something that you know, but you don't actually know it."

Kevin looked at Harmon, not grasping his answer.

"It's like you feel something deep inside. You just have this emotion that pours out of your soul. Sometimes it just makes you feel like, invincible, or like yelling at the top of your lungs in exultation. It drives your heartbeat wild, makes your eyes grow a couple sizes too big, and you want to cry out of happiness and sadness at the same time. You know, in that moment, you will never feel something more real and more enrapturing. Yet if you try to think about how you feel, it goes away. You can't put it into words or thoughts. It's just something you have to feel," Harmon said. "Do you get what I'm saying?"

"I think so," Kevin said. "But how do you know? Like, know know? Like, how did you know with Harmony?"

"Oh, man," Harmon said, sitting one leg on the edge of the table. "Harmony just cleared everything up. She was... She reached past my mind chip and into my heart. The Master says actual love can have that effect, and sometimes that love causes early awakenings."

"Do you think she woke up from your love?"

"She died."

"But the Master said that..." Kevin realized the knowledge of the kill code might not be something that was shared with all members of the group. "Never mind."

"Okay," Harmon said, standing up off the table. "Remember, if you feel love, you'll know it. Deep down. Now eat some of that stew before it gets too cold and tastes bad."

"Thanks."

Stars filled Kevin's eyes as he recoiled from Sarah's strike. Her elbow had caught him in the forehead, square between his eyes. Dazed, he stumbled back and wobbled for a few seconds before taking a knee.

"Focus, Kevin," Sarah chided him.

"Kinda hard right now." He rubbed his temple and pinched the bridge of his nose, trying to get his vision to return to normal.

"What's up with you today? You usually have this elbow-strike avoidance flow down."

"Sorry," Kevin said, blinking, the world around him coming back into focus. "My mind is just elsewhere."

"Well, you need to be here. Otherwise, I'm going to hit you in the face again."

"Sorry. Hey, do you know about Harmon and the girl he loved?"

"Harmony? Yeah."

"Well, he was telling me that sometimes people who find love wake up early from it. I can't help but wonder,"—Kevin stood back to his feet—"well with your dad's kill code. Do you think maybe she woke up? I mean, Harmon thought she died in the dream, but what if that was just the code? Maybe she's alive somewhere in one of the other Awake satellite groups you guys said you broke into. Maybe she's out there somewhere, going by the name Clewy or something, just wishing she could see her love one more time."

"She's not."

"Yeah, okay, maybe she's not in an Awake camp. But what if she is alive somewhere and bringing the two of them together would—"

"She's not out there," Sarah said, interrupting Kevin.

"But how do you know?"

"This isn't the time for this."

"Come on. Tell me."

"Harmon had a nurse who was a sympathizer with our cause. Harmony's nurse..." Sarah paused. "She wasn't one of us. We tried to track her down, but it was too late."

"So she is dead."

"Yes."

"Does Harmon know?"

"He knows."

"Hmm," Kevin let out.

"Yeah," Sarah said. After a brief pause, she asked, "Ready to try that move again?"

"Yeah, I'm ready."

Kevin focused, but the previous hit slowed him down. This time, he ducked, but not fast enough. Sarah's elbow caught him behind the ear, directly in the mind chip. In a snap, Kevin's mind went black. He was pulled into a memory from his last dream.

Anxiety, fear and depression were paralyzing Jaared. His body shook in waves as he sat on the basement carpet floor. His hands held his hanging head, fingers pushed through his crewcut hair. Next to him sat an untouched bottle of whiskey and a letter of notice of tuition past due. Jaared breathed in broken inhales, forcing air into his lungs.

"I'm sorry. I'm sorry," Jaared said softly to himself. He was alone in the basement, yet he was apologizing to himself, to God, and to his family. "I'm sorry. I don't know why, I..."

He stood and walked to the mirror that hung on his bedroom wall. Leaning against the wall, using the support to keep himself upright, he stared into the mirror and studied himself. His eyes were bloodshot. His face, swollen from the emotional outburst. He stood there, just staring for what felt like an hour.

"I'm sorry," he said to his own reflection. Jaared looked down at the flabby gut he had grown out of stress over the last few months. He looked back at his sad face reflecting back at him. "I can't," he said. "I can't live like this. I can't fail. I can't fail anymore." Jaared closed his eyes hard, still murmuring. "I can't. I can't. I can't."

"I can't. I can't. I can't fail," Kevin said, his head hanging low.

"It's okay," Sarah said as she cradled Kevin across her lap, holding his head. "That's what practice is for."

"No. I..." Kevin's mind was still coming back to the present moment from a memory of his past life. "I'm sorry."

"What for?" Sarah asked.

Kevin looked up at her. "I can't fail. I can't let you down."

"You won't. You just have to be faster."

Kevin rubbed his face. "Sorry, when you hit me, you triggered a memory. It's, uh, it's still affecting me."

"It's okay," Sarah said, rubbing her hands through his hair. "Let's get you back to the barn."

"Yeah, that's a good idea." Kevin sat up slowly, a migraine spreading through his mind, originating from his mind chip. "Ow."

"Here," Sarah said, helping him up and putting his arm around her shoulders. "Let me help." Together, they walked to the barn.

"I heard you had an interesting moment during combat training yesterday," the Master said as he and Kevin sat in the bunker.

"Yeah," Kevin said, unintentionally rubbing his mind chip.

"Tell me about it."

"About how Sarah kicked my butt?"

"I was talking about the whole emotional dream-reaction thing," the Master said, smiling back at him. "Rarely does a dream leave a person a mess like that."

"I was back in my last life," Kevin said. "It was during a time of pure disappointment, self-disgust and loneliness. Just pure, utter loneliness. That feeling just overwhelmed me."

"The dreams that we experience both from past sustained dreaming and even from our own minds can be affecting. More important, they can also help us see the truth."

"How so?"

"Well, you are here, training for a purpose. What dream do you experience? You could have pulled any part of your last life out of that storage, but you didn't pull a moment of happiness, or freedom. You pulled a memory of failure, more accurately, the feeling of failure. Maybe you're afraid to feel that again?"

"It's more though," Kevin said. "That feeling, not the failure or the disappointment, but that deep inner loneliness. I felt it before. I know that feeling too well. It's like I can't remember but can remember it. My whole life has felt like shades of that feeling. That's why that dream has been messing with me so much. I'm not afraid of failing just for the sake of failing, but I'm afraid of..."

"Of what?"

"Of losing the feeling that I have here. I feel connected. I don't feel alone. I feel like I belong."

The Master smiled and leaned back in his chair. "It's different when you feel it for real, isn't it?"

Kevin nodded.

"Everyone feels loneliness," the Master said. "The difference is, most never get to experience actual connection. They don't even know they are missing out on the greatest experience of life."

"Thank you," Kevin said, more emotional than he could remember being. "Thank you for saving me."

The Master's eyes grew misty. "You're welcome. I was saved, just like you. I told you I changed too. Something affecting, something deeper than understanding, caused my soul to understand. I found love. Love is the genuine connection. I think you have too."

Kevin sat in silence, lost in the moment.

"That's also why we have to save these people. We have to keep this real thing going. And we need to set up a path for others to escape and find this truth, the one you and I know," the Master said. "Remember that. Use that feeling as a motivator."

"I don't know if I know how. I don't know if I can."

"Well,"—the Master pulled his chair closer to the lawn chair Kevin was sitting in—"then focus on what you can control. Learn the code. Practice here and out there with

Sarah. Then when the day comes, do everything you can to fulfill your purpose, and maybe, just maybe, you can set her free."

Kevin nodded. "Okay."

"Okay," the Master said. "Today we are going to use all the implanted code that you've hidden in our little dream network and practice compiling it to create massive action sets."

"Compiling the small code chains, is that how we're going to use the kill-code program?"

"We'll get to that," the Master said. "But first you have to learn how to compile. Ready?"

"Yes."

"Then let's plug in."

"You know, I think my dad likes you," Sarah said as she playfully shouldered Kevin.

Kevin flung back a pumpkin seed at Sarah.

"Hey!" she said. "I know we're stuck cleaning these pumpkins from the harvest, but that does not mean you should start a food fight. Besides, I'd win."

"Can you win a food fight?" Kevin asked, scraping the innards of a pumpkin into a large plastic trash can.

"You can lose one," Sarah said, smiling and picking up a piece of pumpkin she'd dropped on the floor of the barn.

"Ha ha, alright," Kevin said. "As for your dad, I think he just enjoys having someone to talk about coding with, and to practice coding with. I coded for the system as my job, but it's ten times more fun coding with your own goals. You should have seen your dad the other day. He was like a little kid. He was teaching me how to hide code in lines of other character attributes. Then showing me how to call them out and compile them. It was like he was playing in a sandbox."

"I wish I could see my dad like that," Sarah said, a slight sadness tinting her words. "He's always so serious. I feel like he's getting more and more, I don't know, solemn."

"Solemn?"

"Yeah, like when I was a young girl, even after the incident, he would play games and laugh. He used to make dad jokes all the time, and I'd be embarrassed but still find myself chuckling along with him. Now,"—Sarah put her finished pumpkin onto a small trailer that was attached to the tractor—"now he just, I don't know. I just wish he could laugh and smile and be free. I wish I could see him like that. You know, you're lucky."

"Why?" Kevin asked, having completely forgotten about his pumpkin at this point.

"Well, you get to go into a dream with him and see him at his happiest. I can't. Dreaming isn't a possibility for me." Sarah pointed at the empty place where a mind chip would normally be implanted.

"Right," Kevin said. He reached out and took her hands in his. "But you're wrong. He isn't the happiest in the dream world. The happiest I ever see your father is when he talks about you."

"Thanks. That's sweet, but—"

"No, seriously," Kevin said, "you're the most important thing to him. Every time we talk about you, I can see his eyes change, and he just loves you so much."

"You talk about me?" Sarah asked, a curious innocence in her voice.

Kevin felt with absolute certainty what Harmon and the Master had tried to describe. There, with Sarah's hands in his, he knew. He loved her. An unease in the air. A magnetic pull. A building pulse. Kevin and Sarah stared into each other's eyes. He leaned in. Sarah leaned in too. Eyes closed. Breath paused. Their lips touched and then pressed into each other. A spark of excitement ran down Kevin's spine, and a wave of warmth rushed through Sarah's cheeks. For a moment, the storm raged.

"Sarah!" Diehl yelled from outside.

Kevin and Sarah instinctively separated from each other. Kevin felt her lips leave his and her hands fall from his grasp.

"Hey." Diehl rounded the corner. "Sarah, we need your help with the harvesting. Kevin can handle cleaning these pumpkins by himself for now. The freeze is coming, and we need to get the gourds to storage before it gets too cold out there."

"Right, be there in a second." She turned to say something to Kevin.

"No, not a second," Diehl said. "Let's go. Let's go. Let's go."

"Fine!" Sarah shouted at Diehl. "Bye, Kev."

"Bye." Kevin weakly waved, wishing so badly that Diehl had shown up a minute, an hour, a day, or a million years later.

"Kev?" Diehl asked Sarah as she walked by.

"Shut up," she said.

Kevin breathed a deep breath, allowing a giddy joy to spread through him. He felt his face with his hands, feeling the flush in his cheeks. "Oh!" Kevin said, realizing he just smeared pumpkin innards all over his face. He grabbed a rag nearby and wiped the orange mush from his cheek.

A thousand miles away, Thairn wiped the blood from his face. He looked down at the body of a young woman, in her early twenties, covered in knife-stab marks, her life pouring out of her.

Riiing. Riiing. Riiing.

Thairn raised the phone to his ear with a practiced motion of control, after he had just released all his aggression on the woman bleeding at his feet.

"Sir." He spoke in a calm voice. Listening to the man on the other end only made him angrier by the second. Thairn answered questions with an aggression that his tone did little to hide.

"Yes, sir."

"Yes, I have consolidated the cell that we tracked the last rescue to."

"No, sir, he wasn't here."

"I know."

"They were forthright with information."

"No."

"No, sir, but they tell me that something big is planned."

"No, they kept that information separate."

"Yes."

"I understand."

Thairn felt a chill run down his back at what his boss on the other end of the call had said. He felt his heart racing. "It will work. He has to—" His boss cut him off. Thairn gritted his teeth. "Understood." Thairn hung the phone up. His blood grew to a boil.

"Ahhhhh!" He screamed, his face shaking and his entire body tensing. He took out his anger on the only other person in the room. Thairn kicked the dying body and kept kicking.

Kevin paced in his stall. *Where is she?* A noise outside the stall made him lunge to the door and peek outside. Nothing, no one was there, just the barn stretching and settling in the cold. *Oh, come on.* He continued his pacing. He was so lost in nervous thought that he didn't hear the boot steps approaching. Kevin turned and saw Diehl a split second before he was going to reach out and grab Kevin's shoulder.

"Ah!" Kevin screamed and jumped back.

"God!" Diehl exclaimed, also jumping back.

"Diehl!" Kevin shouted again. "What! What are you do-ing here?"

Diehl was holding his chest. "Whoa. I'm here to come gather you."

"Gather me? What's going on? Where's Sarah?"

"She's waiting for us. Now, come on, let's go."

"Where? Where are we going?"

"Come on. It's time."

"Time for what?"

"The mission."

CHAPTER 7

THE MISSION

Kevin and Diehl entered the bunker to find they were the last ones to arrive. Harmon, Mei, and Sarah were already sitting on a hay bale. Another empty hay bale sat a few feet to their left. The Master was busy writing on a whiteboard that Kevin wondered if he had ever seen before.

"Come on," Diehl said, guiding Kevin to the hay bale.

Kevin sat on the far left side, while Diehl took the seat closest to Harmon. Kevin leaned forward and looked over at Sarah. She smiled across at him, and he smiled back.

"Sorry we're late," Diehl said. "Sleepyhead here kept asking questions."

Kevin glared at Diehl. "Really?"

"Well, you're here now," the Master said, setting down his marker. "Let's get started." He took a step to the side of the board. "Most of you know the story of what happened at the original Awake base. We took a risk, and it cost a lot, but in the end, we got what we went after. We stole the code, special instructions that the Dream States created a long time ago. They came for us, and they almost wiped us out. Now they have been continuing to hunt us down, because we plan to use it. This weaponized code can take down the systems of an entire Dream State. It can shut down pieces of the network, waking up large groups of people early. If we can do this, we can cause a complete cascade of the system. The entire network will shut down."

Kevin looked at Sarah, puzzled. She looked at him with the same puzzled look and shook her head. The meaning was clear. I don't know what he's talking about, or why.

"The plan," the Master continued, "is to take down one private VIP dreaming station, to both draw their attention and also create Awake individuals of high enough status that the corporation can't simply kill them all. If this works, then while they are unsure of what to do next, we will strike at the heart of the Dream States and set free an entire state. It's a game of distraction and movement. This is not a minor attack. This is a full-out, one-hundred percent-commitment effort. I can't promise that, once this starts, we'll be safe."

"It's not like we're all that safe here anyway," Diehl said.

"Oh, nice, Diehl," Mei said.

"He's right," Sarah said.

"How do we do this code?" Diehl asked. "Is it on a USB or something?"

"That's what he is for," the Master said, pointing at Kevin. "Our newest member worked as an editor before we rescued him. He and I have been practicing for this. He has the code for the weapon, and he's almost ready to use it."

"That's the coding practice you've been doing?" Harmon asked.

Before Kevin could answer, Diehl interrupted. "So you're not completely useless."

"Wait," Harmon said, "that's not possible though, right?" He looked at the Master. "You always said that we can't implant code that isn't already there. The system deletes it and the person attempting it."

"That's why we needed the code, Harmon. This code is already there, hidden. Kevin will need to pull it out to activate it," the Master answered.

"But wouldn't he have to implant himself in the dream network first?" Harmon asked. "So wouldn't he be deleted?"

"We've found a way around that," the Master said, dismissing the question. "Now, continuing the plan. Kevin,

Diehl and Sarah will infiltrate DS 8 using the van and the same trail you used when you rescued Kevin." The last part of the sentence was directed at Diehl. Diehl nodded his head. "Diehl, Sarah, you need to drill DS 8's back room layouts."

"Kevin, you and I will need to finish your coding training, so when it comes to the mission, you follow her lead. Until you're out of the van, Diehl will be in command. Is that clear?" Kevin, Diehl and Sarah nodded their heads. "That being said, they won't be doing chores, so Mei and Harmon will have to pick up some of the slack. This is the mission. Remember why we are doing this. Not just for ourselves, but for the freedom of all those currently in the Dream States." The Master pointed at the board, which had two maps drawn on it. Kevin recognized one as the layout of the main lobby of DS 8. He had placed a star at the doors Kevin had seen earlier, marked *PRIVATE*. "Sarah and Diehl, take this board to the farmhouse and start planning. Also, take the portable computer with you to check the most recent 3D scans of the trail."

Diehl stood up and waved for Sarah to go with him. She stood, and they each grabbed a side of the board. Sarah reached one hand out and touched Kevin's shoulder as she passed him, almost causing her to drop the board. "Hey, come on," Diehl said. They marched out of the bunker. Diehl came back inside a few seconds later and grabbed the laptop.

"Mei," the Master said, "I don't think we are going to need to replant these fields. Go now and break down the irrigation systems. I know it's a lot, but if we can preserve the important equipment, we may have to move them and start over."

Mei stood to head out of the bunker.

Harmon stood as well. "Wait! This doesn't make any sense. This won't work! The network will kick Kevin out. The Dream States will reject his attempts to login."

Mei looked back at the Master.

The Master waved her out, and she left. He then turned to Kevin. "Come back in one hour. You and I have more training to do."

"Are you just ignoring me?" Harmon almost yelled.

"Harmon." The Master held his hand out peacefully. "Kevin. Go. Now." He spoke the command with a fierceness that took Kevin by surprise. "Harmon, please sit with me."

Kevin walked out of the bunker, turning to see Harmon and the Master sitting face-to-face on the two hay bales.

It had been the longest hour that Kevin could remember experiencing. Something about the barn, empty and silent, combined with all the upcoming plans, mixed into a nerve-inducing wait. Kevin was glad to be walking in the crisp late-fall air. He blew his breath into a smoky cloud and watched the steam of warmth disappear into the sunlight. He was happy to be moving. As he made his way to the bunker, he spotted Harmon, hands in his pockets, walking with his head down.

"Harmon!" Kevin shouted, drawing his attention.

Harmon looked up, his eyes bloodshot and red, the dirt on his face stained in streaks from crying.

"Harmon?" Kevin asked, stepping toward him. "What's wrong?"

Harmon stopped in his tracks ten feet from Kevin. Kevin watched Harmon's breath puff in ever-increasing clouds of steam.

"What's wrong?" Kevin asked, taking a half step backward.

"Are you for real?" Harmon screamed, taking a step toward Kevin, his face showing aggression like Kevin hadn't ever seen.

Kevin put his hands out. "I don't know what you're talking about."

"Is this for real?" Harmon asked through gritted teeth, taking another step toward Kevin.

Kevin took another half step backward. "Is what for real?"

"Is this real, or are you putting on an act?"

"I don't know what you're talking about. Are you okay?"

"Do you love her?"

"Love who?"

The noise of the farmhouse door creaking open drew their attention. Sarah stepped out onto the porch and looked at them, trying to judge the situation.

Harmon turned his body and spoke more to the ground than to Kevin so that only he could hear. "Do you love her?" Harmon nodded his head in Sarah's direction.

Kevin glanced at Sarah, who folded her hands over her chest. Turning back to Harmon, in a voice just over a whisper, he said, "Yes."

Harmon sent a small wave in Sarah's direction. Kevin followed suit. She waved back, still confused. Kevin was watching her wave and didn't notice Harmon coming close. He jumped a little at the feeling of Harmon's arm being placed around his shoulder.

"Hey!" Kevin said, trying to pull away. Harmon held him with a surprising strength.

"Listen," Harmon said, "I trust the Master. I trust him with my life, but this is something different. This is everything, the future. I need you to be completely honest with me. Right now. Do you love Sarah? No bullshit. You asked me what love is, and I told you it can't be explained with words. Do understand what it is now?"

Kevin froze. The only thing he could do was swallow the dryness that was forming at the back of his throat.

Harmon studied Kevin for the better part of a minute. He watched his facial structure, studied his eyes. Harmon must have seen something he liked. His face grew soft, and a smile formed on his lips. "Okay," he said as he hugged Kevin.

Kevin, still in shock, hugged Harmon half-heartedly.

"Well," Harmon said, "that's that, then." He walked off.

Kevin continued his walk to the bunker, confusion in his mind.

"What was that all about?" Diehl asked from behind Sarah, having watched Harmon and Kevin from the shadow of the screen door.

"I don't know," Sarah answered, still standing with her arms folded.

Diehl snapped his fingers. "I got it. They're lovers. Of course. That's why they're always talking about feelings and stuff."

"What?" Sarah said, turning and shooting Diehl a look.

"What?" Diehl said. "I'm not judging. That's awesome for them. Can you imagine the odds they find each other in this place? It's beautiful."

Sarah pushed past Diehl, shouldering him as she went back inside the farmhouse.

Diehl shrugged his shoulders, dismissing the attitude he had just received.

"Lock the bolt," the Master said as Kevin stepped inside the bunker.

"Okay. I don't think you've ever had me lock this." Kevin's voice wavered, afraid of what the sudden change in protocol meant.

"Come, have a seat." The Master's serious tone did nothing to ease Kevin's nerves.

Kevin made his way over to the lawn chair and assumed his usual position. "So what's the plan, doc?"

"Doc?" the Master asked, turning around in his chair to face Kevin.

"Sorry, I'm just nervous," Kevin said, fiddling with the armrests. "The whole mission thing. Me being the key piece, and then the door-locking thing and Harmon."

"What did Harmon say?" the Master asked forcefully.

"That's not helping."

"What did he say?" the Master asked again, equally forcefully.

"He just wanted to know if I loved Sarah, but he was weird before then."

"Kevin, do you trust me?"

"Yeah. Of course."

"Good." The Master reached to his desk, opened a box, and produced two pairs of handcuffs. "I need to handcuff you to the chair."

"Ha ha ha, what?" Kevin laughed, not believing the Master to be serious. The Master's face showed just how serious he was. "You want to handcuff me?" Kevin asked.

"It's for both our protection," the Master said, still holding the handcuffs but not attempting to force them on Kevin.

"Our protection?"

"Please."

Kevin sat back in the lawn chair. "Okay. Okay." He shook the chair, realizing something was different. Looking down, he found the chair was now bolted to the ground. "Why is the chair anchored?"

"Please, just let me handcuff you to the armrests and I'll answer all your questions," the Master said, opening one end of the cuffs. He calmly but quickly put them around each of Kevin's wrists and the other sides around the chair's armrests.

"Okay, so..." Kevin pulled his hands against the metal of the cuffs, clinking them against the armrest. "I'm hand-cuffed. What is going on?"

"I'm sorry, I need to tell you something I haven't been completely honest with you about. There is something I didn't tell you. Something I have kept secret. Something I have chosen to keep hidden, even from my daughter."

Kevin sat in silence.

"The man who betrayed us. The one who turned out to be an agent. He and I spent time together, coding like you and I have. You know how the kill code scatters throughout the dream, just waiting to compile?"

Kevin nodded his head.

"Remember, that process can be used for other things. Not just in the dream, but also in your mind chip. Memo-ries or even entire identities can be hidden, broken into tiny pieces and scattered throughout the burn-protected pieces of your mind. But if you know the code, you can spot it. There are certain pieces of coding language that are true identifiers. Or they are for me at least, since I helped write the code. The person becomes a Manchuri-an candidate, or a true sleeper agent. It's the on switch that triggers the agent to remember their mission and act on their directive. It enables their real identity to be the primary. Sometimes, all it takes is the right oral trigger. A certain string of words or a phrase repeated several times. His code activated on a sort of timed se-quence that triggered after he had logged into the Dream States. Plugging in started the clock. Then, after a certain period of time,"—the Master snapped his fingers—"the code compiled and his identity restored, taking with it all the memories of the time he shared with us. We got lucky that it happened as fast as it did. You,"—the Master paused for a moment—"you know this already though. You know, because you have been taught about it in your agent training."

"What?" Kevin let out an uncomfortable laugh. "What?"

"Kevin, you're an agent. You are a sleeper."

"No." Kevin shook his head and pulled against the handcuffs. "That's not possible."

"On top of that, you're something different. Someone high up. Programming with you the last weeks has been amazing to experience. The code you use has a signature I've seen before, but not for a long time. I've coded with your family before. Being able to get to do it again, but this time with freedom and a positive purpose, it's been an honor. Your code is buried deep, but during your coding, it comes out."

Kevin was breathing hard, wanting to run but holding himself back.

"I'm sorry," the Master said, placing his hand on Kevin's arm. "I had to be sure before telling you."

"You're sure? You're sure I'm an agent?"

"Yes."

"Then why? Why not just kill me? Why let me live here with you? Oh, God. Does Sarah know?"

"No. Sarah doesn't know. Just Harmon and I."

"Harmon?" Kevin realized why Harmon had been so shaken when he'd seen him last. "Oh, Harmon, he must hate me."

"No, he understands. You can set us all free."

"Why me?"

"You're not just an agent. You are an Eliander."

"I'm an Eliander?" Kevin asked, stunned at what he had just heard. "No, you can't be right. I'm just... just..."

"It's true. When I created the kill code, the Elianders made me program specific delineators of block chain that identified the ruling class so that no matter what, they wouldn't be lost. Their unique code is the only one that can implant code into the entire system and affect the mind syncs around the planet."

"Mind syncs?"

"Elianders sync to the entire dream world, keeping track of everything that happens."

"How? Wouldn't their minds explode?"

"No, because they share the neural load. Strangely, though, I've never seen an agent who is also an Eliander. Usually your family are management or higher. You are an Eliander, and only an Eliander will be able to imprint the kill code, not just into the dream, but into the sync. There is a special security against implanting built into the sync system that you can bypass."

"So, this is all about the kill code? What was all that about shutting down the Dream States at the meeting?"

The Master exhaled and got serious. "Mei and Diehl see the Dream States as one-hundred percent evil. I had to provide them with the hope of ending it all. This mission, the true mission, is not about ending the Dream States. It's about camouflage, invisibility. The Dream States have done and are doing good, but those in power abuse it and do evil with it. When you plant the code into the dream and the sync, you, Sarah, anyone who wakes early and is marked for killing will be able to disappear. The powers that be will have the memory of seeing their dead body burned for fuel, when in reality they will have walked free. If they see your face on the camera or even in person, the second they turn their head, poof, the memory will delete. You and those who are Awake will be ghosts. One moment there, the next moment not even a memory. Freedom while maintaining the good that the Dream States created."

Kevin's mind was spinning. For the first time in the last few minutes, he was glad he was confined to the chair. "Why, why are you telling me this?"

"Because you have to know. I tried with the last agent. I told him and reasoned with him. He understood the need to help us. Logic, it seems, wasn't enough. He helped us, but when the identity code was set off, it didn't matter. The second it triggered, he switched back and ended up almost killing us all. But I'm hoping you can fight that."

"Why me?"

"You have something he didn't. Something that trumps your programming. Something that I can trigger after your identity code is set off."

"What's that?"

"Your desire to be connected to others. You probably have felt that desire at other times, but they suppressed it with dream medication and a sense of purpose. You felt a piece of genuine connection, being an Eliander. Sharing that neural network. But that's not enough. It's not the connection you desired, which is why you always felt unfulfilled."

"You're basing all your hopes on that?"

"I was. But now I'm believing in something else. I'm believing that you have found something here among us I could never teach you, show you, or force upon you. You found friendship. You found respect. Most of all, you found love. Remember when I told you about intuitively programming?"

"Yeah, I've been trying, but—"

"That type of programming comes from relying on emotions to trigger the compiling of code rather than thoughts. It's not inline, and it doesn't go away. Emotions can trump pre-programming, freeing you of all your control mechanisms. Meaning you'll be free to make your own decisions."

"So even if I become myself again?"

"Your emotions can help you remember everything, even the memories that they will have burned away with your identity code."

"So I will snap back to what I'm like, here, now?"

"No." The Master shook his head sympathetically. "You'll be both who you are here and who you were in the past. You will remember the happy times here and the most likely tragic times of your past."

"Won't my mind break with two lives in it?"

"No, for most people, yes, but you, as an Eliander, have had special training to handle multiple memories. To you, it will feel like a long life of a lot of memories, and you'll be able to handle it. Plus, as an Eliander, you can trigger a push update."

"A what?"

"A push update is a way that you can wirelessly connect to everyone in the Dream States or not, and implant or update code. In this case, you'll upload the camouflaging kill code."

"How is that possible? When you're not dreaming or working, you're not connected."

"No, but there is a way that the Dream States can connect to you if it needs to." The Master pointed to behind his ear.

Kevin understood the implication. "The mind chip?"

"The GPS tracker in your mind chip. It has basic programming that allows for send and receive. You can use that to save those who wake up, and Sarah." The Master paused. "Are you willing to be the hero in this story?"

"What do we have to do?"

"Well, my plan is to go into your memories from your last dream and implant feelings there. Then attach those emotional, triggering dreams to code with the Eliander sequence. So when your identity is re-compiled, it pulls the emotions with it. Then those emotions will trigger those past dreams, which will bring the memories back. Make sense?"

"Not even a little bit."

"Well, there's only one way to do this," the Master said, handing the connection cord to Kevin.

"You're sure about this?"

"I trust your heart."

"I don't."

"Lay back, and just relax," the Master said, plugging the cord into his mind chip.

"I don't feel the dream network like before."

"You won't. This time, we're going inside your mind chip."

"What?" Kevin asked just before darkness overtook him.

Jaared opened the fridge in search of milk. He found the gallon jug on the top shelf. His nine-year-old hands could barely control the weight of the full milk jug. Walking over to the kitchen table where his bowl of cereal sat, he focused on not dropping the container. He didn't notice the assailant at the top of the stairs. A man, with muscled arms, sauntered down the steps, his boots making little noise on the carpet as he made his way toward Jaared.

Jaared had just set the milk jug down, proud of his young skill, when the man yelled, "I'm going to get you!"

Jaared turned to see the bald man, wearing camouflage pants and a black tank top, wielding a machete. He froze for a moment, his heart and lungs refusing to work. Fear rose in him and then melted away in an instant. Jaared recognized the man. The person threatening him was familiar. "I know you. You're my teacher, and"—Jaared looked around at his surroundings—"this isn't my house." Understanding dawned on Jaared. "Oh, this is a dream."

"No, it's not." The man advanced, menace in his face.

Jaared closed his eyes hard and opened them. His brother had taught him how to wake up from a bad dream last year. But something strange happened. He didn't wake up, or at least he didn't completely wake up. He found himself in a black room. The floor, the walls, even the roof simply didn't exist. It was just an empty expanse of darkness. Jaared tried to wake up again, but nothing happened. He closed his eyes hard, opened them, and then tried pinching himself. No luck, he was still in the blackness. Jaared tried a trick he'd used before. He leaned forward, falling face-first, but he never hit the ground. Instead, he started free falling. He plummeted for what felt like an eternity, never waking up and never hitting bottom. He gave up on that trick, simply pushing himself off a suddenly tangible ground and standing tall. *Wake up. Wake up. Wake up.* Jaared tried to will himself awake.

"That won't work here," a voice said through the darkness.

"What?" Kevin asked to the blackness.

"I said"—an older man appeared behind three old cathode-ray-tube televisions that were on but only showing static—"that won't work here. You're in my domain."

"This is a dream, my dream."

"You're partly right," the old man said. "You are dreaming, but this is not your dream."

"Yes it is," Jaared said, defiant. "I'm a lucid dreamer. My dad says that's why I can change things in my dreams or wake up when I want."

"Then why can't you wake up now?"

"I can," Jaared said. *Wake up. Wake up. Wake up.*

"Not working, is it?" the old man said, a sickly grin appearing on his face.

"No."

"That's because you're not in control. Your dreams are chosen for you. I program and design your actions and thoughts and feelings. Nothing you have experienced is real."

Jaared sat defeated, his head hanging in acknowledgment.

"No, that's not how that dream ended," Kevin said, taking the young Jaared's place.

"You're not in control here."

Kevin looked up at the Master standing behind the televisions. "Yes, I am. I always was. This dream, you're distorting it. I never gave in to the old man. I fought him until I beat him. I was and am still in control."

The Master smiled. "Good."

"What is this about?" Kevin asked, standing to talk with the Master.

"We need to bury the emotions and desires that you will need to remain yourself in your memories. When they activate your agency code, it will bring your mission to mind. You will mentally only be able to understand that everything you've done, everything that's happened, has been part of the mission. Even me talking to you and telling you you're an agent. Your feelings for Sarah, everything, will be explained as part of your mission, and you will believe it."

"Why would I believe that?"

"That's what the code does. It brainwashes you. But there is a chance to override it, if I bury the emotions deep enough. That's why we're here, back in a dream that affected your last dream at an early age. It stuck with you. It made you feel the need to rebel against control. That is the start of building a set of emotions that can break the brainwashing."

"But if I already had this dream, why would we need to visit it again?"

"You had it as Jaared, a dream identity that can be burned easily, but if you revisit it and experience it now as Kevin, and feel the same feelings,"—the Master made a fist—"it becomes strongly entangled code. Shared emotions from two lives create a messy knot of coding that can't be burned completely, hidden, but still recoverable."

"So you are going to take me through dreams I had as Jaared and make me fix them as Kevin?"

"Feel them, yes."

"Okay, are they all going to be nightmares I had? Dreams like this?"

"Not all of them, no."

"Okay, so what's next?"

"Are you ready?"

"Yeah."

The world turned black a moment later.

Jaared turned the stick he was using to hold his marshmallow over the fire, making sure to evenly brown the sides. A flame burst burned the night sky to his left. "Woah!"

Arthur, his college friend, laughed. He was still holding the bottle of lighter fluid that he had used to douse the snow-covered rock before throwing a match into the fuel. "That was awesome."

"A little excessive," Jaared other friend Jason said as he walked up carrying more firewood he had grabbed from his car.

"Hey, the rock is dry now, right?" Arthur said.

"Do you still have eyebrows?" Jaared asked.

"Look, if there is one thing I know about snow camping," Arthur said, soaking another snow-covered rock, "you always make sure your seat is dry."

"We get that. We're just saying you don't have to light all the Rocky Mountains on fire to do it," Jason said, stacking the wood on a tarp he had spread on the ground.

Arthur sent another massive fireball into the sky as he lit the second rock on fire. This time, the flame singed his inch-long beard. His face showed his surprise.

Jaared laughed.

"Maybe I'll give the lighter fluid a rest now," Arthur said, taking a seat on his newly dried rock.

"Hey, thanks for inviting me with y'all," Jaared said, still turning his marshmallow.

"Of course," Jason said, taking a seat on the other rock.

"Yeah," Arthur said.

"I mean, I know I've busy with school, but still, I should have at least reached out more," Jaared said.

"Stop, man," Arthur said. "We've all been busy."

"Yeah," Jason chimed in. "The best part is, no matter how long we're apart, we always pick back up right where we left off, like brothers."

"Yeah," Jaared said, smiling. "You're right, we do."

"True that," Arthur said.

"Wait," Kevin said, supplanting Jaared. "This isn't a dream. This is a memory, or at least…"

"At least what?" the Master asked, walking in from the edge of the frozen forest.

Kevin shook his head. "I don't remember this dream, but I remember parts of this memory in different places in my last dream."

"You're part right. This is a dream they programmed you to have later on in your last visit to Dream State 8, or at least the camping scene was," the Master said. "But I pulled real memories from your that dream life into it."

"Entanglement?"

"Exactly."

"Why?"

"Well, what do you feel?"

Kevin ate the marshmallow and looked at Jason and Arthur, who had both been sitting and smiling happily. "I feel like I belong."

"And?"

"I like it."

"Good."

Blackness snuffed out the fire and all the light of the dream.

Kevin opened his eyes to the dim lights of the bunker. Everything seemed so much more defined than the dream world he had just been in.

"Welcome back," the Master said, reaching for and unplugging the cord from Kevin's mind chip.

"Thanks," Kevin said, rubbing his mind chip out of instinct.

"Does it hurt?" the Master asked, unplugging his own mind chip.

"No, just feels weird."

"Well, we were just messing around in your brain. It's going to feel strange."

"True." Kevin paused, looking at nothing in particular. "Can I ask you a question?"

"Of course."

"That feeling, that desire to belong. Did you put that in my brain?"

The Master smiled a welcoming grin. "No. I can't implant desires. Sure, I could brainwash you to forget things, believe things, and maybe even do things, but true emotional desire is something you have to create on your own."

"Okay, but—"

"Go ahead, ask."

"I was an agent. I am an agent, I guess. I am part of the system. So shouldn't that mean I shouldn't have a desire for something like that? I mean, wouldn't that be something that would be, well, frowned on?" Kevin asked.

"Ha ha ha," the Master laughed. "Frowned on. Yes, very much so. If you had those feelings and expressed them, you would have been most likely executed for crimes against your status. You don't remember, but most likely, you had these feelings. You either were a quick learner of how to hide them or, more likely, have someone higher up who is watching over you."

"Watching over me?"

"Yes, most likely, someone in a higher position recognized this desire and has helped you hide it."

"Why?"

"Connection and love are impossible to completely program out. Eventually, they break through. Even for those at the top of the food chain. If they are ruthless enough, they will be beyond suspicion, even so, they will feel those emotions. For those people, they either focus that energy into love of the system or find a protégé to protect," the Master said. "It's been a long evening. I think it's best you go back to the barn and rest."

"But—"

"We'll talk more later. For now, it's time for rest."

Kevin nodded his head.

The Master uncuffed him. "Oh, and don't tell anyone else about what we're doing here. Keep our training between us."

Kevin nodded again.

Kevin's head hung as he walked back to his barn stall. He found a small plate of food Harmon had left for him.

Kevin ate it without pleasure or restraint, simply shoveling calories in. He pushed the plate aside and lay on the straw, his head awash with strange thoughts. He attempted to search his memory but couldn't push past his last dream. The only thing that came to him was that feeling, that desire, the need to belong. He fell asleep with that emotion in his heart and mind.

Jaared almost spat out his swig of Jack Daniel's, choking on the whiskey. "Aakcch ca. Come on, man! There is no way that's true!"

"I swear. I swear to God," Dave said, smiling and fighting to keep a laugh in. "Well, I may have embellished a little."

"How little?" Justin asked.

"Well, I met him," Dave said.

"Ha ha ha." The three of them laughed loudly into the silent night, with nothing but the stars, pines and an illegal campfire to keep them company.

"I miss this," Jaared said while passing Dave the bottle of whiskey. "I wish you hadn't gone out of state for college. These times just hanging out are so cool."

"Yeah," Dave said, and took a swig from the bottle. "I'm glad I could come backpacking with y'all this summer."

"I like the hair, by the way," Justin said, putting another stick on the fire.

"Thanks," Dave said, pushing his hand through his plumed hair. "I've been growing it out for my semester abroad next fall. You know, European style."

"Or Bradley Cooper from *The Hangover*," Jaared said, smiling.

"Well, I used to be a one-man wolf pack," Dave said.

The three young men, sitting around a small fire high in the Rocky Mountains, laughed and enjoyed each other's company.

Whoosh! A sudden icy wind cut through their joyous time, extinguishing the fire. The sudden burst of weather took them all by surprise. Dave and Jaared fell off the logs they had perched on, and Justin turned to look in the wind's direction.

"What the—" Jaared started to say before getting cut off by a menacing roar echoing through the trees.

Yeaaaahhharrrrrr. The low-pitched wail poured through the trees, blowing snow into the air and beating Justin's, Dave's and Jaared's faces.

"It's him!" Justin yelled.

"Who?" Jaared asked above the wind.

"Run!" Dave screamed.

Jaared, Justin and Dave ran at full sprint through the forest, jumping over logs and rocks, all the while hearing that voice growing louder and closer. Dave tripped on a root of a wind-twisted tree. Jaared grabbed him, using pure adrenaline and strength, and threw him to his feet ten feet ahead. *Wait, how did I?*

"Bro! Hurry!" Justin yelled.

Jaared started running again, quickly catching up to Justin and Dave, who had run into a dead end. The trees ahead were tightly wound together. There was no way to pass.

"We're screwed," Dave said.

"He's gonna get us," Justin said.

"Who?" Jaared yelled, more than asked. "Wait. This, this isn't real." The realization dawned on Kevin. He was back in a dream as Jaared. He remembered. This was another blend of dream memory and fabrication.

"What do you mean?" Dave asked.

"This is a dream. I can wake up," Kevin said, having mentally become entangled in the dream.

"Then do it! Save yourself!" Justin said.

"Yeah, get out of here. Don't worry about us," Dave said.

"But you're not even real," Kevin said, confused and somewhat sad to say that to two people he could remember having such brotherhood with.

"Maybe not," Justin said, "but if he gets us, he will kill us."

"You can't die," Kevin said.

"Not in life, but we can die in your memory," Justin said.

"We can be forgotten," Dave said.

"But don't worry about that. If he gets you, you could lose your mind. Don't risk yourself for the memories of us," Justin said.

"No," Kevin said.

Yeaaaahhharrrrr. The screech echoed from the trees even louder than before. Their assailant was nearing.

Kevin turned toward the noise. "Get behind me. You may not be able to affect this dream, but I can. Whatever comes, I'll fight for you."

"Good."

The voice was not Justin's or Dave's. Kevin turned to find the Master standing behind him.

Kevin opened his eyes to find the Master sitting next to him in the dim glow of the barn stall's light. Kevin reached up and unplugged the cable that connected the Master and him.

"I'm sorry, but I had to test you and implant dream code when you weren't aware of the process," the Master said, unplugging himself and coiling the cord in his hand.

Kevin stared at him, unsure of what to say.

"Get some actual sleep," the Master said. "I'll see you tomorrow for more training."

The Master stood and walked out of the stall, leaving Kevin to attempt to sleep after just being dream hacked.

The air screeched and cracked as bullets whizzed past Justin's head. His boots pounded the dirt, sending dust into the air as he sprinted at a frantic pace. His helmet bounced with each step, and his lungs burned. He took an extra breath and dove shoulder first behind a rock that could only just barely reach the category of boulder. *Ping. Thud. Ping.* The bullets assaulted the stone. Justin was mere inches from death. He panted, his pupils large as fear rose in his heart. His training took over, letting him keep tracking the moment. Justin checked the magazine on his M4 and cleaned the ACOG sight of dust.

Jaared watched as his brother huddled behind a small gray rock, squirming in the dirt as enemies did their best to end his life. Jaared studied the multi-cam uniform Justin wore. He read the Ranger tab and studied the sword and mountains of his insignia. Then Jaared saw Justin's face. He felt the fear in his eyes, and he felt the pain in his chest.

"Justin!" Jaared yelled.

Justin didn't respond.

"Justin! Can't you hear me?" Jaared looked around. He was there and not there at the same time. No one was shooting at him, but there he stood. Jaared tried to touch his brother's shoulder, to let him know he wasn't alone. His hand went right through him. *I'm dreaming. Of course. Justin is in Afghanistan, and I'm in Colorado, I know that. But what if this isn't just a dream? If something happens, do I have to watch my brother die?*

Justin rolled over to peek over the rock. As he raised his head, Jaared saw a bullet in slow motion, cresting just over the stone. "No!" Jaared screamed, with emotion flooding his body.

Justin bobbed, having second-guessed his decision to look. The bullet passed just over his helmet.

Jaared watched as Justin shook his head in confusion. *Can I affect things here?*

Justin braced himself to survey the battlefield that lay ahead.

If I'm dreaming and I can affect things, I have to stay with you. I'll do anything I can. You need to survive. I need you to come home. I can't. You have to survive.

Justin peeked over the rock, seeing his next cover. A mud-brick wall that led into the village lay only forty feet away. Justin said something into the radio and waved to another soldier close by, whom Jaared hadn't seen earlier. Justin jumped to his feet and took off.

Dear God. Please let me take any pain that I can from him. Let me feel the soreness in his muscles. Let my lungs burn as he runs. If he's shot, let me take the bullet. Please let a force field be put around him, even if it takes all my energy. Even if it kills me, let him live. Jaared prayed as he watched his brother.

Justin ran, with greater speed than he had ever run with. He made it to cover unharmed. He fought for the next hour, risking his life, dodging bullets, and protecting his men. At the end of the dream, Jaared watched as Justin rode in a helicopter to safety.

Jaared woke up with every muscle screaming in pain, bruises all over his body, and a smile on his face.

When Kevin opened his eyes to the dim lights of the bunker, he shared the smile that Jaared had worn in his dream.

Awake Splinter Cell J8

...

Her footsteps pounded on the cement stairs as she ran with all her energy, fear, shock, and grief powering her up the steps. The sound of her pursuer closing the distance pushed her faster. She gripped the small piece of paper in her hand tightly as she sprinted. Skipping every other step, her young legs screamed with lactic acid as her twelve-year-old lungs attempted to keep pace with her feet.

Almost there. Just one more flight. She thought.

She reached the door at the top of the stairs, shouldering herself into the push handle, barely slowing down as she stepped out onto the roof. There was no time. The heavier boot steps pounded on the cement stairs less than twenty feet behind. Covering the short distance to the pigeon coops, she grabbed one and pulled it out of the crate. Tucking the small piece of paper into the leather carrier attached to the bird's foot, she whispered, "Mei," to the bird's ear. Throwing it into the air, she didn't even have time to watch it fly off into the cloudy sky before she felt hands pulling her backward. The hard tar roof scraped her back through her shirt as she slid, the force of the throw sending her sliding. Before her wind could come back, a hand grasped her throat and squeezed hard. Blood vessels popped in her eyes, turning them red.

Her attacker's face stared back at her, hard and angry. She struggled to breathe, flashing white lights popping in her eyes. She squirmed as her attacker reached behind her ear. His fingers closed around her mind chip. With a sudden and violent motion, the device and the wires that led to her brain were ripped out.

Angelica died, her mind shutting down, staring into the eyes of Thairn, hard and cold.

Jaared sat at the end of the bar of an Irish pub. Framed pictures of old beer advertisements and random memorabilia intermixed with green clovers and leprechauns on every wall. One could get lost just looking at the walls of the place for a good length of time. Not Jaared. He was looking at the beaten wood bar top, playing with the condensation ring his beer had left on the lacquered surface. Taking another large swig of a dark stout, he felt the beer pass through his lips. It tasted weirdly sweet. Jaared took another drink.

"Why the long face?" a man's voice asked.

Jaared looked up to find the bartender, a tall man with brawny arms that didn't seem to match with his beer belly, cleaning a mug and looking at him over a pair of loose-fit eyeglasses.

"It's okay," Jaared said, dismissing the man but attempting to be polite.

"Come on," the bartender said. "I'm a bartender. It's what I'm here for. Besides, you know you're dreaming, right?"

Jaared looked around at the bar. The fuzziness of it all gave away the dream world. "Right."

"So there's no harm in sharing here. Heck, you're dreaming of me for a reason, right?"

"I guess," Jaared said, and took another drink of his beer. "Well, I guess I'm just lonely. I mean, I know I shouldn't be. I have friends and everything, but..."

"But what?" the bartender asked.

"Well, I just moved, and I don't have any friends as close as the ones I had at home, and I know that kind of friendship takes time to build. I get that. It's just..." Jaared looked at the bar top again, feeling uncomfortable saying the next words, even to an imaginary bartender. "My brother was my best friend, and he's married now, and it's just different. Not bad different, but I just, like, have to mourn a time passing. But I'm so happy for him. He's with the girl who will be his best friend forever. They are true life companions. They always have each other. I want that. I want my life companion, and I just wonder if, well, what if she doesn't exist?"

"If there is a perfect companion out there for you, how would you know?"

"I don't know," Jaared said. "I guess I feel like there would be a spark and I'd just know, like, deep in me, I should know."

"If you were to find her, if she walked into your life right now, are you ready to meet her?"

"Yeah. I always thought I'd have to have my life figured out and have everything be awesome, and then I'd be ready to meet that girl. But now I want her there as I struggle and grow, and I just want to experience all my memories with her in them."

"Hey," the bartender said to someone else, "come over here."

Jaared was still looking at the bartender when she approached. He felt a hand on his shoulder, and a jolt of electricity shot through his body. He looked up and saw her, a brunette beauty, smiling at him.

"I'm Sarah," she said.

Jaared watched a fast-forward life of memories of Sarah and him pass through his mind. He only remembered glimpses of holding her hand on a beach, cuddling with her and their children, and the sound of her voice telling him she loved him.

"Find me," she said, taking her hand off his shoulder and walking into the cloudy edge of the dream, disappearing.

"Wait!" Jaared yelled, but she was already gone. He turned back to the bartender. "Who was that? Where did she go?"

The bartender smiled. "Remember, you're dreaming. I imagine if you search through some more of these soul-searching bars, you'll find her." The bartender winked at Jaared, making it clear he was instructing him.

"Thanks," Jaared said, running off into the mist of the dream.

Jaared ran into another bar, this time a modern building with clean, sharp lines and a white-stone bar top.

"Is she here?" he asked the room.

A man looked up from a newspaper. Jaared recognized the bartender's glasses. "Not here."

Jaared nodded and ran back into the mist. He ran into and out of hundreds of bars. He searched high-class whiskey bars that smelled of cigar smoke, explored college bars with Jell-O shooters, tried beach bars with sandy floors, drank at dive bars that smelled of must, and even sampled coffee and tea bars whose pastries perfumed the air with sweet, tempting smells.

Weary from his search and unable to find this girl who had sparked such emotion in him, Jaared stepped out of the mist and into a grand train station. He strode up to a bar that was all made of brass with taps out of the steampunk era.

The bartender came up to him. "Still searching, huh?"

"Yeah. What if I never find her?"

"You will."

"When? I've been searching all night. I've been to every bar I can imagine. What? Do I have to search every bar in the world to find her?"

"Would you?"

"Yeah, but I could miss her by a matter of minutes."

"Sometimes the time just has to be right. Sometimes you can search forever and not find what you're looking for. Maybe she'll come to you if you stay in the same place long enough."

"You think so?"

"Absolutely."

"Well then, I'll wait right here. I'll take a beer."

"Sounds good." The man pulled on a lever that dispensed beer through an elaborate tubing system.

Jaared watched the liquid as it winded. "Cool."

"It really is," Sarah said, taking a seat beside him.

Jaared almost choked on his spit.

"You've found me. Now never let me go," Sarah said.

"I won't. I promise."

"I promise." Kevin said the words as he woke from his dream and brought his mind back to the bunker.

Kevin blinked a few times and then looked at the Master. "I remember having that dream, although I remember the name differently. But I can't remember if the face was different."

The Master nodded. "I know. You won't ever remember a different face. Your emotion, it's real, and your love for my daughter is strong. I know this is a strange way for a father to be connecting his daughter with someone, but I'm glad I get to feel your emotions and know it's for real."

Kevin nodded, super uncomfortable. "So what next?"

"I think it's time."

"Really?"

"Yeah. I'm going to have to handcuff you again."

"Okay," Kevin said, leaning back.

The Master secured both of Kevin's wrists tightly to the armrests of the chair. He then took the cord that was still plugged into Kevin's mind chip and connected it to the computer. The Master typed a few commands in and then stopped. His finger hovered over the "Enter" button.

"Do it," Kevin said, noticing his delay.

The Master depressed the keyboard key with a soft click. Code ran across the screen. Commands and files opened and closed, archived and compressed, and executed installations. A few minutes later, the code stopped, and a window popped open.

Complete.
Agent K00004 - Re-identified.

Agent K00004 opened his eyes from a dark sleep. His head pounded, and a burning sensation emanated from his mind chip. He attempted to rub his forehead, only to find himself restrained. He pulled against the handcuffs, testing their strength. "What? Where? Wait. I remember." He turned his head to find the Master sitting a few feet away, leaning forward, watching him close. "You." Agent K00004 rattled against his restraints, his anger causing his muscles to flex.

"Hello," the Master said.

"You, you should be dead," Agent K00004 said, a vein in his forehead bulging.

"Yet I'm not. What does that tell you?"

"That I have failed so far. I won't fail forever, though. You, your death, is my purpose."

"And what will you do after that?"

Agent K00004 just stared at him.

"You don't have plans for your future?"

Agent K00004 tested his handcuffs again, pulling his arms into them hard.

The Master noticed the trace of blood running down Agent K00004's arm. "You're hurting yourself."

"You think I care. I would kill myself if it meant ending you and your filth."

"Why? Why do you care so much?"

"Why?" Agent K00004 said, steaming. "Let me remind you. I was nine years old. I was in DS 2 just learning. It was a simple time for me, but then you and the Awake broke into our Dream State. You murdered everyone. The nurses, the doctors, all my age group. I survived by hiding under the corpse of one of my fellow nine-year-olds. You didn't see me, but I saw you. I burned your face into my mind as I watched you put more and more gunshots into the dead bodies. I saw your eyes flash in the gun blasts. Then you opened into the body on top of me. One bullet went through and hit me in the stomach. I had to not react to survive. I lay there, in pain, bleeding for hours, afraid to move. But I never fell asleep, didn't dare let my eyes close, in fear I would see your face again. No matter what they put me through in training to become an agent, that memory fueled me. I will never stop until I see your eyes close and feel your heart stop beating."

The Master sat back in his seat. "Is it possible?" He turned to the computer and started typing.

"Hey!" Agent K00004 yelled. "Hey. You piece of sh—"

"There it is!" the Master yelled over Agent K00004. "Found it." The Master turned to Agent K00004. "Kevin."

"That's not my name."

"Okay, Agent K00004. I want you to think through your memories."

"I don't care what you want."

"Look, you humor me and, at the end of this, I'll take the handcuffs off. Deal?"

Agent K00004 said nothing but pulled less against his handcuffs.

"Good. Now think through your memories of me. Start with your life as Kevin Altair."

"I don't," Agent K00004 said, "I don't remember much. That's kind of the point of the re-identity program. I know I was an editor. I know it was my mission to perform well and infiltrate your terrorist group, to kill you and your, your, Sarah." Agent K00004's face softened for a moment. His eyes opened wide, and he began shaking. A moment later, Agent K00004 shook his head and hardened his tone again. "Your abomination daughter."

"What just happened?" the Master asked, turning to the computer.

"What?"

"Okay, you don't remember much about life as Kevin. Tell me something. Do you remember a dream you had? One of me? One from when you were Jaared Johns."

"I... yeah. You were in a dark room. I was... I was..." Agent K00004 shook in the chair for a moment. "I was there. That's it."

"Wow. There it was again. I think I know what this is. I wonder why," the Master said, still looking at the computer screen, watching code packets. "Agent K00004 is not your real identity."

"What are you trying, old man?"

"I'm telling you. You were re-identified as Agent K00004. There is another identity before this one. One that is blocked by a different scatter code. One that also has an emotion-masking program."

"You are a terrorist."

"I need to study this code, figure out who wrote it before I can unscramble you. Let me ask you, when you were just thinking about that dream, what did you see?"

"I remembered you in the dark room with TVs. Then they started flashing. Then I remembered you and those gun blasts. The night you changed my life."

"What do you remember from before that night?"

"I remember not having to live in fear that the Awake was going to come kill me."

"Hmmm. That must be the re-identity point, then. That fake memory of an assault by me."

"Fake memory!" Agent K00004 railed in his chair. "No! You don't get to lie like that. I'll tear your head off your shoulders."

"I'm sorry, but it never happened. I can see the memory code. I can even see a false vision coding... but if I—"

"I'm going to enjoy feeling the life leave your body. I'm going to make it slow. Piece by piece, I'll take you apart. I'll make you suffer just like you did to me with your bullet burning in my gut."

"Enough!" the Master said with passion, standing and stepping to Agent K00004. "Listen. I don't kill kids. I don't raid Dream States and murder people. Only your kind do that! Oh, and I didn't shoot you, ever!" The Master reached and pulled Agent K00004's shirt up. "Look."

Agent K00004 only snarled at the Master.

"Look!"

Agent K00004 looked at his exposed stomach. It didn't show any scar from an injury. "What? What did you do to my mind? Why can't I see it?"

"It doesn't exist! They put the code in your mind to make you see an injury that didn't happen."

"Liar! I'm going to kill you!"

"That's enough for now," the Master said, letting go of Agent K00004's shirt and going back to the computer.

"Let me go! Let me out of these things!" Agent K00004 thrashed in the chair.

The Master typed in a few commands, pounding the keys. A few seconds later, Agent K00004 stopped thrashing, his identity and memories re-scrambled into a million pieces of code.

Kevin awoke to the feeling of pain in his wrists. His eyes blinked against the pain. "Aww. Wow. What? Ow. What happened?"

The Master spoke over his shoulder, still trying to calm himself. "Failure. There is something else going on."

"What's that?" Kevin let out a gasp, looking at his bleeding arms. "Did I?"

"Don't think about it," the Master said, still angry, but calm. He turned and unlocked the handcuffs.

Kevin curled his arms into himself and held them close, trying to ease the pain.

"Go, take care of your wrists. I'll find you later."

"Are you okay?" Kevin asked, concern in his voice.

"I wish you could just stay Kevin Altair."

Kevin walked out of the bunker, heading for the barn, his heart sinking, knowing he did some real emotional damage to the Master. *I know it wasn't me, well at least this me. But I don't think I've ever felt this guilty.*

"Oh." Mei let out a little combined whine and relief as she straightened her back out, standing tall. She felt her spine and muscles stretch and release, fighting each other, the pain fading away after a few seconds. Mei turned and looked across the field. She had spent the better part of the last two days turning by hand. She took a deep breath of accomplishment.

A pair of dragonflies flying and circling each other caught her eye. She watched as they played tag in the sky, a mating dance. Mei felt a smile creep to her face. The tandem glided past her and off into the distance, disappearing into the fading light. She was alone again. So alone.

Mei reached into her pocket and freed the glass coin. As she rubbed it with her thumb, a tear crept down her cheek. "This was easier with you here."

The flapping of wings caught Mei by surprise, the messenger pigeon landing on the dirt three feet to her right. The surprise made her jump and drop the hoe she had still been holding, causing it to fall in the dirt along with the glass coin. It felt slow motion as she watched it fall and land on the edge of the tool. With a crack, the glass broke into the pieces that it had been made of. Mei shouted, "No!" The pigeon flapped nervously, sending a few feathers and a puff of dust into the air.

"Sorry," Mei said, turning to the bird that threatened to leave with its message undelivered. "Shhh. It's okay." She reached down and lightly grabbed the bird. "What are you doing here?" she asked. Turning the bird, Mei saw the small scroll protruding from a leather holder strapped to the bird's foot. "What do we have here?" she said as she pulled the note free. Mei tossed the bird into the air, and it took flight, flapping off into the sky. Mei didn't see what happened to the bird. She was too focused on the note in her hand, and the blood drop that stained one edge of the paper. She opened it and read the words the message contained. Every letter turned her face pale, but only for a moment. Her skin turned from white to red, and her jaw went from shocked open to hard. Mei's heart pounded, and fiery blood filled her body as the rage rose inside her. She turned and began marching toward the barn, each step she took digging deep into the soft earth she had just finished churning.

Mei stomped across the field, her breath steaming hot against the cold air. Her face wrinkled in an angered expression. In one hand, she clung to her handgun. In the other, squeezed even tighter, was the small piece of paper that the messenger pigeon had just brought. Her focus was laser-like. She only had one target and one purpose. She was on the hunt, and she knew where her prey was. Opening the door to the barn, she found him sitting at a picnic table with Harmon wrapping bandages on his bruised and bloody wrists.

"Hey, Mei," Harmon said, seeing her walk over and glimpsing her emotion. "What's wrong?"

"Get away from him!" Mei screamed, emotion causing her vocal chords to crack.

Kevin looked up to find Mei's eyes leaking tears, staring straight into his. For an unknown reason, Kevin felt pity for her. A longing set over him he couldn't place. His heart fell into his stomach, foreshadowing what was to come next.

Mei raised the handgun and pointed it at the target of her hatred. The sights lined up with Kevin's face.

"Mei!" Harmon yelled. "Don't!" He jumped in front of Kevin, blocking Mei's shot.

"Harmon, get out of the way!" Mei said, taking an aggressive step forward.

"No! You can't do this," Harmon shouted back.

"He deserves it!" Mei shouted back. "You don't understand. Move now or I will shoot you both!"

"No!" Harmon yelled again. "Don't shoot."

"Harmon, he's an agent!" Mei yelled. "Get out of the way!" Tears were completely pouring out of her eyes at this point.

"I know!"

"I don't care!" Mei shouted first, dismissing what he said without hearing it for a moment. "Wait! What? You know?" Understanding dawned on her. Her face turned from anger to hurt, her heart breaking at the feeling of betrayal. "You knew, and you didn't tell us?" She fought her emotions, trying to keep her wrath, her resolve. Mei's face hardened again. "I hope the Master hangs you for this! Now move. I don't want to shoot you, but I will."

"The Master knows too," Kevin said as he pushed Harmon to the side, moving him out of the way of the shot.

"Kevin," Harmon said.

"It's okay," Kevin said. "The Master knows, Mei. He's the one who told us."

"What?" Mei asked, the feeling of confused betrayal winning the battle of her emotions, the gun drifting to her side.

"He's the one who found it in my code. Harmon and I didn't know until he filled us in. He knows, but he is using that piece of me as a tool to fight back against the system. Look," Kevin said, removing the bandages from his wrists, showing Mei the bloody marks. "He's triggered and turning off that code. He's figuring out how to keep that part of me in control."

"No. Lies." She raised the gun again.

"It's true," Harmon said, stepping closer to Mei.

"Shut up!" Mei said, pointing the gun at Harmon. "You knew about this and you didn't tell me. You didn't kill him the second you found out?"

Kevin stepped forward. "Mei," he said, trying to get her attention off Harmon. "Harmon wanted to kill me, but he understands that this is our best chance."

"Our?" Mei said, her face twisting as she pointed the gun at Kevin again. "You are not one of us. You are evil. I spent years as one of your pieces of meat. Something you lied to, used and abused. You don't deserve to live."

"He never—" Harmon started to say.

"You're right," Kevin interrupted him. "I don't. You should kill me right now. Blow my brains out."

"Kevin," Harmon said, nervous about what he was saying.

"I should," Mei said, her finger squeezing the trigger tighter.

"Or you can let me do actual damage. With my agent code, I can cause unrepairable harm, not just to one agent, but to the entire system. The kind of impact they can't fix. But I can only do that if you don't kill us. The power is all yours. Kill me and lose the war against the Dream States, or let me help. It's your choice."

"You'll betray us the first chance you get," Mei said.

"No, he won't," Harmon shouted.

"Yes, he will. It's how they work," Mei said, her gaze never leaving Kevin. "You know this. What happened, Harmon? How can you be okay with this, this thing?"

"It's not me," Harmon said. "When I found out, I wanted to kill him that instant. But then I learned something. I thought all agents were just mind-warped, pre-programmed, less-than-human, figurative robots that deserved only to be shut down. But that's not true, or at least in Kevin's case, it's not."

"Why?" Mei screamed. "What makes him so special?"

"Love," Harmon said.

This time, Mei shot a look at Harmon.

"He loves Sarah, and his code, his programming, is shattering because of it. He's become human again. Now he could be our greatest weapon against the system."

"Or the death of us all," Mei said.

"I know you can't trust a word coming out of my mouth," Kevin said. "But please trust the Master, trust Harmon, let me do this. Let me try to make the sacrifice of so many worth it. Let me make Cassidy's death worth something."

Mei pushed her gun forward toward Kevin, her face squeezed hard, nostrils flaring. "Don't. Don't you ever say his name again. You don't get to."

"Mei," Harmon said. "This is the plan. This is how we win."

"Who else?" Mei asked. "Who else knows?"

"Just us and the Master," Harmon said.

"You didn't tell Sarah and Diehl?" Mei asked.

Harmon shook his head. "The Master made me swear secrecy. He didn't think Sarah, Diehl, or you could know the truth without killing him, and we couldn't risk that."

"So you just lied to us all?"

"For the greater good," Harmon said.

"For the greater good?" Mei almost choked on the words. "Is that who we are now?" she asked Harmon, her gun lowering.

"It's what we have to be right now."

"That's what they are, Harmon. That's what the Dream States uses as rationalization for everything they do."

"Mei," Harmon said.

Mei took a deep breath, feeling the bags under her eyes and the exhaustion of a life hard, lived weighing on her. "Harmon, I'm tired."

"It's okay," Harmon said. "Sleep on it. It makes more sense with a rested mind."

"No, I'm tired of all this," Mei said, waving her gun in a circle. "This meager existence. The constant fear of death. The loss. And the lying. I'm tired of all of it."

"Mei," Harmon said.

"I miss Cassidy," she said.

"Mei," Harmon said again, tears escaping his own eyes.

"Good luck with your rebellion," Mei said, raising the gun to the side of her head.

"No!" Kevin shouted.

"Mei!" Harmon shouted as he lunged for the gun, his vision a blur of emotion. His reach was too slow.

A blast rang out in the barn.

The pain and loss of life filled the atmosphere of the barn as Mei's corpse slumped to the hay-covered floor.

The emotion and mayhem was replaced with a sudden, strange and utter silence. Time stopped. Kevin stared at Mei's now-lifeless body, in shock at what had just happened. Harmon fell to his knees and wept, his eyes still open and staring at the dead body of his long-time friend. What felt like eternity but was in reality just less than a minute passed.

Sarah came sprinting through the doorway, gun drawn. "What's..." She paused when she saw Mei's body and the pool of blood on the ground. "What happened?" she asked.

Kevin couldn't force words to come out of his mouth, and Harmon only cried.

The yell shook Kevin's words free. "She killed herself," he said more matter-of-factly than he would have wished, but his mind was not embracing any emotion in particular at the moment.

"No, she wouldn't do that." Sarah's mind refused to accept the answer. "What happened here?"

"I . . . I . . . I . . ." Kevin stammered.

"What happened, Kevin?"

"She, she shot herself" was all Kevin could say, still without emotion.

"Why? What were you three talking about? What did you do to her?" Sarah asked him.

"Me?" Kevin asked back, hurt at the accusation but in that moment feeling immensely guilty. *I made her lose hope in the future by being an agent, the person who put her through so much pain,* Kevin thought. "Nothing," he forced out.

"Well, what happened to your hands?" Sarah asked, still holding her handgun at her side but starting to bring it up.

"I didn't. I can't."

"I did that to him," the Master said from behind Sarah, saving Kevin from his inability to find words.

"What?" she asked her father.

He walked past her and knelt next to Mei. "Oh, poor soul," he said under his breath.

"What is going on?" Sarah asked, extra stern.

"Kevin," the Master said, still looking at Mei's body. "Go to the bunker and wait. I'll meet you there."

"No, no one leaves until you explain," Sarah said.

"Kevin, go now," the Master commanded, shooting Kevin an imposing look.

Kevin nodded and mouthed the word "sorry" to Sarah as he walked out of the barn using the kitchen door.

"Answer me!" Sarah yelled at her father.

"Enough!" The Master turned and snapped at her. "You think you're the only one who feels her loss? Harmon! Did she kill herself?"

Harmon nodded, still on his knees but his tears having run out.

"This is my fault," the Master said to Sarah. "I feared this would happen."

"What?"

"With the loss of Cassidy and the long, lonely hours in the field, I feared she may fall into depression."

"She wouldn't be alone if you hadn't sent away so many of us," Sarah said.

"I know that!" the Master snapped again. "I take responsibility for this. Her death is my fault. And that's my cross to bear. I don't need you to remind me of it."

Sarah swallowed for a moment, a mixture of angry, sad and confused.

The Master turned to Mei's body. "Harmon and I will bury her next to Cassidy. It's what she would have wanted."

Harmon looked at the Master with eyes, begging not to have to bury his friend.

Sarah saw his gaze. "I'll help do it, Dad."

"No," the Master said, surprisingly stern. "You will go join Diehl on guard duty."

"Dad? Look at Harmon. He can't."

"He will," the Master said, turning to Harmon. "Are you able to help respect the memory of Mei and lay her to rest with me, or are you going to wallow here in self-pity instead?"

"Dad!" Sarah was shocked at her father's words.

Harmon stood, red anger filling his face.

"Good," the Master said, nodding at Harmon before turning back to Sarah. "Now you go join Diehl on guard duty."

"Just like that, move forward?" Sarah said.

"That's all we can do," the Master said. "We are at war. There are casualties, but the fight must go on."

"This wasn't a casualty," Sarah said.

"Yes, it was," the Master said, making a fist. "She may not have died immediately, but her death is the result of the Dream States. Her wounds have lingered for years. Her mind and body have been suffering from what the system did to her, and now those wounds have finally taken their toll. She succumbed to them and lost her fight. We can't let that cause us to lose ours. Now go. Join Diehl. Tell him what happened."

"Dad,"

"Sarah, just do it."

Sarah wanted to confront her father more, but felt so frustrated at the moment that she just turned and walked away.

"Harmon, let's do this and talk about what happened," the Master said, waving him to Mei's body

The night air's chill had done little to cool down Harmon physically or emotionally as he and the Master dug Mei's grave. With great reverence, they placed Mei inside and piled dirt on top of her. Harmon couldn't figure out how to let words out without screaming, so he had remained silent the entire time they worked. It was the Master who broke the quiet.

As he patted the small mound of dirt gently with his shovel, the Master asked Harmon, "What happened, Harmon? Why did Mei kill herself?"

Harmon clenched his jaw. "She found out about Kevin."

"How?"

"I don't know," Harmon responded, devoid of any care.

"Did she tell anyone else?"

"No," Harmon said, shaking his head.

"Are you sure?"

"She came straight to kill him!" Harmon let out, louder than he intended. "And she came alone! If she told anyone else, they would have helped her. Hell, she thought I was going to help her, until she found out that I already knew. God, how could I have kept this from her?"

"It's good you did. And it's good you were there tonight."

"Are you kidding me? Mei is dead, and I can't help but feel somewhat to blame here."

"Our mission is still intact. That's what's important."

"That's what's important? Not Mei, not the person you just buried in the dirt. Just the mission? This is your fault, you know."

The Master just looked at him.

"You don't think so?"

"I think it's been an emotional night."

"That speech about the wounds that Mei carried, that all of us here carry, was right. But you delivered the kill shot. When she found out about Kevin, she came to protect us, me, you Sarah, everyone. You know what, it wasn't even the fact that he was an agent and we couldn't kill him that broke her. It was the lying. She believed and loved you and me, and we betrayed her. Think about that. I know you want this to stay secret, and I won't tell. But if you don't want to break others, break Sarah, maybe you should fill everyone in."

"Harmon," the Master said, squinting his eyes. "How did she find out about Kevin?"

"Are you?" Harmon said, aghast and infuriated. "No." Harmon took a step away before turning and facing the Master again. "I don't know. I didn't figure that out for you before she blew her brains out with the look of a broken soul in her eyes." Harmon threw his shovel down and stamped off into the night.

Kevin and the Master sat in the bunker in their usual chairs, but the computer was quiet. They sat for a good fifteen minutes, just facing each other in silence.

"I talked to Harmon," the Master said. "I heard she found out about you and couldn't handle it. She's been through a lot."

"This is my fault."

"No, no. Kevin, this is the Dream States' fault. They did things to her that broke her down, and she's been barely keeping it all together since. It's hard to live for years, knowing that the entire system just wants you dead. She just cracked. What you witnessed tonight is the fate of all of us if we don't stop them. Tonight's loss shows us even more why we need to accomplish your mission. We need to help every other person we can to gain freedom and peace. That's what Mei and everyone who escapes deserves. I'm sorry to say, but Mei wasn't the first casualty in this great struggle, and she won't be the last."

"How many?" Kevin asked. "How many have to die? How great a cost must be paid before the end?"

"I don't know. Hopefully not too many more."

"If there is going to be more death on this mission, I think we have to tell everyone the truth. They deserve to know and understand the situation."

"No," the Master said. "They wouldn't understand. If they find out, they will come for you, and more death will follow."

"So, Diehl, if he finds out, are you saying you're willing to kill him? What about Sarah?"

"I know you don't like this, but it's for the greater good of all of them and the others out there. A simple lie, a temporary withheld truth, will give them and generations to come true liberty."

"The greater good? You sound like the people who run the Dream States. Is that what we're becoming here?"

"Go, get some rest. We'll take tomorrow off training and then try the reset again the day after. In the meantime, don't talk to anyone about this."

"I'm sure the agent version of me will understand your plan."

"Look, you need to be better about channeling your emotions."

"Sorry," Kevin said, starting to walk away. "I guess having emotions that break logic means I'm going to have trouble controlling them."

"Then don't control them, but channel it. When you feel you're about to slip, or you feel yourself about to say that you're the bad guy in this story, turn that guilt into something else."

"Turn it into what?"

"Anger usually works. It conveys the passion that can cover guilt. Do you think you can do that?"

"You know this is wrong."

"I know it's necessary."

The following morning, Kevin sat in his stall, a wiped mess of a human. He was staring at a ray of orange sunrise that had found a gap in the barn wall. His mind was elsewhere, completely lost in a mire of doubt and gloom. It took him almost a full minute to realize a large shadow was being cast on him. He turned to find Diehl leaning against the door, framed by light from the interior of the barn.

"Hey," Kevin said.

"What happened?" Diehl asked, a hard tone in his voice.

Kevin just shook his head.

"No. Not good enough."

"What, what do you want?" Kevin let out in a complaining style.

"The truth," Diehl said, "and not a single word that's a lie. For every lie you say, I'll break every bone in your body until you tell me what you're hiding."

"I'm not hiding anything."

"Then tell me what happened. The whole story, not just the end."

Kevin thought for a moment about how he could tell the truth, but also lie by omission. "Harmon and I were sitting at the table. He was helping me with my wrists." Kevin showed Diehl the marks. "Then Mei came in." Kevin cleared his throat, both thinking about what to say next and bracing his mind for having to recap last night. "She was holding her gun and talking about missing Cassidy. She said she was tired, and this existence was hard. She said she was sick of fearing death and losing those she loved, and feeling like everything, all her hope, was a lie. Then..." Kevin shook his head.

"You don't know anything else?"

"I only know when she came into the barn, she was already an emotional wreck. I was in the bunker with the Master for hours before that. This whole thing is just, I don't know."

"What happened to your wrists?"

Kevin felt his investigation continuing. "Turns out that training with the Master on this code stuff can be violent."

"Why? It's all on the computer."

"I guess I shake a lot when we're doing the coding, so he handcuffed me to the chair so that,"—Kevin had to think about how to say what he needed to say without lying—"we could keep working without me flying out of the seat at him."

"Does it hurt?"

"They sting, but not too bad."

"No, not your wrists, the memory of seeing Mei kill herself."

Tears started pouring from Kevin's eyes. He nodded his head, trying to keep his voice from wavering. "I keep thinking back, wondering what I could have said or done different. If I had jumped at her, could I have gotten the gun? If I had been more open with her, could I have maybe connected earlier and kept her from breaking?"

Diehl softened. "Listen, it's not your fault."

"Then why are you grilling me like a criminal?" Kevin yelled, channeling his guilt into anger like the Master suggested.

"Hey," Diehl said. "I had to push you. To see if you had authentic emotion, see if you felt guilt and sadness. Only an innocent man will feel both. It's counterintuitive, but it's true. This isn't your fault."

"How? How can you know that?"

"Everyone has their battles. It's up to them to fight them. You opening up or doing something different wouldn't matter."

"But what if I had?"

"Then you would think that opening up may have caused this. Some people just break."

"How can you tell?"

"Tell what?"

"Who will break?"

"You don't, until it's too late," Diehl said, turning and walking away.

Until it's too late. Kevin was comforted by the thought, though he didn't know why. He felt sleep finally taking him after being unable to sleep the night prior. He didn't wake until the scent of peonies pulled him from his slumber, just in time for dinner.

"Kevin." Sarah whispered as she shook him by the shoulder. "Kevin, time to wake up."

"I'm up," he said, rolling over and into a seated position.

"Come on," Sarah said. "It's dinnertime."

"What's on the menu tonight?" Kevin asked.

"Roasted chicken," Sarah said with a smile on her face. "Harmon has spent the day butchering, marinating and slow cooking, before finishing them over the fire."

"Are you serious?" Kevin hopped to his feet with a new-found zeal.

"Yeah, with Mei gone, I guess my father decided it was time to stop farming."

"Stop farming? What does that mean?"

"It means that the mission is almost here. Come on, let's get dinner."

Sarah and Kevin sat, both enjoying their quarter of fire-roasted chicken.

"Mmm, I don't think I've ever tasted anything so good," Kevin said between bites.

"So good."

"Compliments to the chef!" Kevin shouted toward the kitchen. After not hearing anything for a few seconds, he asked, "Where is Harmon?"

"He's with my father, talking about something regarding the mission."

"Oh," Kevin said, uncomfortable.

"Yeah," Sarah said as she focused on her next bite. "I hope it's something good. I can't take much more bad right now."

"Sarah, I..." Kevin started, before tripping over his own words. "I need to... there's something you... I don't know how..."

"Kevin, I'm sorry."

"What? You're sorry?"

"I accused you of killing Mei. That wasn't fair."

"I don't remember you doing that."

"Kevin, I pointed my gun at you."

"Oh, yeah."

"It's just, sometimes I'm so scared and so overwhelmed with this whole thing." Sarah brushed her hair out of her face.

Kevin studied her face, the rings under her eyes, and the sunken expression. Exasperation showed in the minor features.

Sarah continued. "When you first got here, we weren't sure whether you could be trusted or not. I think when I saw Mei lying there and you with your wrists bleeding, I just snapped back into that frame of mind. Throw in the fact that we have been getting close and our feelings for each other, and I just I couldn't—"

"Sarah," Kevin interrupted. "I'm not going to hurt you. I could never do anything to you."

"I believe you," Sarah said. "At the same time, I'm scared. I know you are on our side, and I know that you're real, but deep inside, my heart is still afraid that you're going to flip a switch and next thing you know..."

"That's not going to happen," Kevin said.

"Kevin, the man who was an undercover agent before, he told me the same thing, and I believed him. You know, when I think back on him, what gets to me the most are the happy memories. Isn't that strange? I can see him killing my friends. I can hear him barking orders to the security forces, and I remember how stone-faced his expression was when he switched, but those thoughts don't make me angry. When I think of him, taking the time to sit with me every morning for a week, teaching me how to tie my shoes, I feel my face filling with red. When I remember him dancing with me, standing on his feet, I feel my fist clench. When I recall his singing voice and how he used to belt out romantic country songs, I can't help but want to run my fist through the wall. Do you know why?" Sarah asked.

Kevin just shook his head, no.

"It's because it makes me doubt all the happy memories I have ever had in my life. All those things that you can close your eyes and revisit that put a smile on your face. A good joke, a beautiful sunset,"—Sarah looked Kevin in his eyes as she said the next statement—"a welcome kiss. If my happy moments with him could be just a fake means to an end, what else is? How do you know what's real?"

They both sat quietly for a long, awkward pause. Kevin felt the need to console and connect with her. He reached across the table and placed his hand on hers.

She didn't pull away, but as tears came to her eyes, she asked Kevin, "Is this real?"

"Yes. More real than anything I've ever felt."

"How can you know?"

"Because I love you."

A short lingering moment of silence filled the air with an energy so thick they could both feel it, the force pulling on them, building, until it finally won out. Kevin and Sarah both jumped up from the table simultaneously and force-fully kissed each other. They reached over the table and grabbed the other's neck. Their lips locked and held them together. They fumbled and bumped the bench seats as they pushed themselves away from and around the table, still connected by their passionate intertwining of lips and tongue. The fire, the heat between them, igniting and turning into a raging inferno. Hay and splinters scattered across the floor as they shuffled to Kevin's stall, holding each other tight, and both entranced in the passion of their embrace.

Kevin closed the door behind him, freeing a hand. Sarah's boot heel caught an exposed board, and she tripped, pulling them to the ground in a rough thud. Kevin had landed on top of her hard, body slamming her into the ground while at the same time catching Sarah's knee to the gut. He rolled off her with an "oof."

She coughed a little as she straightened her back out from the fall. Her coughs turned into a full-bore laugh. The moment having been so unexpected it was all she could do.

Kevin looked at her laughing and felt a wide smile creep on his face. Soon her infectious laugh had caught him. Together, they guffawed on the floor of Kevin's stall. Almost a minute passed before their loud laughter turned into subdued giggles.

They both lay next to each other in the hay, now facing each other, smiling, each staring into the other's eyes, just soaking in the emotion of their current "now."

"I love you too," Sarah said.

That was the spark that reignited the fire that had still been stoking.

Lips locked.

Arms embraced.

Clothes removed.

Bodies intertwined.

In that small hay-filled barn stall, an agent of the Dream States and the illegal daughter of the resistance leader tied their hearts and destinies together forever.

The sunrise was shining a pale-pink light into the barn. Sarah's skin was a rosy shade that made her face glow in a way that Kevin couldn't peel his eyes off her.

He had woken up early and been trying to lie as still as possible to not disturb the woman he loved. Watching the blanket they shared rise and fall as she dreamed, Kevin felt a mixture of emotions.

He felt safety and contentment as he lay next to her, yet he also knew that he had crossed a line, one that complicated things. He could feel himself coming to the understanding that this emotion, this connectedness he felt, he couldn't betray. He would have to tell Sarah the truth about everything, but how could he? Would she still love him if she knew? Would she believe he was telling her the truth, even though he had lied to her about not being an agent?

Kevin felt his stomach turn as his mind raced around the mix of emotions. He felt such happiness and guilt, passion and disheartenment, honesty and falsity, a mix of lies and truths. His heart raced with the stress of the moment. The only thing that could calm him was staring at the beauty peacefully sleeping next to him. He soaked in her energy all he could, searching for peace.

"I think we should tell Sarah everything," Kevin said, closing the handcuff around his left wrist while sitting in the chair.

"No," the Master said as he sat in his computer chair.

"I think I have to," Kevin said. "Sarah and I, we, well, I just don't think I can keep anything from her."

The Master's shoulders slumped. "She can't know." The Master paused. "There is something that I haven't explained yet."

"I'm getting real tired of the secrets. What now?"

"You'll be able to use the code and do some damage from Dream State 8, but for the plan to work, you must plant the kill code in the Z-Bank's mainframe. That server farm feeds out to the rest of the states and the syncs. Only that way will you be able to set her free."

"So why am I going to DS 8? Why not infiltrate the Z-Bank?"

"It won't work. You have to get inside and have access to an editor's computer input infrastructure, with your security codes re-enabled. The only person they'll let in is someone they trust." The Master pointed at Kevin. "Someone who has completed their mission."

"My mission?"

"The one that Klay failed."

Kevin thought for a second. "You want me to kill you?"

"No. I want you to kill the entire movement. Everyone else will die in the minds of the others. But to get you back where you need to be, I have to die for real."

"Why?" Kevin swallowed hard.

"Don't feel bad for me. I've had a good long life, and if my death means my daughter's freedom, I'm okay with that price. I feel sorry for you."

"Me?"

"Yes. Your feelings for Sarah go beyond code. Now, to save her, you're going to have to lose her."

Kevin thought for a couple of seconds before saying what he knew inside. "She will never forgive me for killing you."

"Probably not. But that's the price you have to pay for her."

"I... look, something happened with Sarah. We uh..."

"It doesn't matter. Either you pay this price and set her free because you love her and you want the best for her, or you don't. If not, then I might as well kill you and her now. So, are you willing to sacrifice your connection to save her?"

Kevin nodded his head.

"Good. Now for the other piece of this puzzle. I can't risk her getting killed in this whole charade. Sarah, you, and Diehl will go to DS 8 and plant the code, like planned. But before you go, I will enable your tracking and send them a message from your other identity. First, it will lead them here, where they will find me. Then it will lead them to you after you plant the code. So remember to find a way to get separated. Okay?"

"Okay. But wait, what happens after that?"

"That part of the plan, I can't tell you," the Master said. "I have to tell your other identity that piece."

"You trust him?"

"No. But when he understands he gets to kill me in exchange, I think he'll be all game."

"I don't like this."

"Sorry, Kevin, but it's time for me to talk to your agent identity." He pushed a few keys on the keyboard and watched the code piece itself back together.

Complete.
Agent K00004 - Re-identified.

"Don't thrash," the Master said.

Agent K00004 looked at him, anger brewing and his nostrils flaring, but only for a moment before he calmed down and an almost-sad look came to his face. "I have to kill you."

"You will be the death of me, but someone else will pull the trigger."

"No, it should be me."

"How about we make a deal? If you agree to what I ask, I'll let you free. You can kill me if you want."

"What's the catch?"

"No catch. I just want to show you your real history."

"You want to brainwash me."

"Have you ever seen your own code?"

"It's against regulations."

"That's now what I asked. You other identity planted code to see his past dreams. So I'm guessing you've taken a look at your code. Well, have you?"

Agent K00004 nodded his head.

"Did you ever think something looked wrong?"

"I'm an agent. They put traps in our code to make sure no one can read us."

"That's true, but you know something is not right, right? You've seen the error message, right?"

"What are you getting at?"

"Someone has been in your head. There are memories and programs hidden from you that are counteracting your own mind. I'm asking you to allow me to unlock them. That's it. You remember everything hidden from your mind, and you get to be set free. That's the deal."

"You want to kill me?"

"No."

"Of course you do. If you bring back all my memories, all the dream lives I've had will wreck my mind."

"Oh no, those memories they are gone. They were burned out of your brain long ago. The memories I'm talking about are hidden and encrypted in your mind chip, protected from the burn. I don't know why, but I have a guess."

"What's your guess?"

"No. If I'm right, the only thing that will work will be to let you remember them. So, do we have a deal?"

"Why should I?"

"Well, one option: you get to remember your life and have control over it. Plus, you get to kill me, no resistance. The other way, well, I just leave you chained here to starve to death."

"Not much of an option, is it?"

"No, but you still have to agree to unlock your encrypted memories."

"Why? Why not just force me?"

"The unlock function is coded to only unscramble with your approval. It takes both of us to open the lock in your mind."

"What?"

"I know. It makes little sense to me either. It's like someone planned for you to be here, with me, locked in this chair. So, do you want to know why that is? Or do you want to starve?"

Agent K00004 sat in the chair. Taking a deep breath, he said, "Okay, do it. Before you do, I feel the need to tell you something. I don't know why, but I feel like you need to know that something's different. Different from the last time you tried this. Something inside me changed."

"Then this might just work like we hope," the Master said, nodding his head. The Master typed a command into the computer and watched as the code rewrote itself and deleted. A flush of memories restored and rewrote themselves.

Agent K00004 shook in the chair. After a minute, the code stabilized and a dialogue box opened with a countdown timer that started at 999 and went down by one every second.

998 . . .
997 . . .
996 . . .

"I remember," Agent K00004 said.

"What do you remember?"

"I remember everything. You were right. Someone did plan this."

The Master scrunched his forehead.

"Can I show you?"

"Um."

"I'm not going to kill you. Plug in. He needs to tell you something."

"Who?"

"My father."

The Master plugged into Agent K00004's mind chip. He found a white door standing in an infinite blackness. The Master opened the door and transported to another time, another place.

"Welcome," Alexander said to the Master as he stepped out a white door and into a grassy field.

The Master looked at the man. Something seemed off, like the perspective was wrong. "Why?"

"Listen, I'm currently talking to you in the form of my son. Kevin is nine years old today. I will soon hide this memory beneath millions of lines of codes and scrambles, much like how your scramble works, Mr. Ulbert. I don't know how old you will be when this message finds you, or how old Kevin will be. I hope it reaches you in time. I can hide my memories and feelings from the sync, but Kevin is a child. I will work to protect him and keep you both alive long enough to reach this moment. I don't have much time, so I need you to listen."

The Master understood this was a prerecorded message and observed through the eyes of a nine-year-old boy.

"I know of your daughter, Mr. Ulbert. That's why I know you'll understand. Understand why I'm doing this and why I'm taking the risk. This is all hope. My name is Alexander, Alexander Anders. I am one of the leading members of my family, and I need your help. The Elianders have for a long time allowed some level of leniency with children. When my son was born, they welcomed him as part of the ruling class. Someone to be taught, trained and brought up in areas of science and technology to help us solve the world's problems. Well, things change."

Alexander looked down at his son. "Mr. Ulbert, you've been out of the loop for God knows how long when this message reaches you. We've succeeded. We travel the stars now and are not limited to Earth any longer. We don't need the Dream States to operate at pure efficiency anymore. Yet they provide security, wealth, and freedom from utility for us, so the Elianders have decided to keep them and all alpha protocol active. Thanks to advances in medicine, we are essentially immortal. In order not to create the problem of overpopulation, our children will now enter agent programs, added to the dreaming population, or killed. I don't want any of those things for Kevin. I want him to be able to make his own destiny. This is incredibly selfish and self-serving of me, but I don't care. A father's love doesn't care about the greater good. You understand that, and I'm sure you want the same thing for your daughter that I want for my Kevin. Let me also say I'm sorry about your wife."

"If all my plans work out up to this moment, you will receive this message, but it won't be for a while. As I record this message, it has only been a few days since her passing. I ordered the mission that took her life and almost took yours. All I could do to help you was try to give you a chance. Something inside me broke the day my son was condemned to a life of slavery, and I realized I was controlled as well. I sped up the re-identification of Agent B00003 to give you a chance to get away. I'm glad it worked. Now that you have the code, my son can be the key to both you and your daughter, and his freedom. Please, if this works, and they trained him in the agent program, and you find this memory, help him. He will be implanted with a storyline of you murdering children, but to clean that out, simply tell him, 'X562DF-0983 execute.' This will stop the countdown on your screen and keep his memories of the happy life he had and this talk intact, as well as his last dream. If he hasn't been terrible, give him that. Give him a life."

"Kevin, this will be the last time I can tell you I love you. If you accomplish this mission, I will think you're dead. Maybe my care for you will break that, but if not, you'll only be a stranger. So good luck."

The Master opened his eyes in the dim light of the bunker. "So your name is Kevin?"

"Yes," Kevin Anders said. "Do me a favor, will you?"

"What?"

"Tell me that code. I have a feeling it's coded to your voice."

"X562DF-0983 execute."

Kevin blinked a few times. "Thanks."

"You're welcome. Now remember, when I re-scramble you, you won't remember any of this. So when they re-identify you and all this comes back, act like you don't know of it."

"Be dead inside. I can do that."

"Kevin, I'm glad I got to meet you before the end. The real you."

"You should know, I still love her."

"Good."

"Let's do it."

The Master typed in the command, re-scrambling Kevin Anders' and Agent K00004's mind.

Kevin opened his eyes, unaware of what had just occurred.

"Go back to the barn and rest up," the Master said, unlocking his handcuffs. "I'll come to you in the morning."

Kevin stood from the chair. "How'd it go? No wrist burns this time, so I'm guessing better than before."

The Master smiled at Kevin. "A lot better. I'll talk to you tomorrow."

Kevin left the bunker for the last time.

"Hey!" Sarah said with extra perk in her voice. "How about a run before dinner?"

"Um," Kevin said, looking up from the potatoes he was chopping. He glanced over to Harmon, who was stirring a pot with a brine of some kind in it.

"Go ahead. I can manage here."

"You think you can still keep up with me after all that time you've spent in the bunker?" Sarah said, flirting with Kevin.

Kevin just smiled back. "Let's do this."

Sarah and Kevin jogged and ran, trading the lead position back and forth, more playful than actual racing.

Their watches beeped the drone warning just as they were turning a corner embankment of a dried-out stream. Together, they huddled in the small outcropping. Sweat glistened on their faces, and their hearts beat as they pressed together, hiding from the threat above.

As the beeping of the drone alarm stopped chiming its warning, Kevin and Sarah still hid under the outcropping. Kevin and Sarah were staring into each other's eyes, lost in the tangible emotion of the moment.

Kevin reached and moved a stray hair that had stuck to Sarah's face with the sweat that had beaded on her cheek. He pushed it and tucked it behind her ear, lightly touching her face while doing it. Kevin let his finger fall to the bottom of Sarah's chin and pulled her mouth to his. Closing his eyes, he felt himself consumed by the feeling of her soft lips pressing into his. An image flashed into his mind.

Sarah stood with her back to Kevin, dressed in all black. She was holding a bunch of flowers in both hands as she cried uncontrollably. In front of her stood an engraved tombstone.

The Master
A Father, A Friend, A Leader
Betrayed by the Man His Daughter Loved

Sarah stood there completely broken. Then she looked at Kevin in this imaginary moment and spoke to him. "How could you?" she asked.

"It was my mission," he answered, his heart shattering.

"But why did you have to seduce me and make me love you too? Why couldn't you have just stayed away? I had to lose both of you at the same time. It's too much to bear." Sarah pulled her gun and pressed it to her head.

"No," Kevin said, pulling away from the kiss that Sarah and he had been sharing.

"What's wrong?"

"I," Kevin said, unable to look at Sarah in her eyes. "I'm sorry. I can't. We shouldn't."

"What?"

"I'm sorry, but we shouldn't do this."

"What are you talking about? Kevin, look at me."

"We shouldn't do this. We should focus on the mission, and that's it."

"No. Kevin, you can't go from 'I love you' to 'we have to focus on the mission.' Not after yesterday. Kevin, look at me."

Kevin mustered up all the strength he could and looked at Sarah in her eyes. She was teetering in her resolve but still held strong to what he knew they both felt. He needed to use the nuclear option. Taking a deep breath to steady himself, Kevin hardened his jaw and said, "Yesterday was a mistake."

Sarah felt a wave of emotion run over her, a mixture of shock, anger and grief causing her to tremble. Looking at the man she loved, or did until that moment, she felt a feeling like she had never experienced. Her heart raced, and her body felt somehow more numb to the world around her. She turned and left Kevin there, running as fast as her legs would move.

Kevin watched her disappear into the distance before the dam broke. He held his face in his hands as he wept.

It's for her. He thought to himself. *Let her go. Set her free. She will hate you, but she will live. Better to pay that price now and protect her. Let her go. If you love her, then you'll let her go.*

Kevin had found his way back to the barn after a long walk home. He skipped dinner and instead stayed in his stall, trying to find some sort of peace from the events of the day. He couldn't find it.

A long night later found Kevin and the Master sitting across from each other.

"How are you feeling?" the Master asked Kevin as they shared a meal, bowls of stew, in the barn.

Kevin swallowed a piece of potato. "Well, stew for breakfast isn't exactly my favorite, but other than that, I'm okay."

"I heard about what happened with Sarah and you."

Kevin swallowed hard. "What did you hear?"

"Everything."

"Look," Kevin started.

"Don't. I know you love her. I've been inside your mind. And I get it, losing her is something that's bound to happen, and you're trying to protect her from that hurt."

Kevin nodded.

"I told her I made you promise to say that to her. That I forbid it."

Kevin looked at him, confused. "Why? Why would you?"

"Kevin, your heart is in the right place, trying to soften the blow, but we both know the power love has. You need it, and so does she. This mission has to work."

Kevin nodded. "Speaking of the mission, no bleeding wrists this time, so I'm guessing that your talk with the other me went well?"

"Very well."

"But I still didn't wake up to, well, myself or Kevin or whatever, so the emotion still didn't overwhelm the code like you hoped?"

"Actually, the emotion worked."

"Why don't I remember it, then?"

"Things are in play that I can't explain. You're going to need to trust me on this one."

"You know that's not an answer I'm enjoying hearing so often."

"Kevin, have you ever read any books about time travel?"

"Uh, I saw movies."

"Okay, well, imagine for me I was time traveling, and I met you. Now you're supposed to, or rather you already have, but haven't yet done this one thing that affects all human history. However, if I tell you you're going to do it, then it will cause ripple effects and might even cause the future to change. Do you get what I'm saying?"

"I think you're telling me that if you tell me whatever this secret thing is, the reset won't happen?"

"Or it could happen too soon. I need the moment they flip the switch to cause overloading failure. If I answer your question, then in your mind, the code will assimilate some pieces of the emotion. We need the massive moment. If it's piece by piece, then the overload may not occur, and all is lost."

"You seem sure about this."

"That's the only way to live, Kevin."

"It's a good way to die."

"No, no, I'm taking about the ability to take action with faith. When I first started splintering off and creating a real resistance, I had other partners. They were so afraid to take action without first having everything planned out that we ended up going two different ways. I took action and figured out how to do all of this: the farming, the missions, the power sourcing. I learned as I went. They prepared. Well, we grew and spread. My partners took too long, and when the time came to put their plans into action, it was too late. They drew the attention of agents and died. Action with faith that it will work out, even if that means improvising on the fly, is always better than no action. I had faith in myself, and now I have faith in you."

"Thanks."

"Admittedly, it's a lot easier to have that faith after seeing inside your mind. I've seen glimpses of your emotions, but what I can't see is your soul. However, I know you still have one because your programing is failing. At your roots, you're a good man. Kevin, this is going to be the last time we speak, so now I would like to give you my blessing."

"Your blessing?" Kevin said, a little more nervous than he expected.

"Kevin, you're a man of destiny and purpose. Your heart's desires are pure and well founded. You will find success in your life, and I am glad that I had the chance to meet you before my end. With this Abrahamic blessing, I start the journey you will take without me."

"An Abrahamic blessing. Right." Kevin laughed a little louder before chuckling quietly.

"What? Oh, you thought I was giving you my blessing to marry my daughter?" The Master laughed this time.

"Almost ready," Sarah said, leaning in the barn door.

"Okay," the Master said. "We'll be right out."

Sarah looked at Kevin for a moment. He felt his stomach turn a little in guilt and excitement at seeing her face. Sarah turned away from the door without a smile.

"Kevin," the Master said, "take this." He slid a strangely shaped gun across the table. "Hide it."

Kevin took it and put it under his shirt. "I have a gun." Kevin pointed at the holstered sidearm slung under his shoulder.

"This is a tranquilizer gun. If you need to, shoot Diehl and Sarah, and get away. Keep them safe."

Kevin understood and nodded.

"Look, Kevin. I haven't gotten to code in a long time. It's been... fun."

"Yes, it has. Thanks for everything."

"Thank you," the Master said, pulling out a small hand-held computer with a cord attached.

Kevin plugged the cord into his mind chip.

The Master pushed an icon on the device.

"Is that it?"

"It's done."

Kevin pulled the cord from his chip, suddenly steeling himself for the moment. He looked up at the old man sitting across from him one last time.

"Goodbye, Kevin."

"Goodbye."

"Sir."

Thairn looked up from the handgun he had been adjusting. He reached to the controls of the helicopter's radio headsets. "What is it?"

"Sir," the copilot repeated before speaking. "The drones have finished scanning the farm. They have only found one heat signature."

"Positive identification?"

"Yes, sir. It's him."

"Put us down." *Good work, agent. You did your job. Now I get the pleasure of finishing him.*

The bumpy trek over the black desert landscape was less than a comfortable ride for Kevin, who had the luxury of riding in the unpadded back.

Sarah rode shotgun as Diehl drove. They were all silent, mentally and emotionally preparing for the mission about to be put into action.

Kevin watched a small bolt roll across the floor. He knew he should focus on the plan and study the map drawn in permanent marker on the paper taped to the wall across from him, but he couldn't. Deep down, Kevin knew that out there, past the rolled steel and aluminum, the Dream States agents were closing in on the farm. Closing in on the man who had become a friend to him. Closing the proverbial door on the Master's life.

"Okay, we're getting close now, so listen up," Sarah said, command in her voice. "Look at the map on the wall. While you have been in the dark with my father, we've been planning this mission and drilling it, so rule number one is you do what we say. Understood?"

"Yep."

"Good. If anything happens, and the plan changes, you follow my or Diehl's lead. Understood?"

"Yeah. Look Sarah, I'm sorry about—"

"Don't be. You were doing exactly what my father asked you to do," she said, clearly not over yesterday. "When we get to Dream State 8, we will drive on a back road that leads to a service entrance. From there, we will follow a twisting maze of hallways that leads to the mezzanine. You will follow me. If we get separated, I can't promise I'll find you, or even come for you, so stick on me."

"What happened between you two?" Diehl asked, picking up on the obvious tone shift.

Sarah glared at Diehl. "Just drive the van."

"Whoa, that bad, huh?" Diehl said.

"The Master told me to,"—Kevin paused as Sarah shot him a glare—"he made me promise to do something. Something I didn't want to do. "

Sarah's face softened a little. "Back to the mission," she said. "You stick with me and I'll deliver you to Dr. Flo. If you remember, she's the one who saved your life. She's going to help us get access to the Dream State 8 network. Then you do your thing. Clear?"

"Yep," Kevin said.

"Kevin," Diehl said. "How long will this coding thing take you?"

"Not long," Kevin said. "Maybe an hour, max. I need to spread the code through different emotions and times of my past dream, so it's spread through the network more."

"How spread are we talking?" Diehl asked.

"From five years old to twenty-one."

"That time span in one hour? You can dream that fast?" Sarah said.

"No, I'm going to hop between memories."

"You can do that?" Diehl asked.

"It's like remembering different moments of time in your head. The only difference is that I have to focus completely in on that memory and let myself back into it."

"If I could do that, I can think of a few memories I wouldn't mind being pulled back into, if you know what I mean," Diehl said.

Sarah and Kevin both looked at each other awkwardly for a moment.

"Buckle up," Diehl shouted as he shifted gears and the van lurched over the cement curb that defined the road leading into the service entrance to DS 8.

Kevin was thrown upward, his head smashing into the metal roof. "There's no buckle back here, you dick," Kevin shouted.

"Sorry," Diehl said, smiling.

"You good?" Sarah asked.

Kevin felt his head and found no blood, just a sore spot. "Yeah, just a little more than a second of heads-up would be nice."

Diehl swerved to avoid a rock that had fallen onto the road.

Kevin fell and hit his shoulder on the floor of the van.

"You'd think they'd keep this better maintained," Diehl said.

Kevin picked himself up again.

"Maybe you should brace yourself against something," Sarah said.

"Yeah." Kevin reached over and held on to the back of Sarah's seat. He pushed his head forward, looking out the windshield.

"Hey, Kevin," Sarah said, turning to find her face awkwardly close to his. "Um. I just wanted to say that no matter what happens, I'm glad we pulled you out of here and I got to..." Her sentence trailed off.

"Me too," Kevin said, feeling the same awkward yet amazing energy.

"Okay, lovebirds," Diehl said. "We're on the approach now."

"Right," Kevin said, shaking his head and refocusing.

Sarah took a deep breath, clearing her mind.

Diehl attempted to drive calmly as they pulled up to the service doors that led directly up to the back of the main lobby of DS 8 and the access hallway to the private wing, but he accidentally curb checked the front right tire. He let out a small curse under his breath.

"Let's go," Sarah said.

Sarah and Kevin jumped out of the van and moved with purpose to the service doors. Mounted to the wall to the left of the double doors was a small keypad. Sarah pried it open, exposing wires. She carefully attached leads to them and connected the other end to a handheld device. She punched in a few commands. A few seconds later, the magnetic locks clicked as they released.

"Let's go. Stick with me, and act like we're supposed to be here," Sarah said.

Kevin nodded.

Together, they entered the back door of the DS 8 lobby. The smell of lavender could still be faintly detected in the back hallways that lined the service area.

"Follow me," Sarah said, confidently walking and turning down the maze of intertwined halls.

"How do you know all of this?"

"Please, you think that Diehl and I haven't been training while you and my dad did your computer thing? Every part of this mission has been planned and drilled. Why do you think we could drive in here so easily? We slipped information in to our contacts, which was admittedly more difficult to do since we pulled you out of here recently. They shut down the motion detectors for maintenance and scheduled guard shifts on a specific timeline to give us our window. Why do you think Diehl made the dumb joke about the rock in the road?"

"That was a joke?"

"Not very good with the comedic tone, is he?" Sarah said, smiling at Kevin.

"No."

"Almost there," Sarah said, leading Kevin through another set of doors.

On the other side, Kevin recognized the room. The central bar with the robot bartender of DS 8's mezzanine shined in the dim light. It was yet again empty, no doubt part of the plan.

Sarah led the way to the doors marked private. She knocked on them and waited.

It wasn't more than a second before the doors swung open and the smiling, but clearly nervous, face of Dr. Flo. greeted them. "Hello again," she said.

"Hello," Kevin responded.

"We don't have much time, Flo," Sarah said, stepping past her and into the private hallway. Kevin followed.

"Right, come on." Dr. Flo led them a short way forward and into a smaller, more ornate atrium.

Kevin only glimpsed a light-purple crystalline statue that adorned the top of a buffet laid out to greet special guests before Dr. Flo ushered them into a small room with frosted glass. Inside, two plush velvet couches sat facing each other, and a large dresser stood against the far wall.

"Have a seat," Dr. Flo said, motioning to a couch.

Kevin sat down, while Sarah took position next to the door. "You sure this will work from here?" she asked over her shoulder.

"It'll work," Dr. Flo responded as she opened a drawer in the dresser.

As she turned from it, Kevin saw a small square box with a series of markings on it in her hands. "What's that?" he asked.

"The private clients get to dream from the moment they check in," Dr. Flo said, moving to Kevin's side and joining him on the couch. "Most of them want to get to the dream as soon as possible, and so to cater to their needs, we have these mobile dream hookups." She opened the box to reveal a computerized cuff that had two cords attached. "This unit lets you dream wirelessly until you reach your room, but for us today, it will let you connect to the network without having to go through as many checkpoints."

"More hooking him up, less talking, Flo," Sarah said, checking her watch.

"Right. Let's slip this on you."

Kevin rolled up his sleeve to allow the cuff to slide on. It automatically cinched down, fitting snugly.

"Now we are going to plug this cord into your mind chip." Dr. Flo spoke as she worked.

Kevin felt the all-too-familiar pressure as she pushed the cord in.

"And this tube carries the dream serum so you can stay asleep."

Kevin stopped her hand. "I don't need it."

Dr. Flo, confused, looked at Sarah. She nodded back. "Okay, then. I'm just going to turn this on, and you'll be connected. Are you ready?"

Kevin looked at Sarah and took a deep breath before closing his eyes. "Ready."

Dr. Flo tapped on the cuff, turning on the power and starting the connection.

Kevin felt the dream network as he let his mind slip into the code.

"Jaared? Jaared, I know you're sad, but please take your hands off your face."

"No," Jaared whined, his five-year-old voice squeaking.

"Jaared, come on," his mother said in a soft and consoling tone. "Let's say goodbye to Matthew. Can you give your friend a hug goodbye?"

Jaared shook his head, his hands still covering his eyes, hiding from the moment.

Jaared's mother kneeled down by her son. "Jaared, Matthew is leaving. If you were leaving, wouldn't you want him to hug you goodbye?"

Jaared nodded slightly.

Jaared's mother lightly pulled his hands from his face. The small boy wore a wire frown and scrunched forehead. "Okay, now give your friend a hug goodbye, and we'll wave as they leave."

Jaared hugged his best friend, whose family was being moved by Matthew's father's work, meaning that their young friendship and play times were over. A few minutes later, Jaared and his mother were standing in the parking lot of the school, waving at a gray station wagon driving off into the distance. "Mom?" Jaared asked.

"Yeah, honey?" she replied.

"Why does Matthew have to leave?"

"Well, his family is moving to Tennessee."

"Oh."

"Come on, sweetheart, let's go home."

"Can we go to McDonald's?"

"Sure," his mother said.

Riding to McDonald's, Jaared stared out the window from his back-seat captain's chair, quiet and sad.

"Honey, are you okay?"

"I don't like when I lose my friends."

"Yeah, it's sad sometimes, but you'll make new friends."

"The hardest part isn't the loss of a friend or the lonely feeling that I'm experiencing now, but the feeling that perhaps, sometimes, losing friends or letting them go will be best for both of us. It's necessary to let friends go to set them free, even if it means that I'm left alone and left wanting for connection," Jaared said under his breath.

"What was that, honey?" Jaared's mom asked.

Jaared just sat quietly, watching the glowing white code filtering through the memory. One small piece caught his attention as it assimilated with the door handle. Looking up from the glowing fragment, Kevin caught his reflection in the minivan window. There he sat, a full-grown adult, back in a moment of time from his last life. Kevin closed his eyes on the memory and opened them in another.

Jaared opened his eyes, having finished his prayer. In his hands he held a letter-sized envelope. Inside was the document that would confirm if all his play and practice had paid off. A week of tryouts, dribbling drills and three-point competition had led to this moment. He sat alone in the upstairs bathroom of his junior high, still wearing his basketball uniform, nervously holding his letter. The coach had given everyone letters versus having names listed on a corkboard to keep the cuts more private. Jaared, as an underclassman, was hoping he had done enough to make the team.

Nervously, he peeled the envelope open and pulled the letter free. Unfolding it, Jaared started reading the words on the page.

Dear Jaared,

I would like to first thank you for trying out the basketball program. As you know, there are a number of boys trying out for this team, and unfortunately, we are limited in the number of spots that we are allotted. This means that many of the boys have to be cut. This is not a reflection on work ethic or effort, just a necessary action that must be taken to...

Jaared's heart was dropping with every sentence, word and syllable. He could feel the letter softening the blow.

... ensure that we field both a team of dedicated and talented young men. I regretfully have to inform a number of those who hoped to play with us this season that this will not be the case.

However, in your case, I am pleased to be the first to welcome you to the team and look forward to having you be an Eagle! You have shown the hard work, skill and teamwork that we are excited about incorporating into our team. I and your other coaches expect a wonderful season with you on the team.

Jaared's heart, which had descended into his stomach, leaped into his head. He himself jumped up from the wooden bench he had been sitting on and screamed. "Yeah!" Jaared pumped his fists and read the letter again. His joy and exhilaration carried around the room, celebrating. Jaared stopped in front of the bathroom mirror, smiling and looking at himself. *I did it.* "I did it!" Jaared first thought and then exclaimed. He spun in a circle and looked in the mirror again, this time as Kevin.

Kevin was smiling as wide as Jaared just had.

"You had a goal, a mission that you worked so hard for, and you had moments where you thought you messed it up and failed, but in the end, because of your work, you succeeded. This feeling, this emotion, is the reward. Soak it in," Kevin said. As he did, the lights in the room flickered, white code sparking the electrical bulbs. Kevin smiled, watching the code arc in the room. Kevin closed his eyes, again jumping into another memory of Jaared Johns.

Hearts raced, feet pounded into dirt and sweat beaded on Jaared's forehead as he ran, fueled by adrenaline, from the masked man wielding a chainsaw. Jaared's friend David was a half step ahead of Jaared, also fleeing their horrific pursuer. A noise made David turn his head for a split second.

The rat-tat-tat of the power tool being held by the man echoed in the night through rows of corn decorated with ghosts and tombstones, and grew closer. He was catching them.

When he turned, David's foot caught the root of a near-by cornstalk and sent him facedown on the well-beaten trail. Without thinking, and with a strength Jaared didn't know he had, he grabbed David by the back of the sweater and pulled him to his feet without losing a stride. Side by side, they sprinted their way through the rest of the maze.

Twenty minutes later, David, Jaared and three of their friends crammed into a small Honda Accord, driving home. Jaared was riding in the front passenger seat, while his brother drove, leaving David and their friends Phil and Brian in the back seat. They were all speaking over each other, laughing and joking about their haunted corn maze experience like only young teenage high school boys do.

"Wait, wait, wait!" David yelled over the din. The car got quiet for a moment. "Did y'all see Jaared literally carrying me with one arm, running away from that chainsaw guy?"

"No," Jaared's brother said. "What?"

David said, "He grabbed me because I fell, and ran just carrying me, saving me."

"One," one of the other boys in the car, their friend Phil, said, "you know that it's all fake, so he didn't 'save' you. Two, you would be the one to trip and fall with someone chasing you."

"Oh ha ha," David said.

"Phil, it's more fun if you just go into it and enjoy the fear of it," Jaared said. "And yes, David, I got you. I won't leave friends behind."

"Yeah, don't leave him behind to get caught by the scary amusement park worker," Phil said sarcastically.

"Real or fake, I won't leave friends behind. If you fell, Phil, I would have saved you."

"Well, I wouldn't have fallen," Phil said.

"Very funny," David said, before punching Phil playfully on the arm.

The car erupted into laughter and ridiculousness. While the boys laughed and joked, Kevin looked into the side mirror at his reflection as he repeated the sentiment that Jaared had just expressed. "I save my friends," he said. As he did, the radio glitched for a moment, random code phrases showing on the LED display. Kevin smiled as Jaared's brother hit the radio, trying to get it working again. Kevin closed his eyes, a feeling of loyalty and nostalgia on his heart.

"Acetyl?" Jaared said. He opened his eyes and turned over the flash card. He pumped his fist, yes.

"Hey, do you want a beer?" Jaared's brother, Justin, asked, walking into Jaared's bedroom.

"No, thanks, man. I've got one more final tomorrow. Then this semester is over," Jaared said, turning away from his desk. "Whoever said that sophomore year is more fun than freshman was clearly not in o-chem."

"What time is your final at tomorrow?"

"Eight."

"Well, at least it's done early."

"Yeah, but it's still going to suck."

"Well, we were going to stay here and play games instead of going to the bars, but if you need the house quiet tomorrow, we can go out."

"No, it's okay. I'm planning on studying for this one until late tonight, anyway. Then I'll just rally on a few hours of sleep tomorrow."

"Sounds good. I'll leave you to it, then. You want me to close your door?"

"Yeah, thanks, man."

Justin walked out and closed Jaared's bedroom door.

For the next hour, Jaared studied flash cards and memorized the chemical formulas and bond angles of different compounds, trying to burn into his brain concepts he grasped but hadn't yet mastered. His phone buzzed on the desk next to him. He glanced at it and saw the contact said STEVE LAB PARTNER. Picking up the phone, he said, "Steve, you ready for this final tomorrow?"

If a camera had been pointed at Jaared during that phone call, you could have seen him go through all the emotions of shock, fear, disappointment, disbelief and dismay as the voice on the other side of the phone told Jaared the truth. Hanging up the call, Jaared threw his flash cards in the trash and headed downstairs.

He walked past the game of sectionals, went into the dining nook, and walked straight to the freezer. Not saying a word to any of the eight people less than three feet from him, he pulled a bottle of vodka from the ice tray and poured himself a shot. He pounded two before his brother came over.

Excitedly he said, "Jaared! Are you done?" Seeing his brother's face, Justin asked a different question. "What happened?"

"I missed my final," Jaared said in an empty tone.

"I thought you said it was tomorrow?"

"I thought it was. I wrote the wrong date in my calendar."

"Oh, man. That sucks. Can you take it again or something?"

"No, I guess the teacher said specifically at the final that they wouldn't allow any rescheduling or anything for any reason after the test was given."

"That sucks."

"Yeah."

"Will it... do you fail?"

Jaared nodded his head.

"Are you alright?"

Jaared looked to his left, seeing his reflection in the microwave door. Kevin stood there in that moment, soaking the feelings of shock and self-loathing. He swallowed a burning saliva that had built on his tongue, reacting to the cheap vodka. "I just don't want to mess up like this again. I don't want to fail because I made a simple mistake. No matter what, I have to succeed." The time readout danced as the white code Kevin implanted into the memory assimilated.

"Come on, man. I'll take a shot with you," Justin said.

"Okay," Kevin said. Closing his eyes as the burning alcohol passed his lips, he jumped into another point in Jaared's time.

Jaared rubbed his eyes, trying to remove the burning feeling from them. "Whoa," Jaared said, returning his hands to the steering wheel of his Jeep. "That guy definitely needs to turn his brights off."

"Yeah, that was... bright," the girl in his passenger seat said. "Thank you for dinner tonight." She smiled at Jaared.

"Thank you for joining me," Jaared said back. "I had a lot of fun talking with you."

"Me too," she said.

"I can't believe we talked for three hours."

"Yeah, I didn't realize what time it was until I got a text from my girlfriend asking if I needed rescue."

"You had an escape plan in place?"

"You have to. There are a lot of creepy guys out there. Sometimes you need a friend to 'call and need your help immediately.'"

"Well, I'm glad I didn't make that list."

"No, you've been very sweet."

"It's easy when you're talking to someone that interesting and cute," Jaared said, smiling.

His date smiled back at him.

A few turns and bright headlights later, the girl pointed to a white house with a red door. "It's right here," she said.

Jaared pulled the car up to the house. He hopped out and fast walked around the front of the Jeep, opened her door for her, and offered his hand. She took it, hopping down. He walked with her up to the house, making small talk about the yard and location.

When they got to the front door, she turned and clearly was waiting for something more.

Jaared could feel the tension at the moment, but took no action. His date pressed the moment.

"You know I'm not opposed to a kiss on the first date, or maybe even more."

Jaared felt all of his desires and urges pull against him, but deep inside, he felt something else, a stern, stable resistance. "I'm sorry, but I can't."

"Okay."

"You're great," Jaared said, "but I know deep inside that you're not the one. I promised myself that I would find the one, and I wouldn't want to get in the way of you finding the right guy for you, either. Does that make sense?"

"Goodbye," she said as she turned and went inside.

Jaared walked to his Jeep and hopped inside. Exhaling his stress from the moment, he looked at himself in the mirror. He found Kevin's face looking back at him. "It's okay. You will know when you find the one. When you do, do anything you have to do to get her and protect her. No matter what."

White code rose into the air and disappeared into the stars, and Kevin added his code fragments and reveled in the self-control and determination. A car's bright headlights shining in the windshield interrupted his moment.

He covered his face and closed his eyes, and then opened them in another memory.

Jaared opened his eyes as his head bobbed hard, hitting the window on the side of the plane. He sat up straight, stretching a kink out of his neck. *I hate sleeping on planes;* he thought to himself. Jaared looked at the empty seat next to him. *At least no one is in the middle, so I don't have to scrunch my shoulders in.* He reached to the LCD screen in the headrest in front of him and pressed the airplane symbol. A map came on the screen showing their GPS location. The plane was flying over the southern US. Jaared looked closer, seeing they were currently over Louisiana. The top of the screen read:

2 Hours 25 Minutes to Destination

Phoenix, why can't you be closer to Miami? Jaared pulled his Kindle out of the pocket of the seat in front of him. He turned it on, only to be welcomed by the "low battery" warning. Turning it off and replacing it, Jaared reached to the television screen on the headrest in front of him and found his way to the entertainment section. Most of the movies he had already seen or had no interest in. After turning through the popular choices, he found a title called *Dreams and Their Hidden Code Meanings.* "Interesting," he said to himself. He plugged in his headphones, sat back, and began the video.

"Thank you for watching this documentary. It's made possible by donations from viewers like you."

Something about the public broadcasting logo made Jaared happy inside, reminding him for a fleeting moment of when his mother and he would watch documentaries as part of his third-grade homeschooling. Jaared watched as a narrator spoke over a stream of images of excavated ruins around the world.

"Dreams. The stories we tell ourselves that help us overcome trauma, explore fears and confront our doubts. For many, dreams are quickly forgotten and never explored, yet there are archaeological indications that dream divination and understanding were key elements of many civilizations. So why not ours? Do dreams not matter, or is it that, for many of us, the language of pictures our subconscious uses is too complex to comprehend? What if you could? What if every night when you rested, you could awaken with understanding and clarity? What if you could unravel your dreams and learn the hidden code of the ancients to know their meanings?"

The video turned black for a moment before a legal pad appeared from the dark, hovering in the center of the screen. A pen that flew in from below wrote random scribbles on the paper as the narrator spoke.

"This video is more than just a look at dreams. It is also an interactive learning experience. Get some paper out and follow along to translate your dreams as you watch the video."

Interesting, Jaared thought. Bending over and digging through the backpack he had shoved under the seat in front of him, he pulled out a small notebook and pen. He folded down his tray table and placed the notebook on it. Jaared just finished preparing when the screen went black again and transitioned into the inside of an ornately decorated office. A thin man wearing a pinstripe suit that was a size too large stood in front of an oak wood desk. As he spoke, Jaared understood clearly that this was the narrator of the early intro.

"Welcome! I'm Dr. Emil Harssami, and it has been my life's passion to study the shamans and soothsayers of antiquity to better grasp their intellectual pursuits. This study has led me all over the world, studying nearly every major and rather minor civilization and tribal network. Combining the wisdom of all this human experience has led to my ability to create and teach the hidden code of dream understanding. To fully understand dreams and how we will unravel them, I must take you through my journeys and allow you to discover the truths that I have found. Before we begin, however, I would like you to write on a paper or notepad any dreams you remember. The more details you remember of that dream you can recall, the better. To begin, however, write a few words that best describe to you that dream. Press pause and do this now."

Jaared reached and pressed pause on the video. He thought for a moment and then started writing dreams he could recall. Strangely, there were a few from his childhood that he could recall almost every single detail about. Jaared started writing his list.

Meeting the Dream Master
Camping with Dave and Justin
Saving Justin at War

...

Looking down at his list, Jaared blinked as he swore the ink flashed white for a moment.

"Excuse me, sir."

Jaared turned to find an attractive brown-haired stewardess. He pulled his headphones out. "Yes?"

"Sir, we are expecting some turbulence. Will you please put the tray table up and open your window blind?"

"Yeah, of course." Turning and opening the window shade, Kevin saw his reflection in the glass.

"What are you writing there?" the stewardess asked.

Kevin turned and smiled at Sarah, thinking to himself, *I know I am just masking the appearance of another dreamer right now, but I have to say that it's nice to see Sarah living a normal life. Hmm. I could stay here. I could just make myself and her be here forever. That wouldn't be real.* He smiled and replied while putting the tray table back away. "I'm writing down some dreams I need to remember."

"I wish I could remember my dreams. But, why do you need to remember them?"

Kevin smiled back at her. He closed his eyes, knowing that face would be there when he opened them again.

Kevin opened his eyes to find Dr. Flo pacing the room nervously, her hair bobbing with every step, and Sarah guarding the door. His eyes focused on her. "It's done," he said in a calm tone, a voice that almost didn't feel like his own.

"Kevin? Everything good?" Sarah asked, clearly uncomfortable with how calm he was.

"Yeah," Kevin said, taking a relaxing breath.

"What happened?" Dr. Flo asked. "You've been under for almost an hour."

"I hopped around the memories of my dream life here. I stepped back into the shoes of Jaared again, and I don't know, it's like closing the door on a friend. But, I felt sorry for him. Felt sorry that all those memories he had weren't even real, just pieces of data waiting to be rewritten. I guess I'm just feeling grateful," Kevin said.

"Is the power supposed to go out or something?" Sarah asked.

"Are people about to wake up?" Dr. Flo asked.

"No, there is a time delay," Kevin said. "They will all wake up at the same time, which will cause massive issues, but it's on enough of a delay that it will happen when you're in the clear, Dr. Flo. I can't tell you when or your lack of surprise will be too obvious. Oh, and thank you. I saw, or rather understood, how many people you have helped over the years. I saw your face, and your care for the others who come here, stuck to the memories of so many others I ran into. Don't worry about getting into trouble for this. I'll make sure you are remembered as a hero in the eyes of the system, no matter how many you save."

Tears welled in Dr. Flo's eyes. Clearly, a weight had lifted from her shoulders. "Thank you, Mr. Altair."

"We need to move," Sarah said, checking her watch.

Kevin stood from the couch. Dr. Flo helped him with removing the mobile dream device, replaced the device in the box, and stored it in the drawer. They hurriedly made their way back down the hallway and to the service door on the mezzanine of DS 8. Kevin almost missed it, its design made to look like a section of wall. Sarah walked up to it and pressed on a piece of crown molding, which depressed and opened the door with a hiss.

"Goodbye, Dr. Flo," Kevin said, turning to face her.

She only nodded, still emotional from the moment.

"Flo, I'll be in touch," Sarah said.

Sarah and Kevin were back in the van less than five minutes later, having jogged their way back through the hallways.

"Did it work?" Diehl asked as they drove down the road.

"I think so," Sarah said, back in her copilot position.

"It worked," Kevin said confidently.

"Good. Good!" Diehl slapped the top of the steering wheel. "Hold on back there." This time, Kevin had enough warning to brace himself as the van lurched into the desert. "Now let's get to the rendezvous and tell the others."

"Let's not wait," Sarah said, a wide smile on her face.

"What do you mean?" Kevin asked.

"Let's call Dad right now on the secure line and let him know the plan is working," Sarah said.

"That's not... no, we stick to radio silence," Kevin demanded.

"This thing's not radio," Diehl said, pulling a satellite phone from his breast pocket and flipping it to Sarah.

"No!" Kevin reached for the phone but missed.

"Hey, easy!" Sarah said, catching the phone and fighting off his arms.

"Give me the phone!" Kevin fought Sarah, trying to grab the mobile.

"Kevin. Stop!" Sarah said as she wrestled with him for the phone.

"No, don't call him." Kevin was fighting desperately for the cell phone. He lost.

Sarah had had enough of the tussle and whipped Kevin with an elbow that caught him in the forehead and sent him tumbling back in the van. Now free of Kevin's resistance, she quickly pressed and held the quick dial for her father's private number. The phone rang twice before it was picked up.

"Hello."

The word sent a chill down Sarah's spine. "Who is this?"

"My name is not important."

"Where's my father?" Sarah asked, with an angry determination in her voice that did little to hide her fear.

"Your father can't talk right now." The person on the other end of the line paused. "He's a little tied up, if you know what I mean."

"What do you want?"

"Me? Nothing. Not from you at least. Well, not right now." A moan could be heard through the phone. "Sorry, I have to go now. But tell Kevin, good work. Oh, and Sarah, get you soon." The line went dead.

Sarah lowered the phone to her lap slowly. She pushed the hang-up button in shock.

"What'd he say?" Diehl asked, noticing the sudden disappearance of glee from Sarah's face.

Sarah was staring at the phone, processing the moment. She glanced back at Kevin, tears already pouring from her eyes.

Kevin made eye contact with her. He felt sad, sad for the loss they were experiencing, but even more so that she had to find out this way. "Sorry," he said, just above a whisper, his voice barely working.

Sarah, in that moment, snapped. "Stop the van," she said in a calm yet commanding voice.

"What?" Diehl asked.

"Stop the van!" She screamed this time.

"Okay." Diehl slowed the van to a sudden halt.

Sarah hadn't stopped staring at Kevin.

"Why are we stopped? What's going on?" Diehl asked.

"It was the only the way," Kevin said.

Sarah pulled her handgun from her holster and pointed it at Kevin.

"Wait!" Kevin yelled, raising his hands in surrender.

"Whoa!" Diehl yelled, grabbing the gun instinctively. It went off, ringing loudly in the small van. The bullet went through the roof and into the night sky.

Kevin quickly scrambled out the back doors of the van and fled into the dark.

Sarah pulled the gun to one side, fighting Diehl's grasp. She hit him in the nose with the hard part of her palm. Blood immediately began pouring out of it. Diehl released his grip on the handgun and grabbed at his nose. Sarah turned and hopped out the door of the van in pursuit of Kevin.

Sarah and Kevin disappeared into the night on a mad race of life and death.

"What the!" Diehl exclaimed as he tried to stop his nose from gushing blood.

Lights appeared on the horizon.

"Oh no," Diehl said, recognizing the triangular light pattern of a drone. Frozen, he braced for death as the lights flew closer and then overhead and into the landscape past him. Not waiting to see if it came back, he slammed the gas pedal down and sped off.

Kevin was running full speed through a near-pitch-black landscape. He heard a bang and a whistle as a bullet flew past his left ear. Distracted, he tripped on a rock. His footing gave way, sending him tumbling in the dust. Kevin rolled over, surveying himself, thinking he was dead for a second.

Sarah ran up a few seconds later and stood over Kevin. He could just see the outline of her night-vision goggle on her eye.

"How could you?" she screamed through angry tears.

"I didn't want to!" Kevin yelled, hands up, trying to keep her from ending it there. "Listen to me."

"No!" Sarah pulled the trigger and sent a bullet into Kevin's leg.

"Ah! This is the plan!" he yelled, writhing in pain from the gunshot.

"What!?"

"This is the plan!" Kevin shouted, squeezing his leg.

The lights of the drone were growing larger as it neared. Sarah turned to spot it, but quickly recoiled at the brightness coming through her night vision. She tore the goggles off and started firing at the approaching drone.

"No!" Kevin shouted. Reaching into his pocket, he pulled out the small dart gun the Master had given him and shot Sarah in the leg with it.

Sarah looked at the dart and pulled it out, too late, as the chemical was already making its way into her blood-stream. She moved to raise the handgun to kill Kevin. Her muscles gave way. Sarah crumpled into a pile next to Kevin.

Kevin watched the grief in her eyes slowly fade as the tranquilizer took effect. It was the hardest thing he'd ever done. The drone came and hovered overhead. Kevin's leg wound was bleeding heavily. He passed out there, next to Sarah, sharing the light of the security drone. As consciousness left his body, his mind jumped into a memory a lifetime ago.

Please answer, please answer, please answer. Waves of fear, anger, and grief pulsated through Jaared's body. The click of his mother's voicemail sent goosebumps across his skin. "No. Please, no." Jaared pushed the end-call button on his Nokia. He sat on the epoxy-sealed floor of his family's garage. "I don't even get to say goodbye," Jaared said, both to himself and to God. "Goodbye, Blake. I love you," he said through waves of sorrow.

On a sunny summer day, in the early afternoon, Jaared lost the miniature schnauzer who had spent the last seven years cuddling with him and warming his heart. There on that garage floor, he felt his soul lose a piece of itself.

Thairn sat down in the desk chair, wiping his fist on his shirt to clean the blood off his knuckles. "You know, I hate blood. Just don't like the sight of it at all. And it's always worse when it's not even mine. You're just making this worse on yourself."

The Master, handcuffed to the programming chair, breathed heavily through his bruised nostrils and bloody lips, his face swollen from the beating he had received.

"Look," Thairn said, "I know you have more members out there, in hiding, and even mixed in with controlled Awake chapters. I know you have sympathizers in the nurse and doctor's core. I just want names or IDs. Even initials would be fine."

"Nothing still, sir."

"Nothing?" Thairn turned to a technician who sat on the ground next to the Master.

"Let me check the connection." The man wiggled the cord that was plugged into the Master's mind chip. He then checked the end plugged into his own. "Connection is good. He's just giving me black."

"Well then, hack his memories. If he won't talk to us, we'll just have to see through his eyes."

"I tried that, sir," the technician said. "I can't. He has some old encryption that I've never seen before."

"Give me that connection," Thairn said. The technician unplugged the cord from the computer and passed it to Thairn, who promptly plugged it into his mind chip. He closed his eyes and began reading the code in the Master's mind chip. Thairn quickly yanked the cord free. "Impossible!"

"What is it, sir?"

"We have them, sir." A third man stepped into the bunker.

Thairn acknowledged him. "Bring them here." He turned back to the Master. "I'm going to make you watch."

"No." The Master said.

"He speaks!" Thairn said. "Sentiment will always betray you."

"No. It will save us all. Tau seven... five... two... nine... Jovial F." The Master's eyes rolled back, and his mind chip sparked.

"Wow!" The technician jumped.

"No!" Thairn went to grab the Master's mind chip. A spark shot out, burning his hand. He pulled back and then grabbed at it again. It was too late. By the time he freed it from the Master's head, it was a smoking black husk, and the Master sat dead.

"Sir?" the man from the door asked. "Should I still bring them here?"

"No." Thairn threw the burned-out mind chip across the room. "Have them taken to level 150. Burn this farm to the ground, but leave him and this bunker untouched. Let this be a warning to anyone who comes trying to find hope."

CHAPTER 8
LEVEL 150

K evin awoke to his eyelids sticking to dry eyes. He blinked, trying to restore some level of moisture to them and pull himself out of a drug-induced sleep. His head lolled to one side as he looked around the room. He recognized the built-ins and wood accents. Kevin straightened his neck and fought to focus his vision. The bright light shining in the floor-to-ceiling windows made that difficult.

"He's up," Alexander said from behind the desk.

Thairn turned in his seat, facing to look. "Welcome back," he said, jumping to his feet.

Alexander stood and walked with Thairn toward Kevin. "Congratulations on a successful mission, agent," Alexander said.

"Um." Kevin was still not fully comprehending the situation. "What, what, uh, what happened?" Kevin attempted to raise his hands to shield his eyes from the light, only to find them handcuffed to the metal chair he sat in.

"We did it," Thairn said, smiling.

"We, the Master," Kevin said, still fighting the last effects of the slumber. "Sarah. Where is she?"

"Don't worry," Thairn said. "I saved her for you. Watching the old man's life leave his eyes was so enjoyable. I wish we could both have shared that moment. But you get to kill his abomination."

"I'll kill you!" Sarah yelled.

Kevin turned his head to find her handcuffed to a metal chair bolted to the floor a few feet from him. "Sarah?"

"You! This is all your fault! You, you betrayed us! You killed my father." Sarah started crying through a scrunched face, her emotions running out of control. "How? Why?"

"Sarah," Kevin said, the feeling of betrayal ripping his heart in two

"I wish we never saved you," Sarah said through her tears. "I wish you never came into my life. You've ruined everything!" she yelled as she sobbed.

"Sarah," Kevin said, his body shaking as he fought his emotions.

"Enough of this," Alexander said. "Reset him."

"Gladly," Thairn said. "This is just pathetic." He walked back to the desk and grabbed a small laptop with a cord attached to it. He walked over and plugged into Kevin's mind chip.

Kevin didn't resist, instead just staring at Sarah, watching her crumbling over having lost everything, her father, her love, her hope.

After a few keyboard strokes, Kevin Altair closed his eyes, ceasing to exist.

When his eyes opened again, it was agent K00004 who sat in the chair. He straightened his posture and cracked his neck. He noticed the handcuffs on the chair, looked at the girl crying a few feet from him, and then directed his gaze back to Alexander. "So it's done?" he asked, with no emotion.

"Do you remember, remember the plan?" Thairn asked.

Agent K00004 looked at Thairn. "Of course. We made it right here."

Earlier. Another time. Another life. Level 150.

"They have a coder, probably the best," Alexander said.

Agent K00004 took a confident step forward. "But he knows that if he ever plugs into the dream network again, we'll get a lock on him. They'll never get away with it. Plus, they know they can never get to any of the mainframes they would need to make any major effect. So we need to give them a reason to take the risk. We need to give them the perfect bait."

"Yes," Thairn chimed in. "We give them a high-status editor. Someone with coding experience."

"We give them me," Agent K00004 said.

Alexander began shaking in his chair, his head vibrating side to side.

"Sir?" Agent K00004 asked, more out of confusion than concern.

Alexander paused for a moment and then spoke in a dry, monotone voice. "Yes, and we will make you so attractive to them they can't resist taking action on you. We will make you separate from society in a way that your independence will make them believe they can reach you. You will drive to the Dream States using a parking lot and a car. You'll work in an isolated corner of the editing room, and even put illegal code into the dream network to see your past lives."

"Sir?" Thairn and Agent K00004 asked simultaneously.

"Yes," Alexander said, standing from his desk and walking to stand in front of Agent K00004.

Agent K00004 looked at his boss, sensing something strange in his eyes.

"They will take you. You will learn from them and, when the time comes, put an end to their struggle," Alexander said, turning and leaning on his desk. "Now go, take care of the details."

"Yes, sir," Agent K00004 said.

"Fifteen seconds." Alexander whispered so quietly that only he could hear.

Agent K00004 and Thairn left the office just before Alexander began shaking again.

Now. This life. Level 150.

Agent K00004 cracked a confident smile at Thairn. "I told you this would work."

"He's back," Thairn said. He unplugged the cord from Agent K00004's mind chip and unlocked the handcuffs around his wrists.

Agent K00004 stood and rubbed his hands together. Looking at himself and the dirty jeans he had on, he asked, "What am I wearing?"

"What they gave you," Thairn said, pointing at Sarah, who now sat just staring in disbelief at Agent K00004.

"Right," Agent K00004 said. "This will be over soon," he said to Sarah.

"How?" Sarah half asked, half whispered, exasperated by her emotional output.

"The mind chip. It preserves the truth of yourself," Agent K00004 said. "Thairn, give me your gun."

"Yes. It's time for you to complete the mission," Thairn said, handing Agent K00004 his pistol.

Agent K00004 took it and, without delay, fired a round into Thairn's midsection.

Thairn dropped to the ground, clutching his abdomen. "Ough." He let out a strange sound as the wind left him.

Agent K00004 leveled the firearm at Alexander next. "There is something else I remember. Something you kept from me. Something that the Master helped me realize," Kevin said. "Thank you for this, Dad."

"Dad?" Thairn asked, pushing himself up against the wall.

Alexander started shaking for a few seconds, before standing tall, a smile coming to his face. "Son. I've only got thirty seconds before my mind scrambles again. I'm so proud of you."

"You're his son?" Sarah asked, more confused than anyone else in the room. "Who are you?"

"My name is Kevin Anders," Kevin said, not breaking eye contact with his father. "I never knew my mother, but I had one hell of an amazing father."

"Anders?" Thairn asked, his face turning white from blood loss.

"We need to hurry," Alexander said. He walked to the other side of his desk and typed on a keyboard.

There was no screen. Kevin assumed by the darting look in Alexander's eyes that the keyboard connected directly to his mind.

"Done. I re-enabled your security permissions and gave clearance for Sarah to leave the Z-Bank without issue. Send her to the basement and have her get in the van with her compatriot. I believe his name is Diehl. I captured him last night and have kept him locked there with his van. For the time being, I have removed their wanted status. Once you plant the kill code, we'll remember them as dead. We'll also remember you being killed in whatever way the program sees fit. They'll be free, and so will you. Now quick, give me the gun."

Kevin haltered for a moment and then handed it over.

Alexander walked back around the table. He started shaking but fired two more rounds into Thairn, fighting the convulsions. "Now knock me unconscious, quick. I'll wake and remember shooting Thairn, but only remember you hitting me."

"Dad."

"We don't have time." Alexander was shaking violently now. "Do it now."

Kevin slammed his elbow into Alexander's forehead, crumpling him to the floor.

"What is going on?" Sarah asked, in shock at the turn of events.

Kevin reached to the floor and recovered the keys to the cuffs. He walked over to Sarah.

She lurched away from him.

"Listen," he said, "we don't have much time, and I can't explain everything. What you need to know is this. Your father, he helped me. He set me free so that you can live free. You weren't supposed to be caught up in this. You're supposed to be out there somewhere. But you're here so now, you're going to get away from this place. You and Diehl are going to drive, simple as that. For the rest of your life, you and the Awake, who are still out there, will be completely free. Never worry about drones finding you or agents coming to kill you again. They will be blind to your existence. You will be ghosts. You can live, explore, travel, and someday love and have kids, and they will be safe. That has been my mission the whole time." Kevin reached and took the handcuff in his hand. He unlocked one and then the other. "We need to go before he wakes up."

Sarah ran to the gun, picked it up, and pointed it at Kevin. "I should kill you."

"Please don't."

"Why shouldn't I?"

"I can't ask for you to understand, but I need to make it to that editing room to install the kill code." Kevin teared up. "I know. I know you blame me for your father's death, and I am to blame. But I also know that I remember what life was like before. I remember the loneliness. I remember how much I wished for a purpose. I wished to meet someone who cared enough for others to sacrifice themselves for them. Your father showed me that dream was possible. He loved you so much that he trusted in me. Do you know why?"

Sarah shook her head.

"Because he knew their reset wouldn't work. I should have still rejected anything other than their training. But I didn't, because of you. I remember everything they taught me. I remember the code they implanted to stifle emotion, but I also can feel that code breaking when I look into your eyes. When I think of how your kiss felt on my lips, I feel my mind deleting controls. When I smell that faint scent of peonies, I feel my heart winning out. My love for you is too powerful. When I think of you and me in that barn..."

"Don't."

"I love you. Your father, my friend, saw that too. Now please, I know you may never look at me and not think about the loss of him, but let me finish this. Let me fulfill my promise to him by saving you."

Sarah stood staring at Kevin, the gun still pointing at him. "What happened to Mei?"

"She found out about my mission, this mission."

"Did you kill her?"

"No. When she learned your father lied to her, she lost hope. She couldn't kill me and ruin the freedom I could bring to everyone, but she didn't want to fight anymore either."

Sarah lowered the firearm. "What level do I take the elevator to?"

Kevin let out a breath. "B17"

"I'm leaving." Sarah walked past him, keeping her distance.

Just as she placed her hand on the door handle, Kevin said, "Sarah."

She paused to listen, but didn't look at him.

"I love you. I do. If you feel what I feel and can love me again, if I make it out of here, I'm going home, to the Ranch. Come there."

Sarah pushed the door open and left.

Kevin waited a minute, afraid to infringe on Sarah's escape. He peeked his head out the doors. No one was in the hallway. He walked to the elevator and pushed the button to level 30.

The doors opened to the familiar white marble. Kevin walked to the locker room, making quick work of donning his computing suit, his heart racing the entire time. As he made his way into the editing room, he saw the manager meeting taking place. *Perfect timing,* he thought.

Kevin walked to the stairs that led to his usual programming station. As he assumed, it was empty. Everyone still wanted to gain vision with the managers. Not him. Definitely not today. Kevin climbed the stairs in a half jog. Reaching his orb in no time at all, he climbed inside, closed the door, and quickly plugged into the system. His hands shook with nerves as he connected. If this was a trap, there was only one way to find out. The programming screen opened as he slipped into a half dream.

Kevin programmed at a speed he had never imagined possible. White code and random images flew by as he bounced through the dream network, never letting himself get pulled into a scene. He searched for and compiled the scraps of code he had assimilated in DS 8, replicating them through all the servers. An hour of programming and layering later, Kevin Anders, also known as Kevin Altair and Agent K00004, triggered the push code.

Small fragments of code copied themselves and distributed through the entire dream network. His work was done. Kevin opened his eyes and looked around the programming room. Nothing looked different, only one way to find out if the push code had worked. He unhooked his cord and made his way down the stairs. A minute later, he walked from the programming room and into the hallway that led to the locker room and the train. Kevin walked straight to the train, passing the guard who was currently scanning passengers arriving from the Dream States, and sat down.

The guard shouted, "Hey! Scan in to board the train!"

"I scanned in with him," Kevin said, pointing over the guard's shoulder and down the empty hallway.

"Who scanned..." The guard's words trailed off as he turned and took his eyes off Kevin.

Kevin watched intently, noticing the guard itching the skin by his mind chip. The code was working. It was burning Kevin from his memory.

The guard straightened up and scanned a person passing him coming off the train, not noticing Kevin sitting in his seat.

Kevin smiled as he watched the doors to the train close.

Chapter 9
Ashes & Snow

W inter snow covered the ground by the time Kevin reached the Ranch. His boots crunched with each step as he walked through the frozen landscape. Specks of black ash blew past him in the breeze, burnt timbers shedding pieces of their destroyed exterior. His eyes took in everything, searing the picture in his mind, an eternal memento of his role in the end of the Awake.

"Hello!"

Silence is all that responded.

He swallowed deep, still hoping that maybe someone had heard him. He set off in search of anyone or anything alive.

The barn's roof had fallen in under the weight of the snow, the collapse destroying the entire center area, tables included. Soot and oil fire grime covered the kitchen, and the stalls had been burnt to black crisps.

The farmhouse was gone, reduced to only a few vertical pieces of wood, wall framing that had somehow withstood the blaze.

The vehicle barn was a black stain on the snow. The only remaining identifying feature was the metal frame of the destroyed tractor.

Kevin searched the fields for an hour, scrounging for anything left behind. Only dirt remained.

A burning in his stomach led Kevin to the apple tree Diehl had kept secret from everyone else. On its branches hung one remaining fruit. Kevin picked it and stared at it for a moment before stuffing it in his pocket.

It was then that Kevin knew he had one last building to check. The one that Kevin had wanted to return to least, the bunker.

Of course, Kevin thought as he stood in front of the completely intact bunker. Taking a deep breath to steel himself, he opened the door. The scent of death reached his nose almost immediately, like a force pushing out against him. Kevin recoiled for a moment before stepping inside. Every foot Kevin gained, the stench pressed harder into him. He would not stop. This was something he had to do.

Kevin found the Master's body still tied to the chair, dried blood matting his hair and beard. Kevin cut him free from his bonds and carried him outside, Kevin's body radiating grief, sadness and guilt.

You deserve better; he thought. Grabbing a shovel from the field, Kevin took the Master to where they had shared their picnic and dug. The cold ground, frozen with the snowfall, made the task difficult, but Kevin didn't care. It felt almost deserving. Once finished, he lowered the Master's body into the grave he had excavated, careful to lay him down softly.

"I did it," Kevin said to his passed-on friend. "She's free. I'm sorry you couldn't be here to see it." Reaching into his pocket, he tossed the apple into the grave with his mentor.

Kevin had just finished covering the grave with dirt when his watch beeped the drone alarm.

Beep . . .

Beep . . .

Beep . . .

He stood there and stared into the sky, searching for it. I can't see it, and it can see me, but no one cares.

Kevin tossed the shovel to the side and started walking. His boot steps fell in the same path Sarah and he had walked when he first came to this spot. He tried to let his mind travel back to that moment, but his heart and the pain he felt stopped him. His feet, moving on their own, without direction or cause, led him to the barn.

Kevin stood silhouetted by the orange light of the late afternoon shining through the doorway. The burnt valor highlighted the black ashes that covered the ground of the fire-ravaged barn. Beams marred with burn marks stood as husks of themselves, the fire having turned them to toothpicks.

Kevin took a step inside, the ground crunching under his feet, burned-out coals popping under the weight of his body. He looked at what once had been a welcoming, open room. Now everything was dead. The collapse had destroyed most of it. Anything that had survived the wreckage was burnt and black. Kevin's emotions built as he looked at the room that once had been a happy place, now destroyed because of him.

"AAAHHH!" Kevin screamed as the anger overtook him. His muscles flexed as he yelled, his body filling with rage. He reached and grabbed a burnt chair that somehow still stood, waiting for someone to use it. With all his might, he slammed it into the ground, smashing the back of it. He kept swinging the pieces of the chair until all that remained were the two legs his hands were holding. Kevin threw them into the emptiness of the barn.

Ash and dust covered him, disturbed by his violent assault on the ground. Kevin leaned against the closest beam, slid down it and sat on the floor. He sat on the scorched ground and cried for the first time. Seconds later, he was sobbing. His entire body began shaking in waves of grief as tears ran down his face, creating tracks in the ash that now covered him. The black residue pooled and collected as the tears dripped from his face and fell to the earth. He sat, head hanging, lost in a sea of misery and self-doubt. Every decision he had made led him to this place, this moment, this predicament, this isolation.

Was it worth it? I know I made the right choice, but there had to be a better way. What? How? How can this be my fate? I can't... I can't.

His mind couldn't find the words to match his emotions. The path that had led him here was hard to comprehend.

An hour of crying later, he sat, spent, staring at a spot in the damaged wall of the barn. The sun shined through in a thick beam. Kevin watched as dust and ash particles danced in the air.

I can't... I can't... I can't. I can't be alone.

His eyes, red and blurry, didn't see the shadow approaching. His ears didn't hear the footsteps crunching in the snow. But he noticed one thing. His nose caught the scent in the air.

Peonies.

The End.

A Review Request

Thank you so much for spending your time with Kevin, Sarah, and the rest of the characters in this story. I hope they have entertained you and perhaps let you escape into a world that you enjoyed. Writing this story for you has been my pleasure.

If I could ask one thing, please take a minute or two and review this book. Reviews, particularly on Amazon and Goodreads, are the literal lifeblood of independent writers. I hope this book is the kind that you wish to share with your family, friends, and the world. Please help me share it.

Thank you,
Jonathan DeLeon

About The Author

Jonathan DeLeon was born in northern Colorado and is a graduate of Colorado State University. He now lives in Arizona with his wife, Sarah and their pups.

Connect with author Jon DeLeon. DeLeon shares his interests, his life, and updates on his projects on the following social media platforms:

Instagram – @jondeleonauthor
Website – www.beyondnormalbooks.com

Subscribe to Jon DeLeon's newsletter for updates on new book releases at:

www.beyondnormalbooks.com